THE LAST SEA GOD

BOOK 4

THE BONE MASK CYCLE

ASHLEY CAPES

For Brooke

PROLOGUE

Renasi woke to the sound of his name being spoken into warm darkness — a woman's voice. He sat upright, fumbling through twisted blankets as he reached for the lantern at his bedside.

"Leave it, Renasi." There was an undeniable command in her tone, yet she spoke only softly. Her silhouette rested before open curtains, moonlight slipping in around her. It seemed she wore a hood. The scent of orange blossom filled his bedroom, but he cultivated no such plants.

How had she entered? He swallowed hard as he sat back.

"You will need to dress, little man. We are going to your workshop, and you do not need to arrange for the other Alchemesti to meet us. Two will be entirely sufficient for this task."

"Who are you?" He gripped the edge of his blanket. Why was she here? If she was a thief, she wouldn't have woken him, surely.

"I am your new employer." Again, the tone of voice that expected no argument — and more, it seemed to press upon his very mind, dampening any objections. In fact, the longer she was in the room, the more his shock and fear receded. "And I require your special skills."

"Me? I don't know how special I am, ma'am."

"Oh? Are you not the one called Renasi, leader of the Alchemesti, the one responsible for creating a vitriol that melted the Sea God's flesh from its bones, here in Anaskar?"

"Well, yes, I did, but I still don't—"

She waved a hand. "You will understand soon enough."

"Yes, ma'am."

"Good. Now, a final question before we leave. And think carefully, for your life depends on the answer. You used blood from the Sea God to create your potion – did you save any?"

Renasi frowned. Quickly, think, man, think! Was there any left after all this time? The old vials? Yes. A tiny amount, so small he hadn't bothered mentioning it to anyone other than his fellows. Enough for further testing, if ever required, but what could this strange woman possibly need it for? "Yes, yes. There is a little."

"Good." The word was almost a purr.

"Ah, what will you need me to do with the sample?"

"Replicate it."

"Oh." He took a breath. A dangerous request if ever he'd heard one. "Why, ma'am?"

She did not answer.

The silence stretched, and he shivered despite the pleasant, late-spring weather. "Forgive me, but I find that I achieve better results if I know the purpose behind my research and experiments."

"Very well, Renasi. I mean to restore someone long since lost to me." She crossed the room and leant close. He shrank back, though all he could make out was a pair of smiling lips. "Now, clothe yourself and take me to your workshop – we begin immediately."

"Yes ma'am."

She straightened. "And enough of that. Do I truly seem so old? Address me as Mistress. And make haste."

He flung his blankets aside. "Yes, Mistress."

1. NOTCH

Everything was dry.

The air, his lips, his tongue and throat – the thin blanket on his hammock, the damnable walls of Melosi's creaking tub, everything! Notch wiped at his face. Even his eyelids – shouldn't he be sweating at least? Maybe he was; maybe his hand was simply numb from sleeping on it again.

In the dim quarters below deck Notch tilted his hammock and reached for a nearby pack, rummaging around the bottom for the tenth time. No more fire-lemon. Nothing had changed. Weeks since his fingers slid across the smooth, smooth surface of glass.

He knew as much, just as he'd known the other nine times he'd searched.

No matter.

Ecsoli, the land of the sun, would be *swimming* in fire-lemon and he only needed a little, just to remember the taste, just to brush away some of the fog that lingered. It *had* been receding over the days since he'd been limited to the swill the sailors portioned out – the little they'd been using to bolster their spirits.

Something that seemed to be happening more and more lately.

Still no land in sight.

Food and fresh water running low.

Bad weather looming; a storm that had been threatening for days but which never seemed to break. Always out in the half-distance, black clouds on the horizon or strong winds, continuous lightning strikes like temporary forests of searing light.

But no matter how close it drew, the storms never truly threatened the ship.

And it was all because of Captain Melosi's secret.

Tersi.

Abrensi's son, secret Storm Singer of the *Hawk*. Tersi was the reason Melosi had sailed last winter to retrieve Notch's sword, the blade which even now hung from a post nailed into the door.

Whenever the Storm Singer's clear voice, not unlike his father's, cut through the wind and sent the savagery of nature away, or when Tersi instead chose to harness the wild forces and send the ship tearing across the waves, sails bulging, it was an awe-inspiring sight. And it would have been even more magnificent had Notch been sober for most of the displays.

Now the ship seemed to battle the ocean.

Notch pushed himself from the bunk and stumbled for the door. Movement set his stomach roiling and he gripped the wall. Bad idea. Still, fresh air, even the air from a stormy sea, suddenly seemed worth the risk.

Wind and sleet slashed through his clothing above deck, as if he wore nothing instead of leathers, vest, tunic and heavy overcoat as extra protection from the chill of spring on the ocean. It seemed winter was reluctant to relinquish its grip on the Northern Sea. Perhaps now, after six or even seven weeks of sailing north, they were closing in on their destination, though it hardly seemed the land of the sun would be so near.

Nor that it would be so easy to reach. After all, before the invasion, no ship had crossed the ocean in hundreds of years.

But the *Hawk* was not drawing near land precisely.

Men lined the rails and clung to the rigging, staring out across the dark sea to an enormous green island sequestered in still waters of glittering blue. The storm clouds, the rain and fury of the wind, it all fell into a calm before reaching the shore.

"What magic is this?" Notch whispered as the ship rocked. He gripped the rail.

A huge hand came to rest on the wood beside his own. Alosus.

The Tonitora towered over him, his torso bare to the elements, the skin of his bald head and shoulders dusky – almost the deep red of coals. His expression was difficult to read, despite the weeks of shared lessons in both modern and old Anaskari. If Alosus was surprised by what he saw out in the middle of the vast ocean, he gave no indication. In fact, if anything, it was a preoccupation that Notch detected. The man's son and his family; Alosus held onto the hope that Vinezi had *not* ordered them killed, that his quest would not be for naught.

"Old magic," Alosus said, using the ancient tongue. "We stopped here during our journey, I suspect, though I never saw the land, chained below as befitting a slave." His voice was a low rumble, difficult to hear beneath the wind and hints of thunder.

"Then we're close to Ecsoli. Or heading in the right direction at least," Notch replied. Ancient Anaskari had not been as difficult to learn as he'd expected, but nor was it second nature yet.

"We are. And if your Storm Singer can continue to guide us all by himself, an impressive feat I can still hardly believe, then we should reach the silver shores within four weeks."

"Four more weeks," Notch muttered.

Four more weeks and he'd finally reach Ecsoli, the Land of the Sun, where his search could begin in earnest. He'd failed to save Sofia once; he would not do so again. There *had* to be a way to return her to life. There *had* to be someone in the old land who knew the magic, who knew how to free her soul from the Greatmask.

Gods, she'd deserved so much more. How could death be her only reward for saving the city? For saving all lands, for saving everyone from Vinezi's depraved quest for bones of power?

It was a cruel joke sent down from a bastion of indifferent Gods.

"And no more fire-lemon to blur the days." Alosus' words broke Notch's dark reverie. Again, the big man's expression and voice were hard to read. Disapproval or subtle humour?

"Maybe the island will hold a few surprises."

"I fear it might." Alosus did frown now. "I may not have been able to see, but I heard the sounds of significant struggle. Vinezi and his brothers fought something here when they stopped to re-supply. If we can reach the island, we must warn the captain."

"Agreed." The wind was already dropping as the helmsmen held course, protected by Tersi's song. Notch looked up to the giant. "Who brought Vinezi here, if he had no Storm Singer?"

"I have not been able to figure that out. Something amongst the items he stole from his father, no doubt. Perhaps it no longer matters."

"I suppose not."

Notch asked no more questions about Vinezi – it was a mistake, it always was because his thoughts invariably turned back to Sofia and his failure.

The wind fell away, and the *Hawk* surged forward, before flying across the still waters at a slightly calmer pace. Notch looked back; the darkness of the storm held at bay, waves churning and clouds afire with lightning. Ahead, the lush green of the island drew closer – trees climbing the sides of stony peaks, the faint cries of jungle birds crossing the waves.

Before it all stood a crumbling pier.

And waiting on the boards, a lone figure in a white cloak and hood.

2. NOTCH

The figure was gone when they dropped anchor and rowed to the pier.

And after mentioning it once to Alosus, Notch dropped the subject, since the large man had seen nothing. An unwelcome side-effect of the drink? It wouldn't have been the first time he'd seen something that didn't exist after – or during – long bouts of drinking.

Too bad there was little chance for fire-lemon out in the jungle.

"I'm not saying we won't take heed of your warning," Melosi said as he coiled a length of rope for the pack that lay at his feet. The tiny bird skulls in his beard clinked as he worked, and his black coat had been brushed clean. "But we don't have a choice, do we? We need fresh water, fruit, and I'd even take monkey for fresh meat."

Alosus nodded. "Caution is all I'm asking. Your crew numbers many but none bear a mask." He spoke now in Anaskari; his command of the language was better than Notch's ability to speak Ecsoli.

"The risk is worth it if your land is as rich as you

and Notch claim, and if you can really convince them Ecsoli to trade with us." He grunted. "And since Notch is leading this little expedition, I can always throw him to the lions if we run into trouble."

"I see you still haven't quite forgiven me for the change of course," Notch said.

"No. I haven't forgiven myself for agreeing to your fool plan, but it's easier to be angry with you."

"You can trust my word, Captain," Alosus said. "The Land of the Sun is a rich land – too rich."

"So long as you convince them to trade when we get there."

"I will do my best."

"We'll need better than that, big man," the first mate said. Gappilo held a boat hook and his own pack, his grey beard reaching his stomach.

"Your *lenasi* is rare in my land," Alosus said. "I will come from a position of strength in that respect."

"And your standing as leader among your people," Melosi said.

"Yes," Alosus replied. Again, his expression was even, his voice revealing no hint of the lie Notch had deemed necessary.

And whether Alosus *could* convince the Ecsoli to trade, to prevent them from destroying the entire ship with their Greatmasks, well, that was a hurdle for later. Now, they had to find water and avoid whatever had troubled Vinezi and his group of masks.

With only their swords and Alosus' strength.

Tersi had stayed behind on the *Hawk* with a small crew, Marlosi unwilling to risk the Storm Singer's life on the island. Notch found nothing to disagree with in the captain's thinking there. Crossing the rest of the North

Sea was impossible without Abrensi's son.

Notch led them along the pier, Alosus close behind and Marlosi in turn. The wood beneath his feet was aged, colour drained by the sea, but it did not appear rotten.

When he reached the shoreline, there was only a small, circular beach of white sand before a winding trail. It led into the shadows, out of the bright sun where broad, smooth leaves built the canopy. Vines hung down, thin red flowers blooming along their lengths. The screech of distant monkeys filtered through the trees, chirping too. He caught the flash of movement above; a bird with a striped beak taking flight. Moisture thickened the air and his lungs were slow to adjust. Sweat built quickly.

Alosus seemed not to mind but Marlosi and the others were likewise troubled.

The path led higher, widening as it did. Twice they found parts of the trail where fallen logs, thick with moss and vines, had been cut in half and cleared. Vinezi or Marinus? And where had they run afoul of whatever lurked on the island? It had to be close for Alosus to have heard it... Notch slowed, lowering his father's sword.

A clearing lay ahead, hewn earth and trampled sprouts, sunlight falling across the body of a scaled beast. Had it been standing, it would have been head and shoulders taller than Notch. But its eyes were lifeless yellow orbs, traces of black blood only remaining beside the open mouth, snake-like. The red and black scales formed patterns along its legs and forearms – all six of them. Long, sinewy-looking limbs were tipped with foot-long talons. Enough to rip a man open with a single swipe.

Notch approached slowly, eyes scanning the surrounding trees. "If this is what Vinezi found, I hope it was the only one," he said. There was no strong stench of rotting flesh; the gaunt thing was long-dead and oddly, had not been ravaged by animals or birds.

Alosus knelt beside the corpse. "As do I." He frowned, then pried open the creature's mouth, revealing a shrivelled piece of tongue – most of which had looked to have been cut, rather than chewed by scavengers. "They harvested the tongue, but I cannot guess why."

Marlosi grunted. "I want water first. Fruit and meat is second priority. Understood?"

"Yes, Captain," his men echoed.

They moved on. Notch gripped his blade, blinking away a blurring of his vision. Damnable drink! He'd need something before the shakes returned.

Every new sound in the trees drew his attention, even the trickle of dew pattering from huge leaf to huge leaf. But no creatures attacked, and by mid-morning they found a stream pouring down a gulley. The stone walls cast long shadows, giant vines thrusting up, clinging almost desperately to the rock face.

Despite Marlosi's orders, they'd harvested some of the large, yellow fruit and coconuts along the way but at the first sound of running water, smiles had broken out across the men's faces and even Alosus cupped his hands to drink despite having shown no prior signs of discomfort.

Barrels were passed along to the stream's edge and filled, the sailors chanting an old song as they worked. Notch sat on a moss-covered log and drank from his own flask with a sigh. It wasn't fire-lemon but at least it was cool. He glanced behind, checking on their back trail.

The woman in white stood amongst the trees.

Notch rose.

Her hood concealed all but her mouth and the edges

of dark hair that peeked forth. The robe was more figure-hugging than a typical Mascare garment, which instantly came to mind. Was she an Ecsoli guardian left on the island for some unknown purpose? She wore no mask, of that he was sure, but what other power did she conceal?

She beckoned for him to approach but he did not move.

"Gappilo, do you see her?" he asked the man who stood nearby. The first mate turned, then narrowed his eyes. "I do."

Soon the entire party had noticed the woman.

Now she lifted an arm to point to Notch. "Attend to me. Do not make me wait."

Her tone left no room for refusal; agreement seemed best. A sense of something vast filled the small clearing, smothering the whisper of the stream. The woman was not ordinary – only a fool would think it so. The overwhelming sense of power common to a Greatmask was near, but she wore no mask and her robe did not seem to conceal a bone breastplate. Perhaps she'd stolen some piece of Seto's Greatmask and fled with it, before the confrontation in the Anaskari Temple?

Before he could answer, his leg took a jerky step forward. And then a second. Pain came with the movement. He fought but the growing agony only increased. "What do you want?" he demanded between clenched teeth. Alosus took a step, reaching out but Notch shook his head. If the big man tried to hold him back, Notch's bones would shatter. He couldn't even draw his sword!

Not that it would do any good.

The woman did not respond but his steps quickened as she controlled his bones, bringing him to a halt before her.

She smiled, though he still could not see her face clearly – only her lips. She appeared young, but her presence was that of someone older, more assured. "How convenient that I find tools unlooked for, even here." She paused to regard him. "Dull though they might be."

Dull? A charming woman. "What do you want from us?"

"For you to complete a simple task. There is a ruined temple on this island and within lies a tomb. Bring the bones you find there to the far side of the island – I will be waiting."

"You're obviously powerful enough to do it yourself," Notch said, ignoring the impulse to keep his mouth shut. "Why do you need such a 'dull tool' to do your bidding?"

Her laugh rippled over him. "Then let me hone your edge a little, Notch."

A pale nimbus snapped up around her and his vision grew dim – his mind struggling within a new fog. Was it her? The sensation of being... 'read' followed. There was a cobweb-thin thread between them, and a hint of annoyance thrummed along it; something had interrupted her, something that required immediate attention but not something that would keep her away for long. She meant what she said – the woman would be waiting for him to complete her errand.

The connection broke.

He frowned; she'd used his name. She'd called him Notch. How? Just who was she? A chill followed. She didn't seem to be Ecsoli. Anaskari maybe? Her tanned complexion was the only clue. When the light faded, his vision cleared and he exhaled heavily. Something had changed within him... and it wasn't just the sudden elimination of the effects of his drinking, even the *need* was gone. But something else had happened and the sensation faded quickly as it came.

Yet her magic lingered even as it took no recognisable form. "What did you do?"

"Just enough to ensure you complete the task. Remember, the other side of the island." She tilted her head a moment. "My, my. You know Oseto, don't you?"

"I do."

"If you ever see him again, you will pass on a message. Remind him that he should not seek me."

"Who are you? And how do you know Seto?"

She stepped back, her form beginning to fade into the vivid green of the trees. "I expect you at sunset."

3. NOTCH

Crouched amongst the vines with Alosus and Melosi, Notch looked down upon the ruined temple and its crossed columns with a deep frown. It was impossible to fully drown out the whispers from Melosi's men, who were still sharing curses and wards against evil. And why not? Being frozen in place by a figure in a white robe – a woman who hadn't even lifted a finger – was hardly something to just shrug off.

For most men.

He still muttered a curse; knowing she'd done something to him wasn't as easy to forget.

"What's that?" Melosi asked. His own expression was troubled.

"Nothing."

"Look," Alosus said. His deep voice rumbled.

Shadowy movement flashed between the crumbling columns of the temple. Something big. And fast. Yet it did not reveal itself as it slipped through the overgrown grounds. The walls, vines, dark flowers and spiky grasses burst up from moss-covered paving stones to obscure the creature. But that much Notch was sure of – it was a creature. There'd been a flash of a tail, but he caught it only once and then lost sight of it. Had the thing entered the temple? The main building itself was nearly as deeply immersed as the grounds. The opening was a dark maw.

"One of those giant lizards," Melosi said, his voice flat.

Before Notch could answer, a shape emerged from the temple's opening; long, sinewy, the afternoon light gleamed on black and red scales. Its steps were fast, precise, as it sniffed at the air. A second creature appeared from behind one of the half-collapsed walls and then a third from the temple, this one only slightly smaller than the other two.

The rasping hiss of the silverine from the Bloodwood echoed in his memory; these things would be worse. Notch didn't take his eyes off the creatures. The first started toward their position. "Take your men back to the ship, Melosi."

"And just what do you think you're going to do?"

"Give you time." Notch looked to Alosus. The Tonitora still carried his giant sickle and he rested a huge hand on it now. "Think we can handle three of them?"

"Not truly, no. One maybe, but not three."

"He's right, Notch," Melosi said. "We have what we came for, forget the witch – we'll leave."

Notch shook his head. "I can't. She'll know, and she'll find us. I don't want her to punish everyone because I didn't complete her errand." He hadn't shared all her words with them, but Greatmask or no, she was obviously more powerful than any being he'd ever encountered.

No matter. He had no choice; she would come for him.

And she had offered him something, hadn't she? It

would help, surely. *It had to.* His gaze was caught by the talons that gleamed on the six-legged creatures. He still had his father's sword. "She wants me to succeed. Go, you need time. They already have our scent." He looked to Melosi. "Don't sail off without us – I mean to board the *Hawk* again, Captain."

The man gave a nod, then spun to his men, waving them back down the trail. Notch looked up to Alosus, who was shaking his head. "This is madness. I have a wife and son to find."

"Whatever that woman did to me will make the difference," Notch said. He drew his blade and glanced around. Slabs of old stone, set in a regular pattern, stood nearby, each covered in moss. "See if you can break some legs with those; it'd be a good start."

Alosus moved to the stones and lifted one with no apparent effort, something Notch would have laboured to do if at all, and faced the approaching terrors. The lead creature had broken away from the other two. Alosus lifted the slab, took aim, and hurled the stone forth. Notch felt the wind of its passage from where he stood.

The stone struck the creature square, the snapping of bone following as it collapsed. The other creatures stopped and began to hiss, then the smaller angled away – circling toward where Melosi and his men had left. "Can you stop that one?" Notch asked.

"What are you going to do?"

Notch took a deep breath. "Find out if whatever she did will actually help." Before Alosus could stop him, Notch charged down the hill. He circled the still-thrashing creature Alosus had struck, then hit level ground, approaching the remaining beast.

It spread its forearms, keeping four on the ground,

long black tongue flicking out as it hissed and crept closer. The scales gleamed, and the eyes were dark pools with a slip of yellow iris, tracking him as he held his sword ready. If he could hack through its legs, maybe he'd be able to reach the head without being sliced open.

The huge lizard charged. One arm flew in from the left, the other slashing down from above.

Notch blinked.

Time had slowed. Afternoon light grew... softer, dimmer. The lizard-monster became more vivid as it, too, slowed. Its left arm was still approaching but Notch had time to raise his sword and consider his next move – he was not affected by the strange slowing of time at all. Whatever the woman in white had done, it seemed reminiscent of the magic the Oyn-Dir's used to manipulate the Autumn Grove. But that magic was unique to the leader of the Braonn people, surely? And the witch had seemed tanned as any Anaskari or Ecsoli.

Notch slipped outside of the other talon's reach. He had time to outflank the beast; it turned slowly, slowly – even the pieces of loam it tore with its feet spun into the air at a snail's pace.

Notch swung his sword. Hard.

The blade sliced through the limb with relative ease. He'd recovered to swing at another leg before the splash of blood from the first wound hit the earth. Another clean cut and then he was severing a third leg.

A droning buzz filled the clearing before the temple, but he didn't stop to fathom it. By the time the now-lopsided creature hit the ground he'd already circled to start on its tail, which took a few blows to hack through. Again, time favoured him – the creature's head had not even finished turning to face him when he dashed close and swung at its neck.

The giant lizard-thing died in a spray of blood, droplets spinning, catching the light like rubies as they flew from the edge of his blade.

The natural brightness of the world returned.

The droning ceased, and the creature's remaining limbs twitched as it lay bleeding. Notch stepped back to catch his breath. He hadn't laboured, yet the strangeness of it all... what had the white witch done? Was it a gift or a terrible burden? He didn't know exactly how or when he could slow time but still... such power. On the battlefield he would be unstoppable. If he wasn't surprised, at least. Or shot from afar either – but it was impossible to know the limits of what she'd done.

No need to find out now. Just get the bones and get them to her.

Notch approached the dark maw of the temple, sword raised. Black blood dripped from the steel; he flicked it before pausing on the threshold.

A crumbling stone figure of a man rested above the entry; stern features casting ancient displeasure down upon those who entered. Notch crept within, boots scraping on stone. Light fell into a large altar room at the end of a short passage, a gaping roof open to the sky. Greying plant life littered the empty floor, greener shoots beneath, along with animal droppings. One corner housed a large nest of mud, moss and branches, but he didn't approach it.

Instead, he moved directly for an opening behind the round altar, and no clue as to the particular deity it once served. The opening led down, worn steps visible. He took the single torch from his pack. If it was a long passage... Notch bent to work with tinder and flint, lighting the torch before beginning the descent.

The stair curved back around and under the altar, an arch revealing a dusty catacomb. He raised his torch and flickering light fell across rectangular stone slabs set in the walls. They were evenly spaced, and each bore a pair of iron handles. They numbered in the dozens. At the limits of his torchlight, there seemed a second arch. More tombs. "How by the Gods do I find the right bones?"

Be calm. The voice in his head held more than a trace of annoyance. *Fourth chamber. It is marked.*

"Marked how?"

But the white witch did not answer. Notch growled as he started toward the next arch. More of the same in the room, though the spider webs seemed to have a better hold here. Animal bones, tiny and thin, were heaped across the threshold of the third arch but nothing else was of note. The same stone tombs, the same steel handles, none of which he touched.

In the final chamber, he slowed to search each slab for markings but all were the same until he came to the rear of the room. Here, a bigger, more ornate slab stood in the wall. Large enough perhaps for two or three bodies. But its handles were the same plain steel bolted into the stone. The surface of the slab bore no engraving, nothing to indicate if it was the one the witch sought.

He moved on, searching the next wall.

And there, at chest height, the handles blinked with a white light – totally independent of his torch. He sheathed his sword, then threaded the torch through an adjacent handle before gripping the glowing steel. He braced his legs then pulled. Stone ground as it slid open. Dust sprinkled free at the edges. Notch kept sliding the stone coffin free, pausing once so he could see inside.

Too much farther and it would overbalance.

White and grey shapes lay within, tangled in rotten fabric and dust. He lifted the torch closer. Little of whoever had once been sealed away remained. There was a skull and scraps of cloth and beside them, a longsword broken at the hilt. Something else gleamed in the torchlight – a pair of bracers. They were covered in silver scrollwork that surrounded a leaping lion, and seemed untouched by any tarnish. He lifted both free with an intake of breath. Lightweight, but they did not feel fragile in any way. A power lurked within them; there was a... a pulse that joined his own as he gripped them.

Do not tally with mere trinkets, Notch. Bring me the skull.

He flinched at the command. "I am on my way."

Once again, the white witch did not reply. He hesitated just a moment, bracers in hand, before sliding them on. Notch scooped up the skull and placed it into his pack. "Looks like you're coming with me, fellow."

4. NOTCH

Notch stood on the old pier that clung to the opposite side of the island, exactly as instructed.

The setting sun sent a rose tint across the earth, plants and stone pier alike. The stretching sea was dark but pink brushed across the tips of the tide that splashed against the supports in a gentle rhythm. The sound might have lulled him, but the white witch was not someone he wanted to be surprised by.

He'd encountered nothing more dangerous than a snake or two on his trek toward the second pier, the skull in his pack thudding against his back with every step. Who had it belonged to? More importantly, why did she want it? Vinezi's foul use of bones – and human flesh – was an ugly possibility. Yet the pool of regeneration in the temple back home was empty, wasn't it?

"Well done."

Notch spun. The white witch stood behind him, robes unstirred by even a breath of air. She held up a hand. The sense of her vast power was near-suffocating this time, shrinking him even though he knew he did not stand even half a foot shorter. He delivered the skull, which she did not even seem to glance at – though had there been a slight tightening of her lips? Her hood crinkled, and she looked to his arms where the silver armour rested. "Are you sure you want to carry them off this island?"

"He doesn't need them. And where I mean to go, I need all the help I can find."

She smiled and moved closer. Notch stepped back, reflexively, then froze – had the movement been an insult? But the witch's smile only grew wider. "You show some mettle, it seems." She glided closer again and now he could not move even if he was willing; his bones were locked in place as before. Compelling, just as Danillo had used – something that only Anaskar's Lord Protector should have been able to achieve with the Greatmask Argeon. Danillo or the Ecsoli, anyway. Yet the witch seemed to carry no bones of power. "Should you survive the ocean and then the Land of the Sun, I may just have further uses for you, Notch."

"Uses?"

"Indeed." She removed her hood. The witch was a young woman with dark hair and dark eyes – eyes which did not speak of youth. An unfathomable age glittered within. She was somehow familiar but there was not enough to recognise, merely a vague feeling. He winced as she leaned in, her breath warm against his neck. Her lips brushed his skin; a tingling spreading through him. She opened her mouth...

Pain flashed.

He could not cry out but when she drew back, still smiling, Notch found he could move again. He reached up to his neck – she'd bitten him. Teeth marks were present in two half circles, indents. Only a trace of blood appeared on his finger tips... she had barely broken the skin. But he'd felt it.

"Now you are marked."

"What does that mean?"

Already she was fading. "Be careful with those bracers; they might change you in ways you find alarming."

"Wait, what have you done?" he called after her ghost.

Nothing lasting – and I do hope you didn't grow accustomed to my little trick with time back at the temple.

Gone.

Notch heaved a sigh. He'd survived, but at what cost? He ran his fingertips across the bite-mark and shuddered before letting his hand fall away. Focus! Getting off the island was a big enough problem for now, which meant starting a fire. Assuming Alosus had been able to protect Melosi and the crew, they'd eventually see a signal fire. Assuming also, that they hadn't simply sailed away.

By the time he had a fair blaze going, full darkness had fallen. He stood with his back to the flame and stared out to the ocean. When he wasn't running his fingers over the bite or wondering about her need for the skull, he was examining the bracers. The lion was certainly magnificent, but neither it nor the flowing scrollwork offered any clue as to the potentially disturbing power the witch mentioned.

Was it going to be a mistake to keep them?

But if it was going to offer an advantage, didn't he need to take the risk? In the Land of the Sun, he was going to be overpowered at every blasted turn.

Light appeared in the distance – lanterns on the *Hawk*, its great bulk sliding into view. He waved but his fire had obviously already been seen. Perhaps the action concealed a bit of relief, even if he hadn't truly thought Melosi would leave. They'd obviously bested the lizard-like creature.

A longboat was launched, and he soon found himself rowing beside Melosi's first mate. A man carrying a bow was also aboard, his eyes on the patch of light remaining beyond the pier. "Must say, I'm surprised to see you again, Notch," Gappilo said.

He chuckled. "A warm welcome back."

The first mate rasped his own laugh. "Well, I'm impressed that you dealt with one of them creatures *and* the white witch."

"Maybe 'placated' is a better word," Notch said. "I doubt anything that happened back there was contrary to her plans. How did you fare?"

"Made it back to the ship with most o' what we wanted. One of those things caught up with us but lucky for us that giant of yours cut it near to pieces."

Relief rippled through him. Luck holds. "So no-one was hurt?"

"Well, the big guy took a nasty gash to the arm but he's holding up."

They'd nearly reached the ship. A few faces lined the rails, one of which belonged to Melosi, who was grinning down at them. "Didn't think we'd see you again, Notch."

"Thanks for staying."

"We'd nearly given up, but we thought at least one circuit round the island couldn't hurt."

Gappilo manoeuvred the longboat near the ladder and held the boat steady while Notch climbed. Once on deck, he was greeted with a little cheer. Some of the men now regarded him with a touch of awe. Misplaced, but welcome compared to the more uncertain looks he'd earned when, at times, he'd been too drunk to stand. Now, he no longer felt the urge to seek the bottle – the guilt and self-recrimination hadn't faded, but the white witch had obviously done something good.

Would anyone notice the bite marks in the dim light?

"How is Alosus?"

"Well enough. Why don't you go and see him then take some rest?" Melosi turned to his men. "Let's get my *Hawk* back on the path – there's a fortune waiting at the other side."

Notch passed Tersi while heading below, nodding to the younger man. By the state of his clothing, the Storm Singer looked to have dressed in haste, but his expression was one of determination. Was he pushing himself too hard? Perhaps a word with Melosi wouldn't hurt.

Notch found Alosus resting in his modified hammock, his entire forearm bandaged. He did not appear to be in pain at least. "Notch, it is good to see you alive and well," he said.

"Alive but I do not know how well." He gestured to his neck. "This is from the white witch – I suspect she is not quite finished with us."

Alosus frowned. "You think she means us harm?"

"More that she wants to be able to use me again. Not that I know how. She's obviously powerful enough not to bother."

"All power is finite; there's always a cost."

"I suppose." He fought off a yawn. "How long until we reach the coast now?"

"Four weeks, as before," Alosus said, his voice calm.

Now Notch sighed as he leant against the door. "That doesn't bother you?"

"Each day is a day closer to finding Yolanda and Mane."

"I see." And so it was for Sofia. Each moment took the *Hawk* closer to Ecsoli and the hope of answers. He would not abandon her as her own father had. But Alosus needed help too; Notch had given his word and he meant to keep it. "What will our first move be, when we land?"

"We've discussed this, can you not recall?"

Notch frowned. Much of the trip was a haze, admittedly. They had to convince whatever harbour master awaited them that *lenasi* and their seedlings – along with various other goods that Melosi bore – were worth trading, and also that Alosus was an important figure. But after that? "Not enough."

Alosus leant forward, his serious expression deepening. "You will not survive in the Land of the Sun if you cannot keep your wits about you. You will not be able to help me or Sofia, Notch."

"I know." Notch had to look away. Gods, how quickly he'd slipped back into old habits, wallowing in fire-lemon beneath a dark cloud. But that had changed now; he would not waste the white witch's unintended gift. He met the Tonitora's gaze. "Not another drop."

"Good," Alosus said with a nod. He leant back. "I need to find Vinezi's trail. He claimed to have my family and unfortunately, that most likely means contacting the palace."

Vague pieces of one of their prior conversations were returning. "And Vinezi's father, the king, is he senile? Marinus and the other children were squabbling over the throne?"

"And probably still are. However, something may have changed since news of Marinus' death has no doubt arrived before us. There is another possibility." He paused, and his expression darkened. "The Slavers of the Pine Coast. Vinezi may have sold my family before he left – and if so, I will tear those scum apart."

5. FLIR

"Perhaps you should just tell us why you've really returned, Flir?"

The man folded his arms in the lamplight. His grey, fur-lined uniform stretched across his shoulders as if he had grown into it a little too swiftly. And maybe he had; the lieutenant would have been little more than a boy when she'd left Renovar. A cold draft found its way into the damp basement somehow; welcome home. It didn't bother her body so much as represent disappointment, a stark reminder of the lingering grip of winter which seemed to last an extra three months here.

Chains rattled when Flir lifted her arms into her lap, leaning back in the chair, which creaked. It wasn't the chains that kept her – or Kanis – compliant, but the dozen crossbow bolts trained upon them that had the desired effect.

"I'm surprised anyone remembers me here."

The lieutenant chuckled. "Very droll. Your exploits – the both of you – are indeed well-remembered, if not fondly so."

"I imagine that makes it difficult to think of us as diplomats then," Kanis said with a grin.

The soldier did not smile. "Sent by King Oseto of Anaskar."

Flir linked her hands behind her head, the steel cold against her neck. "Yes. He sent us to reopen relations with the Conclave, which I understand were not precisely rosy, even before the recent attack by certain Renovar ships, ships that the king understands were acting independently of the Conclave. It is an act of good faith that he sent us, not of subterfuge." Not subterfuge so long as she didn't count Seto's instructions to search for the bones of any long-forgotten Sea Beasts, too. Sofia's sacrifice had drained every piece of bone in Anaskar – all save Argeon – and Seto wasn't willing to leave the city unprotected if even a rumour of bone existed elsewhere.

It didn't help that neither Flir nor Kanis could think of a single site in all of Renovar that might hold such bounty. Nor that the Renovar Lieutenant seemed unlikely to believe in the legitimacy of their visit.

"And you have some official documents perhaps, to corroborate your story? Surely your king sent you with something... anything possessing a seal at least."

"If it weren't for the pirates –" Kanis began but the man held up his hand and Kanis fell silent.

"Ah, yes. Silly of me to forget. The pirates – they ransacked your envoy ship and that's why you two and your servant were wandering the coast off Whiteport. Not because you had more underhanded motives for returning home?"

"Exactly," Kanis said.

Flir nodded. She glanced to the heavy oaken door. Was Pevin still alive? He'd been feverish, his skin searing to the touch…

The lieutenant glanced at one of his men. The soldier, an older fellow with greying hair, shrugged. "Stranger things have turned out to be true, Tikev."

"But you're not inclined to believe them."

"Not at the present, sir."

Flir sighed. "This is quite the farce, isn't it? I mean, there's clearly nothing we can offer that you'll accept as proof so I'd appreciate it if you gave up the questioning and either put us on a horse for Enar and the Conclave or put us in your cells so we can break out of them and be on our way already."

Lieutenant Tikev raised an eyebrow. "That's very… bold of you."

"Am I wrong?"

Now he chuckled. "Perhaps not. Very well – you'll visit the governor's cells but remember that anything you try will end quite badly for your servant."

"He's worthless to us," Kanis said.

But the lieutenant had already locked eyes with Flir; she'd given away everything he needed to know without opening her mouth. "I doubt that," Tikev replied before gesturing to the door. "So, if you'd like to lead the way, I'll show you to your cells. And not too quickly mind, my men have their orders."

***

Flir walked the ice-crusted road between low-buildings, the setting sun doing little to warm the quiet streets of Whiteport. The echo of waves and gulls were drowned by wind here, this high upon the hill. Yet when they turned into a narrower street the chill eased, soaked up by the stones. Icicles hung from the eaves like frosty dagger blades overhead.

"Not much of a spring, is it?" Kanis said pleasantly.

"Do you really want to talk about the weather?"

"Well, unlike some, I think talking escape details in front of our captors to be in poor taste." Kanis rubbed at his little finger as he walked, something Flir noticed him doing more and more lately. Ever since the Ecsoli woman placed her bone within.

One of their guards grunted. "Shut up, freak."

Flir added her own glare but Kanis only grinned. Damn fool. "Save it, Kanis."

Flickering light appeared on the walls at the street's end, glinting in the windows. A man stepped from a building ahead, heading toward the light. A Fire Market; Flir almost smiled. How long since she'd seen one. She caught the sharp scent of ginger and pepper mingling on reindeer skewers.

Her first taste had been as a child. Visiting Whiteport from her village to the west. Mishalar, what had it been called? She'd been so young, her father's hand like that of a giant and her mother's smile so bright...

Flir frowned; it was as if the loss were brand new once again.

Had returning been a mistake?

A huge bonfire dominated the market square, lined by braziers with echoing flames. The light almost rivalled the setting sun and the warmth it sent out banished the cold as Flir and her guards neared. Men and women were already milling about the stalls, smiles on their faces as they gossiped and haggled over everything from furs and food to imported fire-lemon or medicines, pouches of the ice-plant with their waxed drawstrings easy to spot and familiar, so familiar.

"Pevin would have liked this," she said softly. Seeing as he was barely conscious in the back of some cart, he'd certainly miss it.

Kanis did not answer, preoccupied with his hand. The white and blue robes of an Ice-Priest splashed with orange firelight caught Flir's eye. The man was paying for liquor, triangular pieces of silver in his gloved hands. The tender was replaced with regular rounded coin and then the man slipped into the growing crowds. A new currency?

"Kanis, I just saw an Ice-Priest using strange new coins."

"Conclave introduced it well over a year ago now."

"Why?" she said, glancing back toward the stalls as the market started to fade.

"Something about needing a stronger currency to maintain national identity. I didn't pay much attention."

"Of course." Change wasn't necessarily bad... she shrugged. There were more important things to worry about; chief among them being how to convince the Governor of Whiteport that they were actually envoys and not spies, as Tikev suspected.

The governor's manor was a dark giant against the sky, its walls climbing to an impressive height – doubled since she'd last been to Whiteport. The guards on the gate rushed the lieutenant through and along the broad path between well-tended gardens, the shaped blue-fir looming in lantern-light. Within the building they were escorted through marbled halls to a large reception room where a single man stood before floor-to-ceiling windows, staring into the night sky.

"Lord Mildavir?" The diminutive seneschal approached his master, lowering his voice when he reached the governor, whose name and bearing seemed familiar. Something about the man's close-cut hair, the way he stood with hands clasped behind his back.

"Very well," the governor said after a moment, turning to face the newcomers.

Lieutenant Tikev went to one knee. "My lord, two dilar were found ashore earlier today. They claim to be shipwrecked envoys from King Oseto of Anaskar."

Mildavir frowned, his frog-like face becoming sinister. Recognition was clear in his eyes. "Do they indeed?"

Flir exchanged a glance with Kanis and she reassessed their list of problems. Staying alive was suddenly a much bigger concern than convincing the governor to hear Seto's messages of goodwill – the man who stood before them was one of the surviving cousins of the royal family they'd accidently displaced from the throne all those years past.

'Accidently' to hear Kanis tell it, anyway.

"How delightful to see you both once more," Mildavir said.

6. Flir

Mildavir leant over to whisper something to his seneschal, who dashed off down a corridor, before beaming across at Flir and Kanis. "If you wouldn't mind waiting a moment?"

"For what?" Kanis asked, his tone wary. Flir didn't blame him; what was the governor up to?

The frog licked his lips. "It won't take long."

"I don't remember you being this theatrical," Flir said.

The governor did not respond, he only moved to Lieutenant Tikev, again speaking too softly to be heard. Flir frowned at Kanis, who was glaring at Mildavir. Footsteps echoed along the hall and the seneschal returned, arms laden with an oiled cloth, which he arranged before Flir and Kanis.

"Please stand upon this."

"Why?" Kanis demanded.

Mildavir waved at Tikev and his second. Each held a crossbow, gleaming steel arms raised. Tikev faced Flir and the other man stood across from Kanis. Tikev's jaw was clenched and his subordinate gripped the stock of his weapon so hard that his knuckles were white.

"Time for a little test."

Flir still hadn't taken a step. "Test what, exactly?"

"I'm going to find out if you're truly dilar as you claim."

"Come closer and let me show you, Lord Governor," Kanis said.

Mildavir smiled again, his wide mouth revealing teeth. "Surely you're not afraid? If you are telling the truth we all know you will survive. And someone will shoot you, no matter what you attempt; whether you attack, simply stand still or step onto the cloth as instructed. For incentive, know that your fate is the same no matter what you choose – but if you choose to make a mess on my marble, your servant will also be given the dilar test," Mildavir paused. "Think he'll pass it?"

Flir stepped onto the treated material and glared at the governor. The bastard knew exactly who they were; this was revenge for what happened to the old king; he'd been a very real chance at succession. But if there was a chance it would protect Pevin, she had to take it.

The problem was figuring out how to escape afterwards. And just maybe how to do it after wringing Mildavir's neck first. So much for diplomacy.

Kanis spat but stepped forward. "Let's hope our positions aren't one day reversed."

Mildavir narrowed his eyes but did not retort, instead, he snapped an order to his men. "Shoot at will."

But both hesitated. Did they doubt the stories about dilar? It seemed unlikely. Dilar were rare but she and Kanis were hardly the only two in Renovar.

Kanis nodded to his soldier and Flir looked to Tikev. "No hard feelings."

"What are you waiting for?" Mildavir screeched.

The men fired.

Pain exploded in her shoulder. She dropped to one knee, vision swimming. Warm blood ran down her tunic but she rose without a sound. Tikev's eyes were wide and his crossbow hung from his hands. Poor fellow. Flir checked on Kanis. He'd taken his bolt in the thigh; blood ran down his pant leg – and it looked like he hadn't stumbled. Wonderful. Flir shook her head – he'd probably try to trot out that ridiculous claim that he was stronger all over again. She reached up and snapped the bolt free before raising an eyebrow to Mildavir.

"Satisfied?" Her body was already starting to heal itself; the pain lessening slightly – though only slightly. Agony still coursed through her.

The man was no longer smiling; he'd obviously wanted a better display of pain. "Not even close."

"Then let's see what else you have in store," Kanis returned.

Mildavir snapped his fingers. "Put them in the cells. Kill the other one if they resist."

And that was that.

***

Her cell was typically cold and dark. Straw and a filthy blanket. Stone walls, no window, no bars, just a serious-looking steel door. Nothing that she couldn't break through in time – if it weren't for the drug they'd given her, and the fact that Pevin's life depended on her compliance. If he was still alive.

Until she knew for sure, that meant she couldn't take a risk.

And that was even *if* the lethargy from the drug wore off before... Mishalar! Her bravado and anger had masked an increasingly dire situation. "We're a pair of stubborn fools," she called.

"I'm happy to accept one of those." The stone wall muffled Kanis' reply.

"So what are we going to do about it?"

"You want *me* to come up with an escape plan?"

"Yes, I do."

"While you take a nap or something, I suppose?"

"I hope that's not your plan."

Barely audible muttering followed. She shifted her limbs as best she could where she leant against the chill stone. No brilliant ideas came to mind. If they were to be fed, that would get the door open without drawing attention but where was Pevin? How could she find him while drugged? If Mildavir planned more torture she *might* be able to take him hostage, but would it be enough to prevent Pevin being misused as a bargaining chip? Or Kanis for that matter? Healing quickly wasn't the same as Godhood – if the governor tried, he could likely kill them.

"Flir?" Kanis' voice was weary. "I have nothing. They've given us *sapper* and it's a strong dose, Pevin will die if we try. We're in trouble."

"I know that."

"Unless..." he trailed off.

"No. I'm not gambling with Pevin's life."

"He might be dead already, and then we're finished if we don't try something."

"I said no. We'll have to come up with something else."

"Fine." Kanis fell silent and she joined him.

Time slid by, dark moment after dark moment.

Nothing changed, and no ideas leapt up to stun her with their ingenuity. She stood and tried to pace the three steps in her cell, but her limbs remained slow to respond. Damn the *sapper*.

She sat again. There had to be a way out, a way to find Pevin and escape. How long would the drug take to wear off? It had been too long since she'd been dosed. No-one produced it in Anaskar and so few people had chased her across the ocean when she first left... she blinked heavy lids. "I'm getting drowsy," she said aloud, but Kanis did not reply.

Darkness pressed down around her.

Steel scraped.

Flir jerked awake. Blinding torchlight obscured two figures. She lifted an arm to protect her eyes and again, her limbs were slow to respond; the *sapper* still hadn't worn off.

"Do not fear," a voice said.

"What?"

The first figure crouched before her, features resolving. A young man with a worried expression. Tikev? "What are you doing?" she asked.

"Getting you out of here but we must hurry."

She frowned. "But why?" Fog still clung to her mind. "Mildavir will—"

"This is Aren," Tikev said. "He has agreed to help you."

She focused on the second figure. Aren was a middle-aged man with silvery hair wearing a guard uniform, still handsome, still in good shape if the muscles in his arms were any indication – yet those details became fleeting when she glimpsed a tattoo on his wrist. A snow leopard. Mishalar cult. How did they find her?

Aren was speaking. "When you first discovered Mishalar's blessing, who helped you? Who taught you, Flir?"

"Kanis." Kanis *had* taught her a lot but before him, she'd wandered, confused and angry – an outcast in her homeland, drifting from village to village. Sometimes she was able to convince people she was not only useful, but that her strength was *not* a mark of darkness. And once, after being found and 'protected' by men like Aren, fanatical dilar-worshippers, she'd been trapped for months. There was one within the cult who had explained a few things... like what she could likely heal from and what she wouldn't, but nothing to hint at where Aren was going with his questioning.

"He wasn't one of Her Surrogates?"

"No. But he knew more than me. About our limits, about things I will never do."

"This isn't the Binding," Aren said. "Though there are similarities." He glanced to Tikev. "Signal the others on my word. And remember what I said; don't fight it, despite the fear."

Tikev's jaw was clenched but he gave a nod as he slipped outside.

"What are you talking about?" Flir demanded. The last remnants of sleep and perhaps even the lingering effects of the *sapper* had left her mind, but her limbs were still heavy.

"To help you escape I need to do something and you have to be a part of it."

"How?"

"In the past when the dilar were rightful Custodians, it was possible to... exchange or lend strength, for a time," Aren explained. His eyes locked onto hers. "However, for the one that lends of themselves there is significant risk. They will appear cold, mute – they will not breathe, they will appear dead. While linked to the beneficiary they will stay in such a living stasis but too long and the transfer of strength is permanent."

"And of life?"

"Yes. The Bequeather risks death."

"And you expect me to lend you my strength so you can break me out of here?"

He smiled. "No. I am offering you my strength, dilar."

7. SETO

Seto did his best to hold his breath while still appearing regal.

It escaped him how anyone could refer to the messenger's aviary with its bags of seed and wire cages as anything other than a stinking trap for flying rats. Of course, that was being ungenerous. Lor, The Royal Messenger, kept his aviary clean enough, and some of his birds were certainly more magnificent than pigeons, but the scents the place managed to ferment were simply so... ungodly.

"Here you go, Your Majesty," Lor said, bowing as he handed over the latest missive.

"Wonderful work as ever," Seto replied. He accepted the tiny scroll and started back toward the door and his waiting scribe. "The moment another arrives, Lor. Send word."

"Thank you, sire. Of course." He paused. "Sire, I can send the message itself if you prefer? That might save you the interruption of a personal visit."

Seto glanced back to the fellow, who was showing

some aptitude for diplomacy, and offered a smile. "Very considerate, but I enjoy the climb, Lor."

"Of course." He bowed again.

In the stairwell Seto slipped the scroll, still unread, into an inner pocket of his orange robe. Had he really been so obvious with his distaste? Perhaps the fellow was simply more perceptive than others. The scribe trailed dutifully.

Halfway down, Seto stepped into a small chamber – it had once been a guard room but he'd converted it into a place for one of his scribes, so communication could be achieved more swiftly. More, it was a welcome resting point for his old bones.

Within, Seto went to the window and unrolled the sheepskin, squinting in the brightness, while behind him the sound of the scribe taking his seat was soft. The man was probably dipping a quill into a little pot of ink already, arm no doubt poised over the next scroll.

Wayrn.

His missive was brief:

Negotiation over bones of last Sea God goes poorly. Elders hold out for higher share of as part of restorative demands. Await your word to make final offer.

The final offer; to train the Medah in the use of Greatmasks. An enormous step. Yet if it was the only way to get his hands on more bones then so be it. Anaskar needed more than Argeon for defence. If the Ecsoli returned or if an even greater threat appeared... well, Seto would not be found unprepared again. His city had to survive beyond his own rule, and that meant securing the bones of power – as many as possible.

Not all would be thrilled with what he, Waryn, Holindo and Abrensi, along with Lavinia and Danillo had planned, but that was just another part of a long price that had to be paid.

Seto turned to the scribe, a young fellow with an unruly mop of hair. "Send a response to Wayrn as follows, 'Make the offer. Inform outcome immediately'."

"Yes, sire."

"Tell Lor to be certain – I don't care how many birds it takes."

"Understood."

Seto hesitated, then added, "And the other letters can wait, take some rest. We will finish in the morning." He left the room, starting down the stairs. All else could wait, truly. Danillo was still in the Bloodwood and word from Flir and Kanis wasn't due for some time in any event. Notch, on the other hand... well, there was little chance of hearing from him. And once again, Seto didn't know if he wanted to. It was as if time had turned back, leaving him furious at Notch all over again. It wasn't the way the man had looted the dwindling treasury. No. It was the sheer foolishness of his flight!

Partially, at least, Seto understood why Notch felt he had to try. He'd been so protective of Sofia; she'd become almost a surrogate daughter.

But it was folly. "We need you here."

Sofia was gone. Her sacrifice meant something; she had saved the city, perhaps the whole of the lands. For Notch to throw his own life away on his mad search dishonoured her act, her memory.

Footsteps echoed in the stairwell.

Giovan appeared, his hard face bearing a hint of worry. He had grown a dark beard, possibly to cover the scar on his cheek, a memento from where the Ecsoli had toyed with him. "Sire. Holindo sends word from the Second Tier. More reports from the Vigil of Ecsoli in the streets."

Seto swore. "More of them? Someone is going to feel my boot heel most keenly." Such occurrences had been growing more frequent of late. They made little sense – all the Ecsoli had been interned, of that he was certain. He'd led half a dozen sweeps of the Tiers himself in between rebuilding efforts – often using already captured Ecsoli as bait. If anyone remained, they were acting strangely indeed considering the armistice Seto had made clear throughout the city.

No, it had to be someone else, someone playing in blue cloaks. But to what end?

"We'll catch one soon enough."

"I hope that is true. Have they attacked anyone?"

"No. So far, they simply let themselves be seen before slipping away again."

"Very well. Assign more men."

Giovan hesitated before nodding. "Yes, sire."

"I know we're stretched thin, but I understand the walls are nearing completion and the harbour has been clear for some time; men seeking work have been arriving daily."

"The vetting always takes longer than we hoped."

"Indeed." Seto shook his head. "The farmlands?"

"Barely enough men to work their own fields."

Giovan glanced out one of the narrow, archer's windows. The square below adjoined the wing chosen to be converted into a veritable prison for the housing of remaining Ecsoli, few of who had been released into the city to date. And no doubt that was who the sergeant was thinking of in terms of extra muscle.

"Where would you send them, Giovan? No-one in the city will work alongside them; they will become a double-burden. Send them into the countryside to help in the fields and we can no longer oversee them. Spread them across the lands as couriers or messengers and I face the same problem."

"The ones you put in the quarry, how have they fared?"

"Well enough, thus far – but full freedom hangs over them still, so I do not know how trustworthy they are."

"Perhaps we need to find out, sire?"

"What do you have in mind?"

"Something like a dead man's work-gang – offer them freedom and land if they succeed, rebirth essentially."

"And if they fail?"

"The sword."

He nodded. "And the task you would give them is to hunt those who masquerade as their countrymen?"

"Who better?"

"Possibly." It wasn't a bad idea, if it could be managed properly. Something Seto realised he ought to have considered earlier. And perhaps he hadn't *wanted* to, hadn't wanted to need the invaders for anything. Still, what was pride but a weight on progress? If he could just find a way to be sure of those he sent into the streets. "Send someone to find Abrensi or Lavinia, then return to Holindo. Tell the captain we meet this afternoon."

"It will be done," Giovan said, turning back down the stairs.

Seto followed more slowly, his legs and back beginning to ache already. While he hadn't exactly lied to Lor about enjoying the exercise, it was not so much a pleasure as one cruel necessity among many.

8. AIN

Ain lowered his hand-saw at a cry from the nearby dunes.

He shaded his eyes with his free hand; Majid's sky-blue, Pathfinder robe – an echo of Ain's own – fluttered in the breeze as he waved an arm. Majid called again, but his words were garbled by the rasp, thump and chatter of the excavation site. Dozens of men and women moved in and around the giant, weathered bones of the Sea God, some carrying slabs of bone, others with stretchers full, and yet more were cataloguing, sawing and digging to free the enormous spine from the sand.

Wayrn looked up from his writing, eyes troubled. He no longer wore his dark, acrobat's clothing but a loose white tunic and brown pants; wisely he'd chosen a cooler set of clothing for the desert, which even now sent the sun pummelling down on everyone. "Is something amiss?"

"Let's find out," Ain said as he waved back to Majid.

But he did not leave at once. Instead, he took a moment to kneel and place his palm against the sand.

The paths were no more audible than usual. They thrummed through his body, the echo of countless feet passing. Hooves, boots or otherwise, Ain felt them all. And here, so close to the Sea Beast bones, fewer paths were to be found than in the Oasis or the Wasteland, and even less need for a Pathfinder to identify safe trails to water, but people had still been visiting the giant bones for centuries.

What Ain could *not* sense, was the sharp pulsing from darklings. Since Vinezi and Marinus' defeat, darkling sightings had become rare. Since he could not sense them now, it seemed unlikely that Majid had seen any. So what was amiss?

Ain started up the sloping dune.

Visitors perhaps? Or the Western Clan? Few stayed in Cloud Oasis after the wave of darklings had been broken. Maybe it was Schan, if the Snake Clan was heading to the Cloud? Only months but already it seemed too long since he'd spoken with his friend. "Trouble?" Ain asked once Majid was within earshot.

"I can't say – but someone approaches," Majid replied as he helped Ain up the final few steps. Ain turned to offer his own hand to Wayrn.

"That's a significant cloud," Wayrn said. "But it doesn't look like a sand storm."

"It cannot be darklings." Majid frowned across the dune. "We'd feel it. What of your king's last message, Wayrn?"

"He did not mention sending anyone."

Ain narrowed his eyes. "They're drawing down from the north – could it be mountain men from the Vakim Ranges?"

Majid frowned. "Possibly, but why? They number few

and have not traded for two generations now."

The cloud slowly drew closer, swirling sands concealing those within. Its speed was not swift, but the progress remained steady. The sand would be upon them soon enough – the sand and whatever it concealed.

And the wind and sand were doing a fine job of achieving exactly that.

"It's no storm – it's too... controlled," Majid said, worry growing in his voice.

Majid was right.

Ain spun. "Sound the alarm! Arm yourselves," he called down to the men and women below. Did they hear him? Wayrn was already halfway down the dune; he'd carry the message. Ain dropped to one knee, driving a hand into the sand once. Majid did the same. "I *still* don't feel any darklings."

"What if we're overreacting?" Majid asked after a nod.

"Then we can laugh about it afterwards."

"Sands, why can't we feel whatever's inside?"

Ain stood, drawing the short blade. Jedda had taught him enough that he wouldn't be defenceless – but against a trained foe, he'd be in trouble, Pathfinder or no. Not that his Pathfinder magic was worth anything here, or so it seemed. Majid was bigger and stronger, better with steel but that didn't mean his friend could stay right beside Ain if they were about to be attacked.

"An ally would have announced themselves before now," Majid said as he ripped his hand axes free.

"We stop them here, whoever they are," Ain said. He had to – not just for his people, but for Silaj and Jali. Having a young family to protect... it changed everything, as he had vaguely suspected it would, during their time apart.

But actually holding his infant son brought a fierceness rushing up within him – it almost engulfed the tenderness he felt when Jali had tried to grip his smallest finger the first time. He held on to that memory now.

Sands, no-one will take them.

A small crowd began to form at the top of the dune. Ain glanced at the nearest woman; she held a bow and arrow ready. Beside her in turn was a large man, Kavi, who Ain had last seen carrying a huge hunk of bone by himself. Now he gripped a large, two-handed blade.

"What lies within?" someone else asked.

"Darklings?" Another voice.

"We don't believe so," Ain said. "But we're going to stop it. The Sands will preserve us."

The strange sand storm seemed to rush up the dune. Ain raised his face coverings and readied his sword.

The sun dimmed.

A rasping filled the air, but its source could hardly be the swirling sand. Majid stood right beside him – yet the other Pathfinder was invisible. At Ain's other side the woman with the bow was gone too. But the storm was empty... no, wait. Shapes were appearing before him. They stood tall and broad shouldered. Each could have come from one of the clans. Perhaps a dozen in total, the figures strode with purpose, but their faces were blank. They wore rags and carried no weapons but seemed unperturbed by the fact and the wind and stinging sand did not trouble them either.

"Halt," Ain cried.

The nearest only walked on.

"Who are you? What do you seek?"

Still no answer. The next man was nearly upon him and Ain raised his weapon, only to have his hands falter.

A deep, deep gash crossed the stranger's entire stomach, blackened blood blending with dark skin at the edges. A corpse? What foul magic drove them forward?

The man raised his arm. Ain ducked, but too slow – a solid blow brushed him aside. He tumbled across the sand, finding his feet, only for something to crash into him from behind. Another walker; Ain caught the same empty expression on the face – only this close the dull green of the eyes was clear.

Plant-like eyes. No pupils, nothing but a sick-looking cactus-colour.

Ain gasped.

Not eyes at all – it was a living cactus plant that pushed through the eye-sockets from within!

Ain swung his sword.

It was no more than a reflex of shock, but his blade still cleaved the walker's forearm. Hand and wrist hit the sand, soundless beneath the rasping in the wind. No blood burst from the stump. The man stumbled but resumed his walk, ignoring the wound. Ain swung at the abomination's back.

His weapon lodged between the shoulder blades.

The walker did not falter, simply striding on, tearing the blade from Ain's grip.

"Sands take you," Ain cried, diving after the thing. He hit at the waist, dragging the corpse down. His head smacked against the walker's back. Blood welled in his mouth – he'd bitten his lip.

Ain grasped for his sword, wrenching it free before the creature could find its feet. He swung down, aiming at the neck. Steel met dead flesh and the head rolled free. Like the hand, no blood followed. The body was still. Ain knelt beside the head, nudging it face-up with his blade.

Sand peppered the man's face but cactus filled the eye-sockets, bulging forth. Ain shuddered. The plant had even taken the place of the man's tongue, green visible in the gaping mouth. A tendril curled from an ear.

Who or what could create such creatures? The dark magic of Vinezi and Marinus was gone – and so were the darklings. Wasn't that enough? If there was a connection, or if something new had risen, then the Cloud had to be warned.

Ain stood – and something caught him from behind. Strong arms wrapped around his throat, squeezing. He dropped his blade, clawing at his captor. Yet whoever held him did not react. Ain's fingernails tore into skin but it had no effect, bright white lights were sweeping in.

His chest tightened.

Darkness.

9. NOTCH

The taste of brine was heavy on the spray where it slashed at Notch.

He sat near the masthead, waves breaking across the *Hawk*'s prow, sun beating down from the spotless sky. The silver bracers taken from the catacombs were still hidden beneath his sleeves, but he had not seen the white witch since – nor had he felt any sense of her in the bite marks in his neck. The bites were only starting to fade now, four weeks after Melosi had set sail once more for the Land of the Sun's shoreline – the final leg of their journey. There, according to Alosus, they'd reach the crown of Ecsoli, the King City Paradisum. The way he'd said it left no doubt in Notch's mind what the Tonitora thought of the idea that the place was any sort of paradise.

Before then, Notch had hoped to unlock the secret of the bracers. The carven lion revealed no clues. A clear symbol for strength, but what else did it represent? The warning from the witch rang in his memory. *Be careful with those bracers; they might change you in ways you find alarming.*

But what did that mean? They had not changed him so far, had not granted strength, speed, or any manner of mastery. They simply existed.

A cry echoed down from the lookout.

The man in the crow's nest pointed west, his arm like a black stick against the sky, sun beaming behind him.

Still distant, an eruption of water speared into the sky. The spout shimmered beneath the sun as it disintegrated. It was difficult to judge accurately, but the height suggested a mighty explosion... nothing any whale might create. Notch spun to the bridge. The helmsman was already shouting for Melosi, and Gappilo stood at the rail, his own spyglass raised.

"It shimmers more than it should for water alone."

Notch joined him as other members of the crew appeared.

By the time Melosi and Alosus arrived, the sea had settled but the glittering waves were rolling, spreading outward. But before the disturbance hit the ship, another shining geyser surged into the sky. It was close enough to rock the *Hawk*. Notch gripped the rail with a shudder. Something dark and *immense* had passed below – he couldn't explain *how* he was sure beyond a glimpse in the water, it was more a sensation. And it chilled him; reminded him just how insignificant he really was.

"Eyes above," Melosi shouted.

Glittering shapes were hurtling down from the spout.

Notch leapt back. Something bright smashed into the rail. He crouched beside two water barrels as someone cried out in pain. Shining objects continued to fall, even as the spout died away. One piece tore a hole in the mainsail, another smashed through the decking – but far more were bouncing from the decks like hail stones. Yet others appeared to flutter down – glimmering, rainbow-coloured shards.

One bounced across the decks to settle nearby. He scooped it up.

A scale.

Hand-sized and a finger's-width in thickness, the surface was hard, like iron but with a pearlescent sheen. More like an opal. Beautiful. But how, and from where? Notch stood. Other crew members were nursing bruises or climbing the rigging to examine holes and tears in the sails. Yet more, including Melosi, examined the scales themselves.

After a moment, the captain's head snapped up. "Collect each and every scale."

"Do you think they're valuable, Cap?" Gappilo asked, hefting one of the larger pieces.

"I mean to find out," Melosi said with a grin. "Repairs next. I want to know what damage we've taken. And someone wake Tersi. Send him to my quarters."

Notch joined Melosi at the bridge. The captain was staring across the waves, toward the direction the vast shadow had disappeared. "Did you feel it?"

The man frowned. "Feel what?"

"You did. Something colossal... passed beneath us – it was probably responsible for the scales bursting into the air."

He sighed. "I fear another Sea Beast. But not a word of it to my men, understood?"

"If they're already thinking so, they're not speaking of it."

"Aye," he said. "And that's just how I'd prefer it, so we'll finish this in my cabin."

Notch set off, waking Alosus and gathering in the

captain's cabin with Tersi and Gappilo. They crowded around the captain's table, charts burying the surface, weights and tiny skulls holding them down. Marlosi lifted a chart only thinly drawn.

"By the calculations we've made from information Alosus has given us, I estimate we'll reach the shores of Ecsoli by sunset. There we will fly a peaceable flag and await whatever response follows."

Alosus nodded. "I will help prepare the message."

"Assuming we have a chance to share it," Gappilo said. "A land full of Greatmasks... I still worry about that."

"I believe that is a small risk," Alosus said. "We will draw much curiosity and that will stay the hand of even the most rash of Ecsoli."

"And the shadow in the sea?" Notch asked.

Marlosi looked to Tersi, who shrugged and spread his hands. "I will be ready to sing if it returns... and if it truly is another Sea Beast, of which I cannot be certain, I will be ready for that too."

"That's good enough for me," Notch said. If Tersi was as powerful as his father he'd be able to soothe any Sea Beast with his songs.

"So there's little else to do but rest now," Marlosi said. "I want you each alert when we dock. I'd wager this is the greatest risk any of us has taken and I don't want any mistakes. Understood?"

Notch returned to his cabin and lay across his hammock, ignoring the clink of empty glass against glass in his pack, and closed his eyes.

When he woke, it was to the sound of feet thumping across boards.

Trouble? He rose and left, checking on Alosus, finding the man's own large hammock empty. Notch paused.

There was no shouting or cries of alarm. Had they reached Paradisum already? "Another step closer, Sofia." He left the cabin and climbed the ladder, emerging into cool evening air. Orange light dusted the boards of the *Hawk* and once more, hushed murmuring came from men lining the rail.

This time they stared across at Paradisum.

Notch joined Alosus.

The King City was a nation unto itself. Glittering walls stretched along a shoreline that had to have been five times that of Anaskar. And the walls themselves, some manner of precious stone caught the light and set a soft orange flame running along them.

A crowd of masts and sails filled the harbour – again, far, far larger than home, but it wasn't the maze of ships that kept him speechless but the way the city kept rising... thousands upon thousands of people had to live within. More. Tens of thousands even.

And atop it all, what he took to be the palace – a place that seemed to sneer down on the rest of the city. An enormous lion's maw admitted entry and domed rooms cascaded down in a mane on either side of the entry. Giant windows made for blazing eyes of pure white light and above the eyes sat what appeared to be a vast viewing platform, resting at the peak of the mane.

"It is enormous," Notch said. "And even that seems like a small word."

"Yes. A world of the deepest corruption and parades of despair," Alosus replied.

He glanced up to the big man. "No need to make it sound so good."

A wry smile. "Very well, Notch. Let me say this then, from the moment we dock we will be very much alone in

a nest full of vipers."
  "That's not much better."
  He nodded.

10. NIA

Nia knelt beside the body.

The warm scent of pollen and the sharp chatter of waxwings filled the forest clearing, sunlight falling freely across the ragged collection of bones and blackened cloth. There was no skin or flesh to speak of, merely the gaunt suggestion of the former – a murky green, an ancient rot. Hanging around the neck was an ivory carving shaped as an arrow-head.

She did not remove her glove to reach for it, to be sure, for she did not need to – yet a sigh still escaped.

"Then it's true?" Lord Protector Danillo stood behind her in his red Mascare robes, his voice echoing from behind the Greatmask Argeon. His presence was stern, even forceful and it seemed to her that such qualities were innate to the man and only amplified by his mask of power. He was taller than she remembered which was saying almost nothing, since her memory was still a thing of patchwork even now, months after her recovery. But Father had expected as much, warned her it might be so. Yet sometimes, a mere moment before her eyes registered Danillo, an image of him as somewhat shorter appeared, only to flicker away. It happened with other people, other places too.

She stood. "Yes. The skeleton bears an ivory arrow-head, just like in the old stories."

"Not stories, Nia. Both our peoples died to stop the Ulag Clan."

"Of course." She shrugged. "But this is no new Ulag; it has obviously been dead for centuries."

Argeon glowed, a flicker of blue in the dark eye-sockets. "Preserved in the marsh beyond the ruins, perhaps. And so the question is, how did it come to be here?"

"A twisted idea of a joke?" she asked. But it didn't seem likely.

Danillo shook his head. "No. This... thing pulled itself from the grave."

Nia nudged it with the toe of her boot. "This sorry heap of bones?"

"With help. I fear you do not recall the darklings, they were most active after you and Notch defeated Efran but before the Oyn-Dir restored you."

"I see." Notch. The name was familiar, yet no face came to mind, no memories attached to the name when she heard it – and she'd heard so many speak of Notch since awakening in the cold stone of Father's cavern. He'd saved her yet Notch had become another missing piece of her memory, so little remained of the time immediately before and around her supposed defence of her people... it was past time for them to return.

Danillo continued, explaining the darklings. "Though this is a little different, since it's not so much reconstitution as whole reanimation. Who saw it walking?"

"Silvya. She's part of the group helping tend the groves.

She said it was coming from the direction of the river."

"I'd like to speak with her."

"Of course." Nia led him away, circling the amber groves, beautiful and deadly as they were, and to low stone buildings with their leaf-stained rooves that had once housed Efran's Sap-Born. Yet of all those that had given themselves over to the strange magic, few remained. Father had one prisoner, a sullen young man who was being kept for study. The others had long-since fled, though trackers were hunting them throughout the forests.

Inside the common room, Nia searched the tables for Silvya – finding her by her bobbed hair and cheery laughter. "Let me introduce you," Nia said, waving to the younger woman.

"Can you tell me exactly what you saw?" Danillo asked after the introductions were done.

Her cheerful expression faded. "I can. It was nearing dusk and I was gathering my tools when I saw the figure approaching from the south. It wasn't moving very easily. I called out, in case they needed help but when I came close enough to see how thin it was..."

"And it collapsed by itself?"

"Yes. Like whatever dark force driving it had been spent."

"And you saw no-one else?"

She shook her head. "No, but we followed its trail far enough to guess it came from the Wilds."

"Its trail?" Danillo asked.

"Not footprints, more... pieces of itself."

He nodded. "And at the edge of the Wilds?"

"That's why I asked Lady Nia to send for someone from the North," Silvya said.

"The bone altar I mentioned," Nia added.

Silvya shuddered. "Everybody is trying not to talk about it. They think the Ulag are going to return."

"In such a remarkably unlikely event, you would have the might of Anaskar on your side," The Lord Protector said. "Thank you for talking to me." To Nia he said, "If there is enough daylight, I would like to see the altar before I depart."

"If we travel swiftly. The horses are nearby," she said.

Outside, they took mounts from the stable then started along the southern path, bypassing the trail that led to the site of the old slave buildings, which had been burnt to the ground, and started toward the Sarough River. Dappled light fell across the path and the loam muffled the hooves.

At the silver banks of the river Nia turned them south along an overgrown trail. Once, it had been a highway to the coast farther south, or the ruins of the watchtowers in the south east – but now it was a path of buried stone, shoulder-high thistles with vibrant purple flowers. Clumps of spiky weed and ancient fences overcome by age and rampaging blackberries that stood like deep green walls – a lost land.

For after the Ulag were defeated, centuries past, all trace of their settlements were destroyed – though *all* was an exaggeration. She'd travelled the Wilds in the past, searching for something she couldn't remember anymore, but she did recall coming across the occasional weapon and once, a bone horn. Deeper into the wilds, where the trees were twisted and black with leaves of crimson and brown, there lurked hints of homes. A wall and a half here, an arch there, sometimes a crumbling chimney slowly being dragged to the ground by vines and ivy.

Nothing she'd cared to examine in any detail.

"What do you think is happening?" Nia asked when they stopped to eat some brown bread and cheese.

Danillo replaced the lid of his flask. "I do not know for certain. Argeon shares ideas, fragments with me. There is something stirring – or something that has been stirring for some time. Does it bring these unnatural things up with it, like the Ulag corpse or the darklings? Before, it was easy to consider Vinezi and Marinus as driving most of the events but every day after that struggle, I have monitored the fragments Argeon gives me and I suspect something greater at play. Something that can conceal its activities even from Argeon."

"You make it sound like some fell God."

"Perhaps. There is much unknown about our own past, our own world."

"But someone human made the altar."

"Indeed."

"Good, because I don't want to have to protect my people from a God."

"An unenviable task," he said, and it seemed he was smiling by the tone of his voice.

"There's still too many unanswered questions," she said. "Why only one Ulag?"

"Agreed. And why send it north, only for it to collapse in the grove – presumably before it achieved its purpose?"

Nia glanced around at the uneven earth. The ground was littered with dips and mounds, small hills between the stands of trees and rolling patches of blackberry and occasional pools of stagnant water. It could have been a verdant plain. "Many of the mounds are burial mounds. Half of the Wilds are a grave for your people and mine. And the Ulag." She paused. "Which is only to say that whoever sent the corpse had no shortage of bodies to choose from."

They rode on but did not have to travel too much further to reach the altar site. A hill rose up beside the road, a cleft around the back led inside to darkness.

"Easy enough to find," Danillo said as he dismounted. "Even without a trail – though I suppose few come here anymore."

"We felt the same. Father wonders if it isn't too easy?"

"A prudent concern," Danillo said. "But I sense no danger – no bones of any living creature that would do us harm nearby. If it is a trap to lure us in, it is not an obvious one. Perhaps it is, rather, an opening gambit. Something to get your attention – or, something to create a more potent adversary than any with sword or bow."

"Such as?"

"Fear," he said. "It had not taken hold in the grove, but you heard Silvya mention that people are already talking about it. Lend too much credence to a wild fancy and it takes on its own power."

"The Ulag are not coming back," Nia said, her voice firm. If her recent memories were merely sketches or absent altogether, there was nothing wrong with her memories of horrific stories told of the Ulag – the worst being the claim that the raiders stole children to cook within giant cauldrons in their ceaseless ships.

"A truth I hope to reassure everyone of when we return," he said as he pulled a lantern from his saddlebags. He lit it and led the way into the barrow.

The scent of earth lay strong within, a welcome scent; Nia breathed in deep as she stooped before entering a large, open cave. Danillo lifted the lantern and light spread around the earthen walls, tendrils of root systems hanging down like pale fingers. Beneath, the bone altar waited; yellowed with age and smeared with dried mud.

It was a complex creation. The base had been set in a triangle; it looked to be made of human thigh bones and other large pieces. It rose up in tiers with successively shorter pieces, until at the top, no higher than Nia's chest, stood a headpiece: a blossoming rose of bone.

Knuckles and other small pieces that looked to have been carved from larger parts were connected in an intricate pattern to create the rose. It was almost as large as a head and its petals were a cleaner white than elsewhere.

Some bore spidery runes, though none she recognised.

When she'd first seen it, Nia had to admit it was the work of a master craftsman, despite its morbid nature.

The altar was soon touched with a faint blue light – Argeon was glowing.

"Is something wrong?" Nia asked.

"Yes," he said. "This is not something that anyone living in these lands could make."

"Do you mean from across the sea? The invaders? Father told me they were your ancestors."

"There is every chance it is the Ecsoli, yes."

"But that isn't all that troubles you?"

The glow faded, leaving only the regular light of the lantern. "No. I am also troubled by the purpose of this altar and by the fact that whoever made it is apparently so confident that they have not bothered to protect it. They think perhaps no-one in this land can fathom it."

"What does it do – does it drive the corpses?"

"No. It is used for summoning."

Nia took a step back, only half conscious of the movement. "Summoning what exactly? What is worse than the living dead?"

"I do not know," he said. "I pray we do not have to find out."

11. NIA

"Father?" Nia knocked on the polished wooden door to her father's rooms but received no answer. The setting sun sent orange light streaming through the dozens of windows in the hallway. They were all kinds of shapes; glass fitted where knots and irregularities in the wood had been removed. She rose to her toes to look through one of the larger windows and into the garden.

There he was, tending to the young cherry trees in their stone pots. She tapped on the glass, smiling down on him.

He glanced up and returned her smile when he saw her. "The door is open."

She went inside, crossing the antechamber with its tranquil dryad fountain and met him in the garden. His yellow robes were dirty at the knees; he'd been kneeling in the garden beds again.

"I am glad to see you returned safely, Nia."

"Don't fuss, Father," she said, but she kissed his cheek. "Lord Protector Danillo sends his apologies. He has already gone to the travel-stone; he suspects Ecsoli involvement."

The Oyn-Dir's expression lost some of its cheer. "He is quite worried then."

"He said he'd send a force to help us protect the altar – he wants to dismantle it but needs to study something in the Anaskar library."

"Did you provide him with a sketch at least?"

"No. Danillo said the Greatmask can remember it clearly."

"Is it safe to leave unattended?"

"We are watching it."

"Ah." He retrieved his watering can and finished the final cherry tree, its deep green leaves tinted by the sunset. He reached out to touch them. "Is it a conceit for me to have such a garden in the middle of our already beautiful woods? To prune and arrange, to change what is natural?"

Nia sighed. "Father, I don't think we should be talking about your garden right now."

"But I am talking about the bones, dear."

"Are you?"

"Whoever is subverting the natural way of the world by making that altar is guilty of the same transgression: they want to remake their surroundings in a way that they find pleasing."

"Then how does that help us find out who is behind it? I refuse to accept the return of the Ulag – in any form."

"Of course, daughter. It may not help; I have been searching the very earth for answers and I taste nothing but... mist. A prescient mist at that, it anticipates my searching and moves to block me, no matter the direction I attempt."

A shiver crossed her body. Things that were outside

Father's ability to see were rare. Such things were always powerful creatures or events. Upheaval usually followed. Danillo's mention of a fell God echoed in her mind.

"Nia, there is one thing that I have gleaned which I might be able to add to the Lord Protector's quest for knowledge."

"I can contact him via the bone charm he left."

"That is well. The rose is more important than it seems."

"That's all?"

He smiled. "Yes. Who is in charge of watching the altar?"

"Pannoc. He volunteered. A dozen warriors support him."

"Good." Her father shifted to a bed of soft pink daisies. "I've felt Gedarow weakening of late. Perhaps you could visit him again."

"Again?" If there was one person she did not want to see ever again, it was the prisoner.

"It has been days. You will win him over where others have failed."

She folded her arms. "I have my doubts, Father."

"Nevertheless, it is my wish."

"Then I'll get it over and done with. Am I fishing for the usual information?"

He nodded.

"I'll report back soon then." She left the garden and her father's dwelling, into the loam-covered trails between homes and trees. The red-tipped leaves were darkening in the falling light, but she found herself in the prison before full dark.

Inside the stone building she was met by the jailor, a burly fellow with a soft voice. "Come to visit him again,

My Lady?"

"Yes." She tried to keep the distaste from her voice, in case Gedarow was listening.

The jailor, whose name she still could not recall, produced a key and moved to the first cell, peering within. "He's still groggy from the dose we gave him at lunch."

"I'll be fine," Nia said. "He likes me, remember?"

"Right." He unlocked the door, then closed it behind her but did not lock it. If it weren't for the drugs, the jailor would have done so but after intensive study, her father and his Herbalists had found something that prevented the Sap-Born from using his power.

Not that he was so strong as Efran had supposedly been, able to turn his very surroundings to amber, but Gedarow was still dangerous.

The young man lay on his cot, a thick blanket covering him. A plain-faced, serious fellow prone to talk, he was quiet now. Sweat covered his furrowed brow – a side effect to the danfel herb. Yet sympathy was hard to muster, after what the Sap-Born did to the forest. That much she had seen; she didn't need memories for that. "Gedarow?"

His eyes fluttered but he did not lift his torso. "My Lady?"

She sat on the small stool. "Would you like to talk?"

"I'd like that." He turned his head, smiling when his eyes focused. "How is the grove? Is it still being tended to? I feel it, I think. It seems well."

"It is," she said. Best to move on from that subject or she'd lose her calm. "Have you thought more about what my father asked?"

He chuckled. "Betray my fellows? No, I haven't thought about it. But may I ask you a question?"

"Yes."

"Is that the only reason you come to visit me? You are not like the others."

Nia hesitated. If Father was right and the man was weakening, was it worth taking a risk? "Gedarow, you strike me as someone who appreciates honesty."

He nodded.

"Then let me say that nothing comes before protecting my people."

"Ah." The hope he had obviously been fighting to hide died in his amber eyes.

"But I admit to finding you interesting." And it was not a lie; she *did* want to learn more about him. Perhaps it was due to a familiarity, something lingered – he was connected to her past somehow. The distant past, not part of her recent blank spaces. "I understand your devotion to your comrades. You have borne our experiments with surprising grace."

"Thank you, My Lady. That is both far less and much more than I expected to hear."

She almost smiled. "You remain optimistic."

"Oh, I know there is no future... that how I feel is pointless, truly. But I didn't want you to hate me. I don't think I could bear that."

"And dramatic," she said, but she lifted his water flask and handed it to him. He was correct, of course, there would never be anything between them, between enemies, but she couldn't find the strength to hate him anymore – not now that she'd started to understand him a little better. And wasn't that the chief source of her reluctance to visit? It was painful to see the Sap-Born as human, as Broann like she herself, when it was so much easier to see them as enemies, evil men and women who had poisoned themselves in a quest for power.

And no doubt Father had known all of that, and pushed her for that very reason.

She leant closer. "Why, Gedarow?"

"My Lady?"

"Why do this to yourself? Did you really believe in Efran's vision?"

He looked to the roof of his cell. "I used to know the answer to that... I am weary, more than I have ever been. Each day is a new struggle with pain and fear. And disappointment."

"That he failed?"

"No." He swallowed. "That no-one has come for me. As far as I know, there hasn't even been a failed attempt to free or even find me."

Nia shook her head.

A look of true pain tugged at his features; something deeper than that which the drugs brought about. "I have been refusing to admit that for a long time now. For an entire season, it seems."

And no doubt it would be a season more before the rest of the secrets of the Sap-Born would be uncovered. Gedarow closed his eyes. She stood. "We'll talk again, Gedarow."

"I'd like that, My Lady."

Nia headed back to see her father. The young Sap-Born had revealed little, but he had confirmed something they had long suspected; there *were* still Sap-Born out there, and more, enough to give Gedarow the hope that rescue might be possible.

12. AIN

Ain woke to cool darkness, moonlight crossing the wall. It fell across a figure that sat sleeping in a chair. Dark hair covered part of her face; Silaj. Her chest rose and fell evenly but a frown was still evident on her brow.

How had he... Ain swallowed, wincing at the tenderness in his throat. The sand-walkers. He'd been saved, but by who? Were Majid and Wayrn and the others safe? At least the Cloud seemed well enough, considering that he was returned and resting. But he had to know. Ain straightened with a soft groan. The door wasn't too far – even if his body seemed stubbornly unwilling to cooperate with any speed.

"That's far enough, Ain."

Silaj was sitting up, smiling at him. There was a fading fear in her gaze too, but by the time she'd lit a candle, it was gone.

He smiled back. "You should be resting in a proper bed, not sleeping hunched up in a chair."

She stood and leant in to kiss him. "I'm not the one who was nearly killed, you fool."

"How is our son?"

"Sleeping – I hope. Mother has him."

He sighed. "Then the Cloud is safe for now?"

She pulled the chair closer and took his hand. "Yes. The things did not come so far – they took all the bone and left. Majid thinks that was their target all long. Wayrn agrees."

"But..." What would such a thing do to the fragile peace between nations? So much negotiation was built upon the bones and their future use. He shook his head – more immediate concerns existed. "Was anyone else hurt?"

Silaj nodded. "Yes. Broken bones and other wounds. But no-one died this time."

"This time?"

"So everyone thinks. I suppose they're right. We have some bone here, after all."

"Then we have to—"

She raised a hand as she climbed onto the bed, sitting on his legs. "None of that 'Ain, Hero of the Cloud,' business tonight. Just Ain, please. You need to rest." She traced her fingertips across his throat, her frown returning.

"Is it bad?" he asked.

"The bruising is already dark. Majid thinks the Walkers only choked you and the others long enough to stop you. Then they took the bones. If the bones weren't what they wanted, he thinks you'd all be dead."

Ain leant back against the soft pillow. Maybe Majid was right. And troubling as it was that such things were not traceable via the paths, at least they could be cut down. But the thought of their return... surely the clans could turn them back. "How many were there?"

"I don't know, no-one said." She shrugged. "Or if they did, my mind was elsewhere."

"And where is it now?"

"On tomorrow, when it should be here with you, in this room," she said.

"Tomorrow?"

"I was foolish enough to think that after everything you went through, after everything that happened back here, after the darklings were defeated, that we'd have a lasting peace." She looked to the dark beyond the window. "I want a different world for our son."

"As do I." Ain reached up to cup her cheek. How closely her words mirrored his own thoughts. "Whatever follows, we are together."

"I know." She gripped his hand then placed it back on the bed. "Now go on, back to sleep."

"Only if you join me," he said.

She slipped beneath the blankets and he drew her close.

***

The council stood around the body.

Ain knelt in the shade cast by the group; Majid and Elder Raila waited beside him. Wayrn, Jedda and others stood across from them, joined by Palan or Wajan of the Western Clan – Ain still couldn't keep the twins straight. But each face was troubled, and with good cause.

"Sands, it's everywhere," Ain said, as he wiped a sheen of sweat from his brow. During the sandstorm and the attack, he hadn't had a chance to really see the corpse-like walkers. But now it was clear once more that the

Clans were facing a powerful magic indeed.

The headless torso had been sliced open, along with the limbs, to reveal green cactus woven throughout the entire body. In many places, it had taken the place – and possibly the role – of muscle and bone.

"We believe the plant reinvigorates the dead," Majid explained. "You remember their strength? It was almost casual."

"Blows did not deter them."

"But what gives the cactus such power?" Wayrn asked.

"And where do the dead come from?" Palan or Wajam added. "This man looks almost preserved... yet he probably died fighting the darklings. He should be sun-blasted bones by now."

Raila looked to Wayrn. "Do you think he will agree?"

"I do. But time will be the factor."

Ain stood. "King Oseto?"

"Yes," Wayrn said. "I sent word requesting aid – and not just aid in retrieving the bones, but in defending the Cloud. But we all know any such help is weeks away at best."

More grim expressions. Ain looked east to where the bones had lain. "They came from the north – do we follow them?"

"We've marked their trail – but the sands obliterate it not far beyond the Sea God's grave. There is no guarantee they continued north," she said. "And more – no guarantee we'd survive what we find."

"I know you're not suggesting we simply wait, Raila," Jedda said as he stroked his white beard.

"No. We can either pursue them or attempt to fortify ourselves to protect the remaining bones. I'm open to other possibilities."

"Send them away," Ain said.

Palan – Ain was sure it was him, now – frowned. "What do you mean?"

"If we really want to protect the Cloud then we send the bones of the Sea God away. To the Wards or further to Anaskar perhaps. Maybe Danillo and Greatmask Argeon can stop these creatures – it is clear nothing I or Majid can do as Pathfinders is capable."

Several voices clamoured in protest. Ain simply waited for the objections to end.

Raila folded her arms. "You know as well as I do that isn't an option."

"I'm only thinking of protecting everyone."

"And I must think of the future too, Ain."

He nodded. The bones were the hinge of all negotiations between the Medah and Anaskar. So much of the possible peace between the two nations depended on differing groups in the clans accepting that the bones and the power they offered was more important than returning to their ancestral home. Ain had stood before them dozens of times to argue for staying in the desert – the only home they had known. Wayrn had offered Seto's hospitality to any who wished to settle in the city, but none had taken such an offer of course.

Worse, an entire new clan had splintered away – they called themselves the Gedaki, the new seekers. Led by Fuasa, a wild man, they refused the idea of peace and had disappeared to the south weeks past, where they said they would find a way to reclaim the Medah's rightful home. How many more would join them if the bones were sent away? "Have we considered the Gedaki?"

"Do you really think those fools have the ability to create walkers, lad?" Jedda asked.

"True."

Majid pointed to the corpse. "Whoever created these will be beyond our ability to face alone, an assumption I think we have to make until we know more."

"Agreed," Raila said. "Which means we must take both paths. One group will seek the bones and report back once they are found, and with whatever information they can glean. The rest of us will work on protecting the bones we have."

"I will go," Ain said.

Raila raised a hand to forestall further volunteers. "Let me decide, Ain. And I'll be doing so over a pot of marjoram tea. Go, eat and return after a meal, all of you. And enjoy it too, you'll have much to do soon enough."

13. FLIR

"You must decide, and quickly," Aren said. His silvery hair gleamed in the torchlight. "Tikev has given up everything to sneak me inside, he cannot return to service and he will be hunted from this day on if we fail."

Maybe it was the best chance. But could she trust Aren? She carried no fond memories of the cultists... yet no-one else had arrived to offer escape. The man was about to make himself incredibly vulnerable to her and to Mildavir. Flir gave a short nod. "I want Pevin also."

"He was in a nearby cell. We will be administering medicine he needs at an inn."

"Fine. What's your plan? How do we make the exchange?"

"We link our body rhythms, much like the Binding. But instead of you directing me, I surrender and then you draw from me. You will feel it."

Rather vague. "And after?"

He handed over a pair of pale roots. "Eat these. They will counteract the drug. Once I bequeath you my strength, it will be added to your own. I do not recommend subtlety here – simply charge your way out. Find an inn west of the public bathhouse – the Ocean Wave. You will be given more instructions there."

"Wait – why don't I just carry you out?"

He shook his head. "I'd only slow you down, and you can't afford to waste any strength. The other guards will find me and Tikev, and assume you and Kanis killed us during your escape, leaving no trail back to either of us."

Flir blinked. "But they'll bury you."

"I have done this before. Everything will be fine so long as you return in time."

A mighty risk indeed. "How long?"

"A full day, no longer," he said. "You will be able to feel a thread of me. Now we must begin. Take my hands. Breathe with me."

Flir clasped his hands, which were warm, aligning her fingertips with his wrist so she could feel his pulse. Then she closed her eyes and breathed in and out, calming herself as best she could despite the hum to her own pulse.

"Focus on me," Aren said.

It took longer than she'd expected but their breathing was soon in sync.

"Say as I do," he said. "Temir, tkma hu movan."

"Temir, tkma hu movan." *Surrender, I trust you with my strength.*

She spoke with him, matching the pace and inflection of the simple chant until the words lost meaning and became sounds only.

Warmth bloomed in her hands, spreading up her arms and into her chest. It infused her entire body – a welcome rush of strength and power. The lethargy vanished from her limbs; a new energy simmered.

But Aren's hands had grown cold.

His eyes were still closed, and his body began to slump, even as heat continued to pour forth. "Aren?" Flir found herself supporting him and then the man toppled to the stone floor in his guard uniform. His face had already taken on a deathly pallor and his chest did not rise or fall, his stillness was complete. Was he alive as he'd claimed? If not, she'd just killed him. Flir paused, despite hearing a voice from Kanis' cell, seeking calm as adrenaline surged within her, trying to locate a sense of Aren.

And there, faint, but the whisper of silver. Of firmness. Determination.

Go.

Flir ducked into the flickering torchlight of the corridor. Each step was effortless, every movement one of suppressed power. She could have sprinted back to Anaskar, across the very waves.

No guards in sight, only a stretching row of steel doors for the cells. "Kanis?"

He stood over the prone form of Tikev, eyes a little wide. "I never knew this was possible."

"Nor I. Hurry up." She started for the exit.

Kanis' footfalls followed. "Will it work? Their plan – it's madness, isn't it?"

"Then let's make sure it works."

At the dungeon entrance Flir paused on the final step, listening a moment. No sounds lurked beyond the steel door. Should she exercise just a little caution, despite what Aren suggested? She flexed her shoulder, no sense of the wound from earlier, and truly she was aching to break something.

"Knock it down," Kanis said.

Flir shrugged, then rammed the palm of her hand

into the steel. The door burst from its hinges, crashing into a bright guard room. Shouts followed. Flir leapt after the door. Two men were struggling to draw swords from where they'd entangled themselves in chairs and a table. Playing cards lay scattered across the stones.

She charged, backhanding one man. He flew into the opposite wall, bones shattering. The next she kicked; more bones breaking and a scream that became a gurgle as the fellow's ribcage was crushed behind his breastplate.

Kanis had already dealt with the remaining guard, a fellow she hadn't even seen. A crossbow lay in pieces nearby. "And now?" Kanis asked. "Once we get out of here, how do we find that inn without being followed?"

A window let in soft morning light between narrow bars. She stood on a chair and looked outside – a narrow alley between tall buildings. Good cover before it led to... somewhere. She stepped down. "Help me." Flir faced the wall and lifted her knee up to her chest, and then the other, performing a few stretches. She'd certainly broken through walls before, but this seemed a lot thicker than the last time. Even with Aren's added might, would it work? "Together, right?"

"Good idea." Kanis took a moment to kick out any kinks in his own legs.

Flir counted. "One... two... three!"

Stonework exploded. The very building shook within the dust-cloud – but it worked. Light beyond, and the vague shapes of a wall opposite. Faint cries of alarm rose from somewhere in the building, but she paid them no heed as she leapt over the rubble and into the cold alley.

The stones were slick with ice but she kept her footing as she jogged down the alley and into grounds that seemed not to be aware that spring was passing into summer.

Brown patches of grass were dotted everywhere, and the plants were little better, their branches bearing few leaves. The main buildings of the mansion loomed behind them. Off to the left was what looked to be stables and beyond that, the tops of the gates.

"This way," Flir said. She ran, and it was effortless; she'd be able to run half a day, easy. Kanis joined her, his eyes alert, gaze sweeping the grounds as they thundered toward the exit.

Shouts echoed from behind.

Flir glanced back. Guards were spilling from the alley. One took a knee and lifted his crossbow. She shoved Kanis even as she angled away. "Split."

A bolt whirred through the space they'd occupied.

Ahead, a man burst from the stables, horse brush in hand. When he saw Flir, he dropped the brush and pulled a belt knife. His hands were trembling as Flir bore down on him – he was young, too young to be chasing down fugitives. He spread his arms, as if to stop her, and Flir leapt into the air – clearing him easily. Air rushed over her face and then she was coming down again – she hit the ground running, ignoring his shout of shock. Kanis re-joined her as they bore down on the gate.

"Showing off?"

"Just didn't think I needed to crush a stableboy, is all."

"Growing soft, I see."

"Shut-up."

A paved stone thoroughfare led to the gate, where guards were lining up into formation. Six in all, and four with crossbows – two held long spears. Kanis slid to a halt and grabbed her arm. "Give me some time," he said, then started driving his fist into the stone beneath him.

"How?" Flir checked on the gate. Four crossbow bolts

were about to tear into them.

Kanis was already standing, arm poised to throw. He stepped around Flir and hurled the first piece just as the snap of bolts echoed.

His throw was faster than the crossbows – the hunk of stone tore one man's head clean from his shoulders in a spray of red. Before his body hit the ground, a bolt struck Flir in the shoulder – opposite to her previous wound – the other projectiles narrowly missing. She swore as blood soaked her tunic. She snatched her own piece of broken stone and flung it at the now scrambling line of guards.

Her stone clipped one man's leg, shearing through and severing the limb at the knee. He fell to the ground, voice tearing on a scream.

More crossbows snapped. Kanis grunted. A bolt flew by her leg as she spun. A shaft protruded from Kanis' side but he only ran for the gate. Flir gave chase – her strength in no way diminished, despite the blood and dull pain of her new wound.

Kanis reached the heavy-steel gate first. He swung his fist and blew the door off its hinge without breaking stride. Flir slid through the wreckage and charged after him, glaring at the spots of blood on the stones. It'd make a fine trail on their way to the Ocean Wave if they didn't bind up first, quick healing or no.

But for now, she was happy enough to put a bit of distance between them and Governor Mildavir's men, even as a new sense of foreboding began to fall over her.

Just how powerful had Aren made her with his stunt?

14. FLIR

Ocean Wave Inn was set off a back street, black ice covering the steps leading to its closed door. Walls of dark stone muffled the sound of a flute, a slow melody, lilting like the sea. There would have been words to go with it, a story about a love lost to jealousy and the ocean but while she could have hummed the melody the words escaped her. Too long since she'd been home to hear such a song.

Flir led Kanis up the steps and knocked lightly. A booming followed, and she muttered a curse.

"Closed until noon," came a curt reply.

"Aren sent us," she said.

The sound of a chair scraping over wood followed and the door opened; a short man in a paint-splattered smock appeared. His eyes widened when he saw the blood-covered bandages and the broken-off crossbow bolt in her shoulder. "Come in, quickly."

Inside the inn the scent of paint fumes stung her eyes and nose – it came from the walls and the roof, a pale tone with a hint of blue, almost like ice. But why replicate the image of the most unpleasant part of home?

"Dilar." The man knelt before Flir, then stood to face Kanis. "Dilar." He knelt again.

"That's enough," Flir said with a sigh. More cult members – she'd expected as much but it had been too long since she'd had to deal with their misplaced adulation. At least Aren hadn't bothered with all of that.

He rose. "Yes, dilar."

Kanis rolled his eyes. "Don't ruin it for him, Flir. It makes him happy."

"He'll have to get used to it. What's your name?"

The man smiled. "Gravateka. I assist Aren here at the inn. We have your servant upstairs, dilar. Would you care to see him?"

"He's recovering?"

"Yes. The fever is fading. Shall I show you the way?"

"I can manage."

"Of course, dilar. Up the stairs and first door on the left. We will discuss Aren as soon as I am able." He looked to Kanis. "Dilar?"

"I'm sure Pevin's fine. How about some food – what have you got here, Grav?" Kanis said as he took one of the only seats not covered in cloth.

Flir glared over her shoulder as she started toward the stairs. Damn fool. No good could come of his taking advantage of the poor folk who'd deluded themselves into thinking dilars were truly blessed of Mishalar.

She missed Anaskar.

Flir entered the room at the top of the stairs and found Pevin abed, sleeping. His chest rose and fell in an easy rhythm, and though his hair was dark with old sweat, his skin was no longer hot to the touch. She sat on the chair beside him and exhaled slowly. At least something had gone right. Water and cold broth sat on a nightstand beside the bed.

Flir tapped her foot. Hard to sit still; Aren's energy still hummed in her veins. "Let's hope our luck holds, Pevin."

Before long she left Pevin and joined Kanis at his table.

The flute player was gone but now there were more cultists in the inn. Some sat at other tables, additional folk worked in the kitchen while yet more tidied the room. All cast she and Kanis glances as they worked, several going to one knee the first time they passed. Few seemed inclined to speak to them and she had little to say to Kanis while he ate; meat, potatoes and gravy.

Instead, she watched the cultists.

Some bore the snow-leopard tattoo, small markings on their wrists or for those wearing vests, on their shoulders. Flir had to shake her head at the vests; a silly imitation. Without furs, they'd probably freeze in winter. Though it didn't appear to be much of a summer so far either. The capital would probably be worse.

"Timid, aren't they?" Kanis asked when he finally slid his plate aside.

"Maybe you could Bind them all then."

He folded his arms as he leant back. "I thought you'd gotten over all that by now."

"All of what?"

"The Binding. It's just a part of who we are, another way to stay ahead of bad luck."

She shook her head but did not answer. Grav had approached, a steaming plate of food in hand. "Dilar, it is my honour to serve you."

"And you don't have to do that," she said, as she

accepted the food.

Grav sat near them and spread his hands. "Would I be correct in assuming neither of you possess full knowledge of your heritage?"

Flir pointed her fork at him. "If this is more of that rubbish about being Mishalar's Chosen you can save it, Grav. Just tell us how to restore Aren and Tikev and we'll be on our way."

He raised a hand. "No, dilar. I mean knowledge that we Surrogates have passed down and protected. I am sure, had you met the right Surrogate in the past, you'd be more aware of this."

Kanis nodded. "They do know some things, Flir. How do you think I learnt of the Binding?"

"You said it was some girl you met."

"True. And who do you think told her?"

She gnashed at a piece of meat. "Well, the Surrogates who took me in were not exactly interested in sharing lore. They wanted a weapon."

Grav cleared his throat. "Yes. Well, such... unfortunate times are well-behind us now. You will see, Aren has changed much about the Order."

"He is your leader?" Kanis asked.

"Only after Mishalar."

Kanis waved a hand. "Of course. I will say, it's impressive that he's taken such a risk for us."

"It is a risk we would all take," he said, not a trace of hesitation in his voice.

"Let's get to the point, Grav. Aren told us a little of what's possible. He also said we only have a day. Shouldn't we be preparing to recover him? And Mildavir will have people searching for us, you know."

"We are watching the manor. Rest assured, we will

mark the gravesites and once darkness falls we would welcome your help in rescuing them. As you say, the governor will have people searching so it might be safest to remain inside the Ocean Wave until then."

"Agreed," Kanis said as he stood. "I think I'll go lie down. Can someone wake me when it's time?"

"Of course, dilar," Grav said. "I will show you to your room."

Flir did not follow. Instead, she waved to a young woman in an apron, who dashed over and took her order for spiced wine, which she sipped at with a frown. Her dark mood wasn't just Kanis' old willingness to take advantage of the cult members. Nor was it wholly the changes in her home, or that for now, Seto's mission had to fall by the wayside. It wasn't even the frustration at being captured, or that she was remembered by the wrong people in Whiteport – for that she had expected.

No. It was the undeniable chill that came from what Aren had shown her.

And he was still present, if she focused. That thin, silver thread of determination. Was he even now being placed in a cellar, limbs arranged just so and a shard of granite placed beneath his tongue, to protect him from the Ice-Walker?

It was a thing of evil.

How simple it would be to abuse such power. The Binding was bad enough, but this... Bequeathing was far worse. And, of course, Kanis seemed unperturbed but that was him just being a self-absorbed fool as usual. What he should have asked himself, as Flir finally did now, was just who had Aren been practising on? What other dilar or dilars were involved with Aren's band of cultists?

By the time darkness had fallen Flir was upstairs, pacing her austere room, stretching, trying to keep moving and wear off the extra energy – though it had been fading. There was still more than enough time to retrieve Aren and Tikev, but it seemed there was a limit to just how long she'd benefit from the additional strength of a Bequeather.

When Grav knocked on her door she was ready.

She, Kanis, Grav himself, and two other cultists whose names she hadn't caught, set off into the chill of night, shovels in hand.

"What's our story if Mildavir's men stop us?" Kanis asked. His breath steamed. "Five people walking the streets with shovels at night isn't exactly the stealthiest group, you know?"

"We must not be seen," Grav said. "In fact, if we are – we will surrender and detain the governor's men so you two can escape and finish the task."

"Very well," Kanis said.

Flir strode along at the rear of the group, her gaze flicking from alley mouth to darkened doorway. At intersections with blazing torches she examined the faces of those they passed, but no-one paid them much attention. She watched for the smart uniform of the governor, focused beyond the laughter and sea songs from the taverns as they climbed the hill on the edge of the city, beyond the haggling of the Fire Markets, but there was no tread of booted feet.

Not until the cemetery came into sight.

In a pool of light from ancient braziers, a pair of guards, armed with axes and short swords, were escorting an older woman from the iron gates. Only a few steps from the entry and she collapsed against the low wall, a sob escaping.

Grav had already brought them to a halt beside the last building. Flir fought the tension rising in her body. There was little threat from two guards. They'd be silenced quick enough if needed, but there was no way she was going to go digging through freshly turned earth to drag up a coffin with Tikev's mother nearby – for that was who it had to be. Had the poor woman stayed in the cemetery so long? When had the funeral taken place?

One soldier was tapping a foot as he waited, but the other man took the woman's arm and spoke soft words to her, helping her up. She stumbled on and once they'd left the light and their footfalls faded, Grav started across the street.

A hush now filled the cemetery after the woman's sobbing. Only the sound of their feet on the stone pathways between triangular headstones. Many loomed tall, others stood only knee height. She avoided them all easily enough, since they'd fallen into single file with Grav in the lead. The graves wound around the hill, occasional skeletal trees spreading their net-like branches up to the starry sky.

Another low fence sectioned off the graves for soldiers and despite the cold air, the scent of freshly turned earth led them to new graves. For now, there were no headstones.

"Here. Quickly now," Grav said, hefting his shovel.

Kanis rested a hand on his shoulder. "Let us. We'll tell you if we get tired."

He went to one knee. "Of course, dilar." He motioned to the other men, who took up watch positions.

Flir stopped before the grave on the left – Aren was within, the thread had grown slightly stronger. Doubtless it was the same for Kanis. She drove her shovel into the earth and started digging.

Beside her, Kanis had already made a fair hole and was glancing across at her – if he thought it was a race he was going to be disappointed. She heaved another shovelful to the side. Her strength was holding as she knew it would; even if she'd used everything Aren lent her she was still dilar.

The piles of dirt beside the hole were tall when she hit wood.

"Finally." She dug around the edges before tossing the shovel up and gripping one end of the coffin and heaving. Something slid against the bottom of the wood; Aren. Flir lifted him easily enough, setting one end atop the grave and pushing the coffin free. Then she followed it up and out, checking on Kanis while Grav and the others started on the wooden box with their bars.

"You finished, Kanis?" she asked him over the sounds of splintering wood.

He looked up from his hole, a shrouded figure in his arms. "Of course. Here, catch." He tossed Tikev. She caught him with a curse, then set his body down. Grav's men started working on the shroud and she hauled Kanis free when he reached up.

"That's a person you were throwing around," she snapped.

"Not until we do whatever it is they want," Kanis replied.

"Dilars?" Grav stood nearby. "We are ready – did Aren explain the next step?"

"No," Flir snapped. Then she sighed. "Sorry, Grav. Tell us."

"Simply take their hands. Focus on the thread and

repeat the chant, you will feel the transfer. You will know when to stop."

Flir nodded, then knelt beside Aren's near-corpse, which had been placed on the earth. The men around her were pacing, muttering prayers to Mishalar. Aren's features were pale, tinted blue in the night. Or by the closeness of death. Or both. But the thread remained and when she took his stone-cold hands it was easier to focus on. She evened her breathing, shutting out the chill beneath her knees, any small sounds made by the cultists as they worked on something unseen, and the soft chanting from Kanis.

She started on the words herself. "Temir, tkma hu movan."

When the old words finally merged into naught but sounds she felt a coldness seep into her – but no, coldness was wrong. It was warmth *leaving*. It flowed from her chest, running down her arms and hands, spreading into Aren. His skin was already growing warmer to touch.

The borrowed life continued to flow until he jerked upright with a gasp. His hands convulsed, gripping hers. The warm continued to flow – too much! She pulled back, reclaiming what was not Aren's, and broke his grip. He slumped back to the ground, eyes wide, breathing hard.

"What by Mishalar was that?" she asked him.

But Aren did not answer. His eyes fluttered closed. He was still breathing and his colour, as best she could tell, seemed better. The ritual was a success.

Grav appeared beside her. "You have done well, dilar. He is returned. He needs rest now but by tomorrow he ought to be fully recovered." The fellow gestured to the two other men. "Bring the stretcher."

Flir caught Grav's wrist and he winced.

"Dilar?"

"What was that?" she asked. "When he woke — it was like he was taking more than his own strength back."

Grav nodded; his face sincere beneath the pain. "So it is. That is your signal to stop, the Bequeather is restored."

"You should have warned me." She let go. "Sorry about your hand."

"No, forgive *me*, dilar."

She glanced to Kanis, who was standing nearby, his own expression a little concerned. He was rubbing his little finger again. Flir joined him. "Well, we'll help you get Aren and Tikev back and then I have a few questions for your leader."

15. SETO

Seto gathered his few advisors in a small glade near the old King's Hideaway, seating them around a stone table set with cool wine and chilled figs and grapes, which Abrensi was already shovelling into his mouth. His Storm Singer robe, with its somewhat gaudy golden lightning bolt on the chest, was no less ruffled than usual, but his hair was mostly under control. He had even shaved somewhat recently.

"So, why the little picnic, sire?" he asked. "Afraid of eyes and ears and more ears in the palace walls?"

The king looked back across the lawns to the white walls of the palace and its glittering balconies. "Since Danillo finished his purge, I've given that little thought – any such eyes ought to be friendly now."

"How goes his rebuilding of the Mascare?" Holindo rasped from where he sat. "I didn't get the chance to speak to him before he left." He still wore breastplate and sword and seemed to have half an eye on the surrounding pines – never truly at rest, a good soldier. A cup of his herbal drink to soothe his throat rested before him.

"Well. Vanepa is gathering new recruits to replace those who chose exile."

Abrensi straightened, a look of consternation on his face. "Exile? Am I missing something?"

Seto sighed. "No need to play at being offended, Abrensi. You were undertaking your own recruitment search at the time, as I recall. Danillo felt that having the Mascare holding allegiance to individual Houses was no longer prudent, considering past history. Those that would not renounce their Houses were exiled and new Mascare – men and women from the Second and Lower Tiers –have been undergoing training."

The Storm Singer nodded. "Prudent? Perhaps. The Mascare now swear directly to the Lord Protector – or to you, my king?"

"To me."

"So much power in one man's hands," he said, making a 'tsk, tsk' sound, finishing with a grin.

"We all have burdens to carry," Seto said. "Now, to the business at hand. Reports of false Ecsoli continue. I want to know why and who is behind it all. Giovan suggested we might offer freedom to our own prisoners, in exchange for their help."

"I see," Abrensi said. "And you wish to use them while manpower is short."

"It is an option," Holindo replied. "They will be ideally poised to assist. It does not need to be a large group, especially while the sightings remain non-violent."

"So. Objections?" Seto asked.

Abrensi took a drink, then stood, pacing in and out of the sunlight. "No specific ones, I suppose. Will you be including the Tonitora?"

Holindo shook his head. "Not unless we must."

"I will send someone with your man... Giovan, was it?"

"Who do you have in mind?" Seto asked. He was yet to discuss Abrensi's own search in any detail. "One of your finds from the villages then?"

"Yes. She is but a girl; Fiore. Yet in her I may have found evidence of two possibilities. Either Singing may not simply be hereditary as long thought, or my predecessors tended to... look beyond the noble families for comfort."

Seto leant forward. "Then there may be more – her father or mother?"

"Possibly. Lavinia and Stefano are still searching, but both Fiore's parents succumbed to sickness, some years past," he said. "It was said, however, that her father bore a most commanding voice. He was well-regarded; an influential speaker."

Holindo was frowning. "Hope for more Storm Singers is a good thing, but do we really want to send a child into such danger, Lord Abrensi?"

"She is not precisely a child, twelve or thirteen summers at my guess," he replied. "But I am confident more so, due to other factors – Vinezi being one of them."

Seto raised an eyebrow. "Vinezi?"

"Yes. We discussed it briefly, not long after his most timely passing," Abrensi said. "You were rather preoccupied as I recall, my king, but I noticed Vinezi very rarely touched I or Lavinia, as if he was... conditioned not to do so. Upon investigating this, I learned from Bethana and her fellow captives that in the Land of the Sun, Storm Singers are never to be touched. Violence against them is done under the pain of death. They are sacred," he said with a rather pleased grin.

"And you believe that sending Fiore with Giovan's team will serve as a further hold over their behaviour."

"Yes. I have also taught her the Song of Sleep as a last measure. In fact, I am looking forward to discovering the true extent of her abilities."

Holindo crossed his arms.

Abrensi turned to the soldier. "Is that so different to what you do with your own new recruits? No blade must go untested, surely?"

"True enough," Holindo said. "I will have Giovan watch over her, if King Seto permits it."

"I do," Seto said. "It is a risk, but so is every move we make."

Abrensi had already turned to the trees, expression pensive. "I regret that in all the years before the invasion we never thought to widen the search. Foolish, foolish."

"Times of trouble brew strange miracles," Holindo said heavily.

"Aye."

16. FIORE

Fi looked up to the stern-faced Shield, his breastplate gleaming in the sunlit courtyard, his orange tunic so bright. Not like the dull brown and greys of home, not like the deep blue of Canto's robe. The Priest of Ana always smelt of herbs and his missing tooth made him look a little scary, like a pirate. But he'd been kind, even if he went on and on about Ana's grace and how lucky everyone was to have her watching over them.

"I am Giovan," the soldier said, scratching at his dark beard. "You must be Fiore?"

"Fi. I don't like Fiore."

He grinned. "All right, Beanpole, no problem. Did Lord Abrensi explain what we're doing here?"

She gaped. No-one had called her 'Beanpole' since Father got sick. Somehow, when Giovan said it, it didn't make her angry – unlike the older children in the village. They always laughed, but this Shield was asking her a question and offering answers, something Lord Abrensi hadn't bothered with. "He said something about, ah, helping the kingdom."

He nodded. "That's a start. We're looking for people in blue cloaks – they invaded the city. Did you hear of it in your village?" More soldiers appeared nearby, herding people in chains into the square, though they were apparently being set free.

"Everyone's heard of the invasion," she said. Was the Shield a bit of a fool? Didn't he know how quickly news spread through the villages?

He only smiled at her tone. "Good. Well, we're trying to find some more – or, at least, people who are pretending to be Ecsoli."

Fi gave him a look. "I'm not a child, you know. You can skip to whatever I have to do. Is it about Singing?"

Now Giovan laughed. "Yes. Abrensi told me you know the Song of Sleep?"

"Every word. I've been practising on myself at night. One day, he said it won't work on me when I sing it."

"Well, I need you to use it if I say so."

"On who?"

"If anyone attacks us." He glanced over his shoulder at the smiling men and women who had once been in chains and who were now speaking amongst themselves, the words having a similar feel to the song Abrensi had taught her. "Or if *they* try something."

"You mean... they're Ecsoli?"

"Yes. The ones who surrendered." Now Giovan's tone had turned dark. He didn't like the Ecsoli, she realised. But why would he? The stories spoke of the Ecsoli as murders, all armed with Greatmasks. It was hard to believe, that was for sure, but she'd seen the melted stone on the way in.

"I understand."

"Good. Now, there's only one rule when we're in the

streets. Do as I say, understood? I don't want you getting hurt."

She frowned up at him. "I've been taking care of myself for a long time now."

"Well, you can continue by filling this, then, Beanpole." He tossed a water-flask to her and headed for the Ecsoli, who were now gathering to hear a man in a fancy robe speak – Lord Abrensi. His words filled the courtyard, his voice rich and commanding. It was like hearing Father speak again and she shook her head.

But it wasn't Father; she'd never hear him again.

And she did not understand the words. Not all of them. Just something that sounded like 'freedom'. Lord Abrensi lifted something, a scroll of some sort. Now when he spoke, whispers broke out between the Ecsoli. Some looked hopeful, others as if they didn't believe what they were hearing. But all listened until he stopped speaking.

Then Lord Abrensi pointed to her and spoke again.

Several dozen faces turned upon her.

She took a step back, fumbling with the empty flask. It bounced across the stones and she snatched it up.

"Dearest Fiore, I have just informed our loyal prisoners that you are a Storm Singer like me, and while I certainly adore you in that colour, I must say, do attempt to act the part while you're out there."

Before she could answer he had already turned to motion to the Shield, who were handing out small packs to the Ecsoli. Giovan was one of them, his expression not cheerful. But since Giovan had told her to find water, that's what she'd do. It seemed best to do so before he finished.

She searched the square and found a water barrel

beneath the eaves and jogged to it, dunking the flask. Bubbles rose and burst as she waited, the water cool where she'd submerged her hand. It was nice, especially since the morning was already warm. Sweat had started to form at the small of her back while she'd stood listening to Lord Abrensi.

Giovan barked an order and the group of Shield and Ecsoli headed toward the exit. He waved her over as he neared. "Stay close."

She nearly trod on his heels as they funnelled into a narrow passage. The clatter of footfalls filled the space, which grew darker. So many bodies pressing in around her. Not like the quiet, open air of home. Canto would have told her to stay calm, let Ana surround her, but it was hard when she didn't know what to expect. Exactly *what* were they going to do out there?

The corridor eventually opened onto well-kept lawns, green beneath a beaming sun. If only she could have kicked her shoes off to walk on it barefoot. It looked so soft. And there were tiny white flowers in circular beds too. But Giovan was striding across the lawns, heading for a giant gate. She had to keep up.

More Shield stood guard there but they were already opening the gates when her group arrived. No-one looked happy to see the Ecsoli. But Giovan and his own Shield only rushed them into the cobbled streets of the Second Tier. Here, Giovan paused to order the searchers to split into smaller groups, directing them into different parts of the Tier.

But his words were almost lost – she caught herself gaping.

Entering the city and the palace late at night, clouds covering the moon and few torches lit, did not prepare her for what she saw. The buildings were all so tall, the stones so clean! Many had ornaments on the eaves or in windows, the black tiles gleamed in the sun. Even the people! Did everyone wear bright silk? Just how rich were they? The few times she'd been to the Lower Tier was nothing like up here.

One little girl even had a servant trailing her, carrying a kitten in a woven basket, feeding it pieces of fish.

"We're starting with a nearby inn," Giovan said to the five Ecsoli. The other Shield watched the prisoners, a hand on his sword-hilt. "How well do you follow my words?"

One of the Ecsoli, an older man, shook his head. "Little, Anaskari."

Giovan sighed and switched to the Ecsoli language. When he spoke, there were more nods and he soon waved them into the street, where they started down toward the distant harbour. Fi kept close to Giovan, who was frowning as his eyes roved around the street. It seemed he never stopped.

"What's in the inn?"

"The innkeeper. She saw the supposed Ecsoli. I want her to tell her story to this lot," he gestured with a thumb, "and see if it rings true."

"Do you think she's lying?"

"No. I think the imposter might have given something away in their behaviour."

Fi frowned. "Couldn't you just describe what the innkeeper saw to the Ecsoli while they're still in jail?"

"Yes." He smiled down at her. "But nothing beats actually seeing something for yourself."

"But we won't see what the innkeeper saw, will we?"

"I hope we will get a chance to see something just

like it, Beanpole." He raised a hand before she could ask another question. "Now, let me watch the streets."

The crowds grew as they moved deeper into the Second Tier, their voices louder than every Harvest Day she could remember. People with carts, armfuls of food or parcels, musicians and hawkers, so many sounds. Her head began to ache. When Giovan pointed to the inn, a four-storey building with a shining silver name, she could barely concentrate on the words.

But inside the door, which did not even squeak when Giovan opened it, the noisy street faded enough. Fancy chairs and tables, each set with a candle and bowls of rosemary, all stood empty. A cold fireplace waited beyond the bar. She inhaled deeply while Giovan called for service.

The kitchen door opened and a woman with black hair appeared. She had rosy cheeks and was smiling, but it fell a little when she saw the Ecsoli. It seemed she recognised them, but to Fi, they looked the same as everyone else. They wore similar clothes and maybe their skin was a little darker and *maybe* their hair was too, more so than she'd first thought and cut shorter above the ears but still...

"Welcome back to the Silver Scale, Sergeant."

"Thank you, Rosai." He gestured to the Ecsoli. "These are the men I told you about. Would you tell your story? I will translate, and they may have questions."

She nodded. When she spoke, her voice was not as friendly anymore. "I have seen a man several times over the last two weeks. He is dressed in the blue cloak of the invaders. He usually stands across from the inn and watches. Sometimes he pours powder in a circle before the inn." She paused, letting Giovan catch up. "It is not *acor*," she added. "I had the Alchemisti confirm it."

Even before Giovan finished the Ecsoli were shaking their heads. One man, thin of face, answered.

"What did he say?" Rosai asked.

"That he knows of no Ecsoli ceremony or gesture like the one you describe."

A second Ecsoli spoke and again, Giovan translated. The conversation was slow and Fi only half-listened to the rest; instead she drifted across the floor to the unlit fireplace. Something glittered within – but not fire; a green light. She leant closer... there it was again! A green wisp, flickering from black ember to ember like a lizard across river stones.

Fiore.

She flinched. A voice had whispered in her mind!

Don't be frightened. I'm here to help you.

Fi glanced back at Giovan and the others, still engrossed in their conversation. It didn't seem they'd heard the voice. Was she imagining it? Imagining the green light too?

No. They cannot hear me. Only you.

Was it even safe to answer? She lowered her voice. "Help me how? Who are you?"

Someone who can help with your singing.

"Like Lord Abrensi?"

Yes. Only I know some songs he does not.

Fi frowned at the flickering green as it grew brighter. Singing always took away part of the sadness since Mother and Father died, new songs would be wonderful... Still, it was all a little strange. "But why me?"

Because you have great potential, Fiore. You could be very powerful; you could help many people.

"I do?" It was something Abrensi had already told her,

but it was still a little hard to believe.

Especially coming from a talking green light.

Yes. I can show you. Just stay with me a moment longer. Focus on the light, Fiore. Only then can I truly help you. Don't be afraid.

17. AIN

Jali squirmed in his arms, wailing and wailing.

"Don't fret," Ain said softly, rocking the baby gently. The little fellow was starting to take on, ever so slowly, the features of his mother it seemed. Same dark eyes. He smiled, despite the shouting.

Silaj looked up from where she was frying lamb on the stove. She was adding paprika, the smoky scent filling the room. "Let me take him. You can finish up here," she said as she crossed the room. He handed Jali over and almost immediately the baby stopped crying. Ain sighed as he took up the tongs and turned the meat.

"Don't worry," she said. "He's just fussy."

"I know." Ain glanced out the window. Lately, Jali had become so uneasy in his arms. He couldn't even get the babe to accept milk. Every time his son was upset, nothing Ain tried made a difference – whereas Silaj soothed him nearly every time. It was as if his son couldn't bear to be near his father... was it all the time he'd been away while the babe was still in the womb?

"Try not to look so downcast," Silaj said. "He's still

so young. One day, you'll be the most important thing in his life."

"Mmmm."

She set Jali in his crib then wrapped her arms around Ain, resting her cheek against his back. "Trust me."

"I do." Even to his own ears, his voice sounded flat.

She squeezed him. "Is that all that troubles you?"

"It troubles me plenty but so do these walkers."

"I know. You want to stop them."

"If I protect the Cloud, I protect you and Jali too."

"Can they be stopped? The women are saying that they are unstoppable corpses, like the darklings but of flesh."

He turned the lamb again, meat sizzling. "They do not seem as bloodthirsty." He hesitated.

"But?"

"But we cannot feel them on the paths; they are silent. They bring with them a sandstorm – or at least, the others did."

"You will find a way, you always do. I believe in you."

He exhaled and some of the tension slid away. "I love you."

"And I you," Silaj said. "Let's eat, forget about all that for the moment."

After the meal he rejoined the council in Raila's home, squeezed in around her small table. The sweet scent of marjoram tea filled the room; had she bothered to eat? It seemed she'd only stopped to meditate on the problem.

"This will be brief, as I want you to work immediately. I believe our course of action must be as follows. Jedda, you will lead Majid, Palan and three of our best warriors after the walkers. Do not engage unless you must, we need information. Where do they lie, their number, who controls them. The rest of us will stay here and continue to fortify the Cloud."

Ain met Majid's eyes. It was clear why she'd chosen him; he was the better warrior. And the walkers did seem to be vulnerable to brute strength. When Raila sent everyone to their tasks Ain lingered.

"Elder?"

"Ain, I know what you will say. But this time, you can do more good here. You have Pathfinders still to train and we must devise a way to hide the bones. Should darklings come again – something we must not rule out simply because a new threat appears – I want you here."

"Apprentice-Taod is more than capable, Elder. The others are not so far behind."

She smiled. "Be that as it may, *you* are the hero. People will rally around you if we are attacked. That is not something I would overlook."

"I understand." He knelt before leaving.

Majid was waiting beneath the bright sun, his expression one of understanding. "I would take you with me. You know that."

Ain rested a hand on his friend's shoulder. "I do. And I understand her choice. Be careful out there."

"Only if you look after things here." He turned for his own home.

Ain glanced to the far end of the square, to the pair of spreading olive trees that flanked the entry to the 'stronghold' as the squat building was called. At times it had housed criminals, visiting clan members and even more rarely, Elders themselves but now it concealed the two or three ribs that had actually reached the Cloud.

Enough for dozens of Greatmasks, but useless in their present form. Pitiful that the very thing the walking corpses would come for, in the right form, was likely the only thing capable of stopping them. How to prevent even that much bone being stolen? To protect the people who would be asked to protect the bones?

Ade stood watch on the stronghold's door, her arms crossed and her bow resting against the stone beside her.

"Pathfinder," she greeted him, speaking softly. She was older than Silaj but not so old as Raila, known in the Cloud as strong and fast, a steady shot. A fine choice for guard, but she'd have others helping soon enough, no doubt.

"Ade. You've heard about the walkers."

She nodded.

"I'd like to see the bone; we have to figure out a way to protect it if the walkers come again."

"Of course." She took a key, unlocked the door and admitted them to the stronghold. Cells lined the opposite wall, a guardroom set nearby. The first had been stacked high with worn lengths of rib, cut to smaller pieces. Some still bore the markings of scratched names, those Ain had seen when he'd started his quest as Seeker.

"Here they are, then."

"Quite a sight," he said.

"So they tell us," Ade replied. "Haven't seen them do anything myself; they're just bones."

"Until they're not – but I know what you mean," he said. They did look innocuous indeed.

"Surely this is the safest place in the Cloud, Pathfinder?"

He nodded. "And how do we make it safer?"

"Ain?" A third voice spoke from the doorway. Wayrn stood waiting. He did not react to Ade, who bristled at the sight of him, instead waiting for Ain to wave him inside before entering.

"Any ideas?" the envoy asked.

"None." Ain shrugged. "Save sealing up the cell, I suppose."

"Not a bad idea," Wayrn said. "It will slow them at the very least – they were tireless but they didn't strike me as creatures able to shatter stone."

Ade leant against the wall. "You're both thinking about this the wrong way. Attack is the best defence, everyone knows that."

"So we need a way to kill the dead?" Ain asked.

She frowned at him. "Yes."

"Or at least stop them," Wayrn said. "What's the one thing we know for sure, about the walkers? Aside from their state of living-death."

"That plants somehow fuel or direct them," Ain said.

"Right. And how do you stop a plant growing?"

"Tear it out at the roots," Ade said. "Then salt the earth after."

Ain scratched at his head. "Would salt be enough – I mean, that takes time with normal plants."

"Let's find some salt," Wayrn said. "Test it on the body."

"Right." Ain dashed from the building and across the square to Emasi's stall, where he borrowed a small pouch then joined Wayrn at the body, where it still rested before Raila's house. There, Ain sprinkled salt across the corpse's eyes. "I don't think this will work, Wayrn. It couldn't be this easy, could it?"

"Let's see."

Ain watched. The cactus did not react. He sighed as he stood, only to crouch once more.

Something *was* happening. The plant had started to shrivel like a slug. The salt seared it down to a shrivelled black nub, spines falling away. "An unnatural response," he said.

"To an unnatural creature," Wayrn replied.

Ain was nodding as he stared at the thing. "This could work. How can we use it on a large scale?" There was more than enough salt available, with the not-too-distant rock-salt plains, but that wasn't enough by itself. He could hardly charge the walkers and hurl handfuls of salt at them.

Wayrn was smiling. "I've already thought of that."

Ain laughed. Maybe there was a way for him to protect the Cloud after all, even if he couldn't be part of retrieving the bones. "Aren't you clever, then. How?"

"What's the quickest way to get the most amount of salt onto the highest number of walkers?"

"Wind. Throw it into the storm."

Wayrn chuckled. "That's quicker than I was thinking, actually, but not quite right, I think, since we can't control the wind."

"Very well. What was your idea?"

"On the ground. We cover the ground before the stronghold with salt. They'll walk right over it without a moment's hesitation – you saw them, they don't like to stop for anything."

"True."

"And if we rough up the ground before the salt, make it jagged somehow, the creatures will cut and scrape and tear their own feet before they reach the salt. We won't have to do anything except collect the salt then drag away the bodies."

Ain slapped Wayrn on the back. "You might have solved the problem before it happens."

"Let's hope so, but it's only a plan at this stage," he said.

"Things always change when you actually get out there on the ground."

18. NOTCH

The old language washed over the rails; unfamiliar words leaping out at Notch, while the words and phrases Alosus had taught him over the course of their long sea voyage were mostly familiar. Somewhere, a woman asked for directions to the *Pale Maiden*. Other voices brimmed with curiosity – did they stare at the *Hawk*? Two men argued over... something, was it birds? Their rough voices blended with laughter from another ship, then competed with the gulls overhead.

But it was the words of the blue cloaks that lined the *Hawk*'s decks that Notch focused on now.

They bore their usual bone masks, pale shapes covering their faces, eye-holes dark. Many wore bone gloves and beneath one open cloak, a breastplate of bone, carven with the image of a shark. The sense of power bore down on his very shoulders, his mind; an oppressive presence with its own vague sentience. It would take little but a single thought, a single command for any of them to snap his own bones.

Notch gave no reason.

He simply stood and listened, having pushed his sleeves down earlier, finding himself holding his breath while Alosus spoke to the leader and Marlosi watched on with a frown.

The conversation had started out simply enough – orders to throw down weapons and the demanding of answers. Alosus had introduced himself not as a prince as he told Melosi, but as a 'free Gigansi' on a trade ship, bearing news from Anaskar for the Royal Children. A gamble, if ever Notch had heard one – and not exactly as they'd planned but perhaps the right move. The conversation slipped away from him when they began to speak too quickly. If only they'd slow down!

From that point, Notch caught only occasional words; 'princess' several times and 'lying' once. Vinezi and Marinus were mentioned also, the leader of the Ecsoli soon folding his arms. His voice contained equal parts doubt and challenge, depending on Alosus' responses.

Finally, the Ecsoli snapped his fingers, gave final orders and strode back across the gangway. His men he left behind.

"What is happening?" Melosi asked. He spun to Notch. "If you've lured me into some fool's errand after all, you know I'll have your guts on a plate, Notch."

"No need for that," Alosus said. "The soldier is fetching a superior. We are to remain here until he returns."

"And then what?"

"Then I convince the captain, or whoever comes, that you should be traded with and that Notch and I be allowed on our way."

"That one seemed a little unsure." Notch stared after the man as he weaved through the crowded dock. "How will you fare with the next one?"

"Better," Alosus said. Again, Notch wasn't sure whether to take comfort from the man's confidence or let worry settle more.

An uneasy silence fell over the *Hawk*.

When a new figure finally appeared, Notch exhaled and stretched his shoulders. The original Ecsoli leader now trailed a heavyset man wearing no mask. His head was shaven so close that not a single hair appeared. He was frowning as he walked, rich purple robes fluttering around his legs. Once aboard, he waved to Alosus with a hand gloved in white.

"This is he?" he asked, and Notch followed better. The fellow had an odd drawl that actually made him easier to understand.

The Ecsoli soldier nodded.

Alosus stepped forward and delivered a speech, that while not short exactly, did not take as long as Notch expected. He followed well enough; Alosus would only reveal news to the royal children or the king personally. In exchange, Alosus expected that Melosi would be free to trade and to leave – and further, that Alosus would be free to pursue his own goals and that Captain Medoro, War-Hero of Anaskar, be given a chance to speak with the 'Library of Souls'.

"You ask for much." The man in purple offered a smile. "It is clear by this ship and its sailors, by your knowledge of events in the New Land that you bear further investigation at the very least. You and he will come with me, where you will be taken to the palace at dawn. In the meantime, no-one from this ship sets foot on land. No attempts will be made to leave."

"Understood, Inquisitor," Alosus said.

The Inquisitor turned to the blue cloaks. "A silver

stalweight from my own purse for any lawful execution of these orders."

The Ecsoli straightened at this and Notch nearly reached for his father's blade. But no-one seemed inclined to force Melosi's men to stay put; there was simply an additional vigilance to them. Alosus took Notch and Melosi aside while the Inquisitor tapped his foot. "Things are going well," Alosus told the captain.

"Is that so? What's the purple one saying then?"

"That Notch and I are to see the king and that no-one can leave the ship. It is favourable," Alosus added when Melosi narrowed his eyes. "If they had any true concerns about us, the *Hawk* would already be kindling floating in the harbour."

"Then I'm expecting you both to return."

Alosus nodded. "Prepare your wares, but do not attempt to leave or head ashore – you can trust me still, Captain. We may not return swiftly but we will return."

"Come now," the Inquisitor said, impatience clear in his voice as he turned for the gangway.

Notch followed Alosus, glancing back at Melosi. The captain was stroking his beard as he frowned. The man had no choice – nor did Notch – he had to trust Alosus would deliver on his promise.

Beyond the gangway, the docks were as busy as the voices suggested – mostly sailors disembarking, or dock workers cursing beneath heavy loads of crates and bolts of cloth. Not so different from home. Yet there was something amiss – the way people glanced at each other askance. As if... to check on the progress of their fellows. But why? Was it some manner of jealousy?

When he asked Alosus about it, the man answered softly. "No. Here it is more a case that if one man realises his fellow has unloaded more boxes than he, then that man may not receive a bonus from his captain. More, if he unloads the least, or performs similarly poorly in some capacity, he will have a portion of his pay withheld."

Notch blinked. Such competitive fear... "You said, 'here' – is it different elsewhere in the city?"

Alosus shook his head.

The Inquisitor paused. "Gentlemen, please. I cannot have you murmuring away with those clipped words of yours."

Notch looked to Alosus, who nodded once more. He took a breath; he had to try using the old tongue with strangers sooner or later. "I was remarking upon the impressive efficiency of the docks here," he said slowly, hoping he'd been clear enough with the inflection. The old tongue was much more rigid than Anaskari.

The man took a moment before comprehension dawned. "Ah. It is so, yes."

They continued on, approaching a sprawling building set beneath the walls. This close, Notch was able to make out patterns in the city-walls. The pearlescent coating seemed to be opal and it was arranged in sweeping waves, building to a crescendo near the still distant gates.

However, the building the Inquisitor led them to was not so grand, though the pale stone was by no means smeared with generations of smoke from torches either. In fact, it was the cleanest stone Notch had ever seen in a city. No torch rings or alcoves for lamps – instead, a crystal rested atop a tall pole. Was that the light source?

Their guide – or captor, perhaps – led them within. He was not challenged by the officious-looking men and women arranged at various desks before lines of people – merchants by the look – but instead the man in purple had them in a small room with a single desk and chair quite quickly.

A skeleton-hand sat on the desk, palm facing up. Its bones were yellowed with age, not unlike a Greatmask.

"You first, Alosus."

Alosus placed his hand on the skeleton. The fingers moved, and Notch drew in a breath. The skeletal hand gripped as best it could, considering the difference in size, but Alosus showed no pain or alarm. "It is to read my past," he said. "To help prove that I am who I claim to be."

The Inquisitor was humming to himself – holding a bone charm in one hand. When he stopped, he looked to Alosus, expression unreadable. "Reported as royal property 'misappropriated by Vinezi Mare'. Very curious."

Alosus offered no answer.

The fellow continued to tap and toy with the charm. A thoughtful expression crossed his features, but he did not speak to Alosus again, only glancing appraisingly at the Tonitora. Alosus appeared to be waiting for more, as if the man would speak further, yet the fellow instead turned to Notch.

"Now you, new-world man."

What would it reveal? Notch placed his hand on the skeleton, standing close enough so his sleeve did not ride up and reveal the bracers. With the prominent lion of the palace, it didn't seem wise to reveal any possible link between bracers and royalty. Skeletal fingers gripped him, and he swallowed – not at the force, but at the strange, internal tapping sensation that followed. Almost as if someone was gently tapping against each and every bone in his body with a small hammer – one bone at a time.

When the grip eased, he drew his hand back quickly.

The Inquisitor sat. "Difficult to read. Warriors in your line – perhaps mountain folk. And yes, impressive feats in significant battles. War-Hero indeed... and something else, Captain Medoro. Something I cannot quite fathom."

Notch did not answer either – if the man was speaking of the bracers, Notch wasn't going to volunteer anything.

The Inquisitor waved a gloved hand. "No matter. For now, you will be shown to some admittedly rough accommodation and tomorrow it's off to the palace and then you are someone else's concern."

Two blue cloaks appeared, and Notch sighed. They had an unmistakably humourless air about them – jailors. "Imprisoned again, I see," he said.

"Not for long, Notch," Alosus replied as he started after the lead Ecsoli.

"I hope you're right about that, but who's to say the palace won't be worse?"

He chuckled. "In many ways it is but we have passed the first two hurdles more swiftly and simply than I'd hoped."

"I take it you aren't going to be reported to the palace as 'stolen property' then?"

"It is already done – but I am hoping that my role as your guide will afford me some time before being reassigned."

"Can you be sure?"

"That they will eventually come for me? Very sure. The question is when, and it may not be all bad news even if it happens soon."

"How?"

"Sometimes it is good for the mouse to keep company of the bear."

"I see," Notch said. "A dangerous game, but at least

we'll be approaching them from a position of strength and not as prisoners in all but name."

"Trust me, Notch. I will find a way."

19. SETO

Seto slid a glass of fire-lemon across the polished table. "You're looking old all of a sudden, Danillo. You need to rest."

Sofia's father smiled, raising a hand to the additional grey at his temples. The afternoon sun streamed through the window, setting the liquor afire. Danillo leant back in the armchair to move his face from the glare. "And I see you've forgotten the saying about the pot calling the kettle black."

"Perhaps. But perhaps, when you get right down to it, that is precisely why I wanted to see you right away," Seto said. He met the man's eyes. "We both know I will have no successor of my own."

Danillo lowered the glass. "If you are asking what I think you are, I refuse."

"I've missed your tact."

"I mean what I say. You must find someone else. I am not the man for the job."

"Then who is?" Seto said, leaning forward. "Despite the toll of your grief, you are younger than I. You are the only one who can use Argeon — truly, who better?"

Danillo said nothing.

Seto pressed on. "Would you have me approach the

ruins of Casa Cavallo? The dullard who heads Tartaruga? Or perhaps the untried boy of Stallion House? You must admit, Danillo, you are the logical choice."

"That I accept," he said. "But it is a burden I do not seek. I have enough responsibility rebuilding the Mascare, helping forge your peace."

Seto nodded; he'd expected no less. But the world was oft a bitter place, and there were few chances to choose the quieter path. "And I hate to pile more weight upon your shoulders, even though, admittedly, I am not dead just yet. Nor planning to die."

Danillo drank. "Good."

Seto hesitated a long moment. "You leave me little choice, but understand it offers me no pleasure in saying this; I wish I did not have to suggest it at all—"

"Then let me stop you. No." Danillo's voice was firm.

"The state of the Kingdom does not afford either of us any luxury. You know that. If you will not take the mantle when I am gone, you must be Custodian until your issue takes the throne."

The Lord Protector stood. "I have no issue."

Seto pushed himself out of his own chair. "That I know."

Danillo shook his head, eyes dark with repressed fury and pain. "I will not do that to another woman, simply for the sake of keeping a noble line on the throne. We are not animals fit to rut whenever it takes our fancy."

Had he pushed his old friend too far? It was unkind of course, but necessary. Seto kept his voice soft. "It is not about a noble line. It is about stability, Danillo. I cannot have my city fall into ruin again."

His old friend exhaled heavily. "This is not the answer."

"Then I require you to help me find another."

"Fine." Danillo sat again. "But not today."

"Very well," Seto replied. "What of the Bloodwood and the Oyn-Dir?"

"The Amber Groves are coming under control and the Sap-Born do seem scattered. Three more breeding camps have been uncovered and liberated but they found few like Catrin."

"And that troubles you?"

"Perhaps more assassins like her exist and are en route to Anaskar now. Or have been since last winter. Or earlier, perhaps several are already in the city and have been for months?"

"We are watching."

"Of course," Danillo said. "That I am aware of. The Oyn-Dir has people searching out rumours of seemingly resurrected Ulag Clan. I personally examined a corpse myself and it was certainly old enough... yet the woman who saw it move, at least the one I spoke to, was not convincing."

Seto frowned. More strange occurrences? "You think she was lying?"

"No. Only that she had little compelling evidence – something about it made me think *she* was being duped into believing the Ulag were returning. There was a bone altar involved and it seemed quite sophisticated, I fear an Ecsoli influence."

"Something similar may be occurring here," Seto said, outlining the Ecsoli sightings. "Is it simply an unhappy coincidence, I wonder?"

"You suspect something larger afoot?" He sighed. "We haven't even had a season of respite after the greatest threat to the world in centuries and you're already looking for another dark motive behind the two events?"

"Well, let me say that I would not be surprised if it were so."

Danillo took another, longer drink. "Sadly, nor would I. It has been a bleak year. In any event, Nia will keep us appraised – about the altar too, which I mean to disassemble soon. Your other concerns, are they going well enough?"

A rapping on his door echoed.

"A message, Your Majesty. It is most urgent." It was a page, and the lad's voice seemed to have climbed a register or two. Probably afraid to interrupt – Seto almost let a flash of guilt come to the fore; he'd been quite terse with the last servant who'd interrupted for something rather trivial.

"A moment." Seto crossed the heavy rug and reached the door.

Outside, a page in orange and grey waited between two Shield, a sealed letter in hand. The wax seal was a vibrant green – most unusual, and the seal was a pair of wings. Not of any House he recognised. Seto accepted it and sent the lad away, returning to Danillo, where he opened the letter. Seto handed the seal over. "Do you recognise this?"

"No-one uses wings like that," he said. "And the wax is... gaudy, isn't it?"

Seto lost the flow of Danillo's words.

The letter was a reply from the Son of the Crown of the southernmost lands, Jin-Dakiv. At the top of the letter, a dark pair of wings spread wide, wingtips pale.

"Seto?"

He gestured Danillo come nearer. "Read this; it's from Jin-Dakiv. I did not think they would even reply to our missive."

King Oseto,

We would welcome a closer relationship between our two nations, certainly. I am comfortable speaking on behalf of my mother the Queen, when I say she appreciates your overtures. Please consider sending a deshi *to further open discussion and perhaps even, if the Nine Gods will it, a state visit. Many are the wonders of Jin-Dakiv and I am personally most keen to see the famous city by the sea and its dread Greatmasks.*

If this is agreeable, please send any such envoy to the Crystal Gorge, three days south of Mattehus. A guide will await you on the caravan trail in anticipation of your arrival.

Shinsal

Son of the Crown

Seto placed the letter on the table. "A warm, if eager response."

"Too eager?"

"I cannot say. Can you? Have you travelled so far?"

Danillo shook his head. "No, not to the Crystal Gorge, though I have heard it mentioned by merchants given the required pass to travel so deep. All of the trade I witnessed happened within sight of the border."

"The merchants I spoke to and who agreed to take the letters were rather reticent to say the least, about what they had seen. One of the conditions of their access, so I did not push them. But one did pass on a rumour. Nothing he had seen with his own eyes, of course."

"And so such rumours multiply and distort to something far beyond their former selves."

"Of course. But even a kernel of truth must lie somewhere within. This one spoke of a mythical bone cradle, hidden deep in the ruins of Jin-Dakiv's Sand

Temples."

Danillo raised an eyebrow. "A cradle made from bone?"

"Said to be the one used to soothe the first child of the Nine Gods, their hero; I cannot recall her name."

"A slim chance."

"Yes," Seto said as he sat. He spun the letter in a slow circle with one finger. "But the expansion of trade and allies is not a poor consolation."

"Who would you send?"

"I do not know. I feel we are spread thinner and thinner... I might have once sent Notch; he has worked on a caravan to Jin-Dakiv before."

"Hmmm." Danillo made no mention of Notch's foolhardy quest. In fact, he had barely spoken a word about the loss of his daughter either. Seto assumed the man had searched the Greatmask for her and found nothing. "I could recall Emilio?"

"From Hol City? I do not know if we ought to wait so long. Especially as his last letter suggested some progress in his own search."

Danillo nodded. "I may have someone else."

"A new recruit of your own?"

"More of an old recruit whose talents had been long overlooked. Though 'old' is misleading – he is in his prime."

"Good. Send him to me when you are ready, and make sure he's prepared for a long journey."

20. FLIR

Flir sat across from Aren in the rear of Grav's Ocean Wave, the chatter of cultists and possibly even regular customers blending with the soft flute. The musician had returned and was playing a song about two lovers fleeing into the night. The small table was a little crowded with Kanis beside her and the wreckages of their meals before them. Aren had four helpings of deer and chicken, his appetite finally sated.

"Thank you again for upholding your end of our arrangement," he said. "I'm sure Tikev will feel the same when he awakens."

"*If* he awakens," Kanis said, his expression not so friendly.

"He will. It is his first time; it always takes longer the first time."

"And we must thank you," Flir told the man. "But I hope you understand, we have questions."

"Of course. That is my role as Surrogate."

"Who taught you to Bequeath? It is not common lore," Kanis said.

He nodded. "Certainly not. Mishalar's Surrogates have long protected such knowledge; I was not aware of it until several years past now. It was contained in the writings of Hevlad – I trust you have heard of them?"

"The Snow Cleric?" Flir asked. She folded her arms. "Surely only children believe in him and his writings." Perhaps such knowledge would have survived the centuries, but she'd always been taught that a greed-stricken group of ancient dilars had been burned alive along with the actual writings.

Aren did not bristle at her tone. "I have copied from what survived, high in the spires of the ruined outpost. He was indeed a real figure. Whether he could heal others as completely as claimed I do not know, but surely you must believe in some mystery to healing, given your own gifts."

"And you carry such writings with you now?"

"No. They reside in our monastery in Tiramof."

Tiramof, a modest town west of the capital. It was one of several holdings that supplied Enar with its produce but hardly a hotbed for cult activity when she'd left. Yet a lot had obviously changed since then; that was the price she paid for her absence. "Tiramof is not on our route," she said.

"I would not presume to direct your paths, dilar."

"But you nonetheless have a request, don't you?" Kanis said.

Aren did not bat an eyelid. "If you imply that I risked my life to save you in order to make you feel indebted to me, I assure you it is not true. It was both my duty and honour – any here will tell you the same." He paused. "But I will request your aid in something and I do so with no expectation."

"Such as?"

Aren waved to get attention from the serving girl before continuing. "Something is afoot here in Renovar. The Conclave does not see it; they are too busy squabbling over their petty reforms. I fear some... force is building its power here."

"How so?" Flir asked.

"East of Whiteport, at the point of land where the First Lighthouse still stands, there have been reports of thefts, disappearances – most of them Ice-Priests."

Flir glanced at Kanis, whose expression had become troubled, though the fool was trying to hide it. "People are killing priests?" It didn't make sense. No-one else could hold back the creeping ice.

"Yes. Or so we fear. A trail was found outside the village of Ithinov but we have not been able to penetrate the tunnels in the hills."

"And you want us to break in," Kanis said.

"We have tried, dilar. Believe me, we have tried. Even *acor* – yet nothing will open the path."

Kanis scratched at his cheek where pale stubble was coming in heavier than usual, but did not offer a response – which was odd. He was usually the first to give an opinion, asked for or not.

Something was amiss.

"Our task is pressing," Flir said. But she could not simply close the door on what might be a serious problem with the Ice-Priests, especially with such a lingering winter. And more, how could she turn away from more answers about herself? "When we complete it, we will seek you here."

Aren inclined his head. "Seek us to the east, in Ithinov."

"No promises, Aren," Kanis said as he stood. He

turned to Flir. "I'm going to get some supplies. Wake Pevin and meet me on the Northern Corridor."

Flir waved him off as she stood. Aren again offered no response to Kanis' antagonistic behaviour. An impressive calm really. "You're taking his lack of gratitude quite well."

"He is dilar."

"And that makes you undeserving of gratitude?"

Now he gave one of the damnable peaceful smiles that all cultists tended to wear – the fool was worse than Pevin had been. "We are here to serve Mishalar and her First Servants."

Flir shrugged; there was never any use trying to talk to them. "Well, thank you again for what you've done."

She slipped through the tables, up the stairs and to Pevin's room, where she found the man sitting up, brow furrowed as he prodded the bandages wrapped around his torso.

"Do you think we took a few ribs out?" she asked.

He chuckled, then winced. "No, just testing. I don't remember... what happened?"

"Pirates happened."

He closed his eyes as he nodded. "Ah. The dead of night – the fire. I assume someone found us. We're in Whiteport then?"

"Yes. After a brush with the governor we've been taken in by cultists. Kanis is collecting supplies, think you can travel?"

"Find me a cart and I'll manage, dilar."

"Right."

Pevin straightened. "Wait. Did you mention the governor? Mildavir?"

"Yes. Distant relative to the old king, as I recall."

"He has not forgotten you or Kanis."

"True."

"The past haunts, does it not?"

She nodded. "So it does, though the ghost is closer now."

"Do you sometimes wish things had been different?" he asked.

"I never took you for a sympathiser for the monarchy, Pevin."

He stood slowly, replacing his tunic as he shook his head. "King Chaak and his ilk were hardly ideal. Even before you and Kanis got involved with the first Conclave there were dark rumours about his plans for Renovar. No, I'm just making an observation, dilar."

"Which is?"

"That your life would be easier right now if the coup hadn't taken place."

"That we'll never know, though you're probably right," she said. "But I'd probably still be a fool too; my mistakes simply would have been different."

"Very philosophical, dilar."

"Thank you. Now let's finish up with all the history and get our sights back on the future; namely Enar. They're not going to move the city closer just for us."

21. FIORE

There was nothing to do.

Fi paced the room. Five steps from the door to the silver-lined mirror on the opposite wall. Giovan lay on the big bed, propped against the wall, his eyes closed. The fabric itself was like everything in the Second Tier, richly-coloured and expensive-looking. The blankets even had tassels – useless but pretty things.

The Ecsoli man sat on a chair near the window, looking down into the street. He was watching for fake Ecsoli, yet nothing had happened in who knew how long? Even the voice from the green light had abandoned her.

"This is pretty boring, Giovan." She sat on the bed with a sigh.

"If we catch one of the imposters I'll let you kick him. How does that sound?"

"You're being ridiculous."

"Yes, I am." He had not opened his eyes yet.

The Ecsoli rose, speaking as he did. As before, Fi did not understand but Giovan did. He answered as he approached the window, and they continued to speak in hushed voices. Fi crept closer.

Down in the street, a figure in a blue cloak stood watching the inn.

He didn't move. Even his mask seemed too still – at least, until two real Ecsoli burst from the inn to charge across the street. The man in blue spun, fleeing down an alley.

"Ana's Hide," Giovan snapped. He started for the door, nearly dragging the Ecsoli on the chair with him. "Stay here," he shouted over his shoulder, then it was only his footsteps clambering down the staircase.

Fi frowned after him. Did he think she was useless? She could help if he let her. Wasn't that what Lord Abrensi wanted?

Fiore?

She froze. There was the voice again!

"Yes?"

There's a friend of Lord Abrensi down in the common room. We need your help.

Fi frowned. Just what sort of friend? "How?"

He is called Enso; he will be wearing black. He has a message for Lord Abrensi.

"And you want me to deliver it? Not Giovan?"

He is quite busy, don't you think? Enso will explain more but you must hurry, he has another meeting after seeing you.

Fiore frowned; it wasn't right to keep people waiting. Wasn't that what Father Canto used to say? But why did the voice need her? Was it because she was a Singer? Green flickered in her mind; easing her doubts. Yes, that was why. She was a Singer; Giovan might not understand.

She started down the stairs, pausing at the bottom. The inn was busy. Most people looked just like everyone else, only a few seemed to be real Ecsoli, sitting with a pair of Shield. Almost hidden in a corner was a man in black. He was thin, and he was wrinkling his nose at the drink before him. He sat alone.

It had to be Enso.

Fi slipped through the tables and chairs, sitting before the man. "Hello."

"Ah, Fiore. Thank you for seeing me." His smile was... unpleasant somehow, she couldn't put a finger on exactly why.

"You have a message for me?"

He reached into a pocket in his robe and bought forth a thin scroll, which he handed over. "Learn this, please – but do not sing it for anyone but Abrensi."

"Is it dangerous?"

"Only for people who are *not* Singers. Abrensi told me to make sure you understood that. You're safe; the song doesn't work on Storm Singers."

"What does it do?" she asked as she unrolled it. The words were unfamiliar – old words like the Song of Sleep – but she knew, with just a little practise, she'd get it right.

He shrugged. "Lord Abrensi didn't say, he just told me it was important." The man stood. "It took me two whole months to find this, Fiore, make sure you don't lose it."

"You can trust me," she said.

"Good girl." He smiled again as he left.

Fi rushed back upstairs and closed the door behind her. She hopped up onto the bed, twisting her feet into the blanket and began sounding out the old words.

By the time Giovan returned – alone – she knew the song well enough. Like the Song of Sleep, it wasn't long or difficult but it was somehow... *deeper* and the words were longer. It was difficult to sing quickly. It seemed to demand a slower pace even than the Song of Sleep.

"We're heading back to the palace," he said, anger in his voice.

She sat up. "What happened?"

"We lost the fake, so we split up but the real Ecsoli never came back. I explained exactly where we had to meet up and they understood when. I was sure."

"You think they ran away?"

"Looks likely." He collected his short bow. "Come on, Beanpole. Let's go back."

She jumped down. "What about the others?"

"They have their orders."

This time Giovan moved quickly through the darkening Tier and back into the palace. She had to half-run to keep up and so black was his mood that he did not even smile when he sent her off with the nearest servant. Eventually, she reached Lord Abrensi's chambers. Silver lamps burned either side of the oaken doors – marked with the same lightning bolt as his robe.

Fi hadn't even needed to knock – since the servant did that before bowing and disappearing back into the maze of chilly halls.

The door eventually opened, Lord Abrensi poking his head out. His hair was a mess, as before and when he saw her he blinked. "Fiore, you have returned early."

"Have I?"

"Possibly." He opened the door wider. "Come in, how did Giovan's search go?"

"Not very well," she said, explaining further as she crossed the heavy carpet. It was a bright blue and so deep that her feet actually sunk into it a little. What flower or rock could make such colour?

"Hmmm," Lord Abrensi said as he moved to a long

table and began arranging papers. "And what of your own role, did you need to Sing?"

She shook her head. "No. Giovan left me in the room just as the chase started – but I did meet your messenger. He said he found an important song."

The Storm Singer stopped. "My messenger?"

"Yes. Enso. He said I had to keep the song hidden, because it might be dangerous but that it wouldn't hurt Singers."

"I see. Can you describe this messenger?"

She did so, handing over the scroll. "Here is the song."

Lord Abrensi frowned when he unrolled it. "Are you sure?"

"Of course, sir."

He raised an eyebrow as he returned the scroll. It was empty! Fiore peered closer and there wasn't even a trace of the sharp writing anymore. "But it was there before."

Lord Abrensi sighed. "Could you write it?"

"No. But I memorised it." She opened her mouth, singing the first word but Lord Abrensi raised a hand. She stopped.

"Best to learn a little more about this Enso, I think – and not before tomorrow." He returned to his desk, hands flashing as he set things in order much more quickly than before. "For now, it's best you found quarters of your own, your own indeed. I will arrange for the kitchen to make you something nice too."

Green flickered, near-blinding.

Fi started to sing – her mouth moving of its own accord. She couldn't stop it, couldn't explain her shock, couldn't even frown. Lord Abrensi spun. "Halt." The command echoed around the room, rattling the window.

But her song flowed on.

She raised her hands, meaning to cover her mouth, but her arms stiffened and locked, halfway to her face. What was happening? Was the voice forcing her to sing? But why? Lord Abrensi reached for her but the final line was free and silence followed.

His eyes were wide and his mouth agape as he twisted his torso. It was as if he could not move his feet. And now Fi could move – she stumbled back from the shock on the Storm Singer's face.

"I'm sorry," she cried. "It wasn't me."

Lord Abrensi spoke – but his voice was silent, only his lips moved. A sad smile now replaced his shock and he shook his head. Was he saying that she was not to blame? Or that she was useless? What? What? What?

"What can I do?"

Again, Lord Abrensi could not answer. He shrugged and by the time his shoulders settled he had grown completely still. He did not even appear to be breathing – and worse, a grey colour was creeping up his throat. When it reached his cheeks and then muted his bright blue eyes, she choked out a gasp.

Every part of the man was solid and hard as stone – right down to the folds in his robe, like a perfect statue.

What had she done?

It is the Song of Stone, Fiore. And you sang beautifully.

"But I didn't want this. He could have changed my life! Why did you do that? Why did you use me?"

Don't worry. It is for the best.

"How?" she cried. "For you?"

Of course for me, but do not worry. You will benefit too. The voice paused. *Now go and report this news but know that you will not be able to mention me or the Song of Stone. For others, it is as if I do not exist.*

"Who are you?" Fi demanded.

I am Vipera.

22. NOTCH

The King City Paradisum spread beneath the palace walls in a mighty swarm of stone and marble; a harrowing display of power and wealth. Even its thoroughfares were set with patterns, to distinguish street from street. The sheer manpower to have paved such a mammoth place was unfathomable. Beside it, Anaskar stood as a poor shadow – yet a sudden urge to return struck Notch as he stared across the viper's nest, as Alosus called Paradisum.

But return wasn't an option. Sofia needed him.

Alosus pointed left of the harbour to a quarter of the city that bore water for streets. It glittered in the sunlight, small boats sliding along between vine-cloaked buildings, roof gardens a riot of flowering shrubs. "Remember, if you head within there is only one way out: the mouth."

"Will I need to know this, Alosus?" he asked. "We don't have plans to go there, do we?"

"No. But if we are separated I want you to have a passing knowledge of the city, of places to avoid."

Notch nodded. "Very well. What of the ruins?" Not too far below, set off to the right and half-concealed by a wall in some disrepair, was what looked like a palace. Soot and shadow clung to the crumbling walls and windows. It was smaller, far lesser than the lion-headed monster that reared up behind them. A coldness seemed to emanate from the silent parapets and the central tower, despite the hot sun.

"Abandoned by the Second Leo Family after a fire. Rumoured to be started by the jealous Silver Wave. Entry is forbidden in honour of the victims. There is nothing within of note – but it is worth avoiding." He pointed to a more central row, directly beneath the palace, where an enormous square stood lined by what looked like Guild Halls. They were not bright marble, but a darker bluestone and while they lacked the grandeur of the rest of the city they bore a humility that Notch preferred. "If you are seeking shelter, the inns will require exorbitant fees so seek the Steel Guild. Ask for Desaphilus, he owes me a favour."

A voice echoed up from below. "The Royal Mare will see you now."

Finally. They'd been waiting half the day already. Notch started down the stairs, Alosus close behind. At the base of the wall, a pair of blue-cloaks – or Os-Bellator as they were named here – waited to escort them toward a narrow wooden path. Notch was able to translate the name to 'war bones' though he was probably a little off.

Almost like the planks of a pier, the wooden path was conspicuous, being surrounded by flagstones as it was. It led away from the wall and directly toward the main buildings of the palace, whose arches were cast in shadow from the lion's mane and other upper storeys.

The moment both Os-Ballator reached the wood they stopped, gesturing for Notch to join them. Alosus did so too, only he wore a deep frown. "Stay still," one blue-cloak said as he stomped a simple pattern on the planking.

Grinding sounds came from below and the planks began to move. They slid toward the palace as if by magic, carrying everyone closer and closer to the arches. "What magic is this?" Notch asked.

"No magic," Alosus said. "My enslaved countrymen toil below us to provide such luxuries to the palace."

Notch looked down. The boards were too close together to see anything – but he started to step free of the planks anyway. There was no way he would let a slave carry him when his own two legs worked. Alosus caught his shoulder, his heavy hand pulling Notch back. "It would not do well to insult the Mare's hospitality."

Notch answered in Anaskari. "That's not the insult here."

"I know. Believe me, Notch."

The walkway soon delivered them beneath the first arch, marble carved with gold. If anything, the wooden walkway was more out of place where it cut a perfectly straight line through the marble floors. They passed exotic plants with long, gleaming blue and purple leaves, each settled in huge ceramic pots, and paintings of epic battles on canvases that covered entire walls. The frames bore silver scrollwork – mostly lions or waves.

It was all so unnecessary. So much wealth in one place... the frame of a single painting alone would have been sold for more than he'd earn in all his years as a soldier.

The walkway stopped at a narrow staircase with ornate hand rails.

At the top, a woman waited, watching as they began

their ascent. Her dark hair was arranged atop her head, held in place with jewelled netting. She wore a charcoal-coloured robe open at the throat and split at the knee – the tanned skin of her leg revealed when she shifted. The closer he climbed, the more striking she appeared; fine features, dark eyes ringed with kohl and a generous smile.

But it was the smile that gave him pause. Was it welcoming alone? Or did something else lurk within, something predatory?

"Welcome to Paradisum," she said, her voice soothing. "Alosus of the Gigansi and Captain Medoro from the New Land, please follow me to a place where you can be comfortable while you wait." To the blue-cloaks she said, "Thank you, gentlemen."

Their new guide started along another marble hall. She did not offer a name or even speak again as they walked and Alosus seemed inclined to silence also. Notch followed suit until they reached an alcove. Empty weapon racks lined the walls, each set with open skeleton hands, and the woman gestured to them. "You will have to leave all weapons and bones here."

One at a time, Alosus placed his sickle and belt knife in the rack, the bone hands clasping the grips.

Notch hesitated, not only due to the disturbing bone magic. "It is my father's sword," he said, once again doing his best to use the old language properly. And more, he did not wish to give up the bracers either. Could they even be considered weapons?

The woman only smiled at him. "None shall take it, I assure you – simply touch the hands when you place your sword within and they will only open for you, thereafter."

An impressive promise and it would have to be enough. Notch added his sword and belt knife and dagger to the rack, touching the bones as he did, and followed Alosus into the next room. It was as opulent as the others, but this one bore plush furniture and a large balcony. The guide showed them to chairs, where chilled lemon-water had been placed, and then turned for the door.

"The Royal Mare will see you soon." Her gaze lingered on Notch, a thoughtful expression on her face. "As I hope to also, New Land Man. You are causing quite the stir here in the palace."

And then she was gone, her parting gift a faint sense of unease that settled over Notch. "Who was that?"

Alosus switched to Anaskari. "As a precaution, let's avoid the old tongue while we are alone."

"Is that enough? Some Ecsoli learnt Anaskari during the occupation."

"Few, yes. And so we must be careful no matter which language we use."

Notch nodded.

"Our guide was Lady Casselli. A dangerous woman, though one perhaps better to have as a potential ally."

"But she's not a member of the royal family?"

"No. Her House is certainly well-regarded, however. Second in influence."

Notch exhaled. Already he was making in-roads. "Will that make it easier for me to visit this Library of Souls? Or for your search?"

"Perhaps. So long as the wrong people do not have a chance to use you too often as a piece in their endless struggle for power."

"You don't make it sound like something we can avoid."

"If we keep our wits about us, it should work out."

Notch took a drink, the tart water refreshing enough. Not enough to dispel his concerns, but still welcome at least. "And what is the Library of Souls?"

"A place where the most knowledgeable Greatmask users have stored their lore over the generations."

"They'd let me use such a place?"

Alosus chuckled. "No. But I believe they'd let you pose a single question – and no more, but it's a good start."

"But only if I remain a novelty?"

He sighed. "I believe the royal family will actually have questions for you. They may not be ones you wish to answer."

"I bet you're right about that, Alosus." He finished the water. "Who will come for us?"

"It's hard to say. The Mare number in dozens."

"Dozens?"

"Acknowledged. Doubtless more exist, but Vinezi's father – the king – has taken many wives, nearly all who have borne sons and most of whom now have their own families."

"Then succession is a problem, even before Marinus died."

Alosus nodded. "It is worse now with his children no doubt squabbling amongst themselves even before they begin to contend with their uncles, aunts and cousins."

"Who do we want to talk to, then?"

He spread his large hands. "Those most removed from Marinus perhaps; depending on what we share with them."

Notch straightened; something that should have troubled him before became apparent at Alosus' words. "What of his immediate family? Are we in danger if we reveal our role in Marinus' death?"

"Publically his sons might seek to punish us, but

privately they would be pleased. We have cleared a path to the throne." Alosus sighed. "It is hard to read the situation. As I understand it, the old king did not approve of his eldest son's ambitions."

"Private approval of our actions doesn't mean we wouldn't be publically beheaded."

"True. But revealing the full extent of what we know to the right rivals might buy us allies."

"Only if we can be sure everything hasn't already been shared by the Ecsoli who left before our ship," Notch said. "This is becoming more of a gamble than I'd expected and I wasn't exactly expecting an easy path before."

"Let me lead; I will gauge the situation, depending on who agrees to see us."

Notch laughed. "That I will gladly do. And feel free to smooth over any mistakes I make if you have to translate. Even before having to wrestle with the Old Tongue, I'm not one for matching words with vipers."

"I will do my best."

Footsteps approached. Alosus turned back to the door and Notch followed suit. A page, dressed in silver and blue, appeared and announced their visitor in a high-pitched voice. "Prince Ren Mare, Third Son of the First Son of King Walerian Mare."

Notch glanced to Alosus. The man mouthed the words 'be wary' before bending to one knee. Again, Notch took his lead from the big man, sucking in a breath as he did so.

Time to roll the dice.

23. AIN

Two weeks had passed with no word from Jedda and Majid.

Ain knew the only thing that kept him from pacing every moment was juggling the bulk of the apprentices and coordinating the collection of rock salt, among other duties. And still Raila wouldn't send another party – though concern was clear in her own agitation, the way she looked north continually, or her shortness with the other Elders.

A wagon bed crunched to a halt before him.

Ain wiped at sweat on his brow, then hauled a block into the wagon. It settled with a thud. Back at the Cloud it would be crushed into much smaller pieces, but not everything they took would need to be broken down. Other men and women worked the plain with shovels, loading huge hessian bags which would then be man-handled into one of the other two wagons. So far, they'd collected enough to comfortably salt the square and protect the stronghold, but nowhere near enough to ring the entire oasis. Nor would they seek to do so; it would take too long.

"We should head back, Pathfinder," one of the men said. "Sun is starting to dip."

"Sands, already?" Ain dumped a few more pieces into the bed and pulled his gloves off, then put his fingers to his lips and let out a piercing whistle. Workers across the white plain turned and started back toward the wagons, others lifted their final shovel load into the bags before gathering to lift them.

Ain jogged to the lead wagon, climbed atop, drank deeply from his flask and started the camels moving.

Time passed swiftly, the sun starting to slide toward orange just as they reached the oasis and its precious water. As he steered the wagon to the makeshift quarry nestled behind the stronghold, Ain examined the homes. Faint glimpses of smoke from cooking fires, parents calling children home – all seemed well.

Warm light glowed in his own windows. He worked quickly to unhitch and lead the camels to the grazing pens, then he unloaded the salt before crossing the square to his front door, where he hesitated. How would Jali react this time? Another screaming fit? Or utter indifference – both seemed likely based on recent behaviour. "Sands, stay firm beneath my feet."

He opened the door.

Silaj smiled at him from where she was tending to the herbs with a cup of water. Half were flowering, little reds, yellows and pinks mixed in with the green. Jali was sleeping in his crib, his expression one of peace. "How go the plants, Herb-Master?" he asked with a grin, keeping his voice low.

"Wonderfully, actually," she replied, also speaking softly.

He kissed her forehead. "How are you both?"

"Better than you, I think," she said. "A dark cloud has followed you in. I saw your expression as you opened the door. It has only been two weeks, Ain. What if Jedda and Majid had to travel all the way to the Ranges? They could be weeks *more* from returning."

"You're right, of course. It's hard not to worry."

"I know."

He moved over to the crib, its wooden frame quite a luxury in and of itself, and leant over to check on his son.

Jali's features transformed into a frown, though he did not wake.

Ain swallowed and moved away without a word.

"Is Jali well?" Silaj asked without looking up, her attention fixed on the rosemary.

"Still sleeping."

"Good. Why don't you rest a while?"

The peal of a bell stopped his words. It echoed across the Cloud, dark and booming. "The storm bell," he cried.

"Is it really a storm?" Silaj asked, dashing to a window. Ain joined her. The darkening skies were clear – it was no monster storm. But people were gathering to the east. Where the Sea Beast bones had once rested.

The storm bell was being used to sound an alarm.

The walkers were coming for the last of the bone, just as feared.

He took Silaj by the shoulders. "Take Jali below, bolt the hatch and take the tunnels if I do not return."

She gripped his hands. "How do you know it will be safe?"

"There's no bone here," he said. "They'll head for the stronghold and our trap. This will be over quickly. I hope."

"Don't be a fool out there, Ain. Come back to us."

Jali started to cry and he kissed Silaj. "I promise."

In the streets, he charged to the edge of the Cloud. A low-lying sand storm approached – much wider than the last. His pulse doubled. Just how many cactus-infested creatures lurked within? And how had they approached so swiftly, without being seen sooner? He wasn't going to be able to ask them. The creatures would soon hit the jagged mess of stone that had been spread before the Cloud, but would the plan work?

Raila and Wajam were urging people into their homes, to be prepared to use the tunnels, the old escape routes from ancient clan struggles. Warriors were preparing themselves and heading to the stronghold, while others, led by Wayrn, were spilling salt through the streets and the square – most of it concentrated around the stronghold. Bowmen lined the rooves.

"Ain, to the stronghold," Raila shouted.

He nodded, dashing toward the building. There he helped Ade spill more salt, spreading it generously.

"Think this will work?" she asked.

"I want it to."

"As do we all, Pathfinder."

When the last of the salt had been poured he turned for another bag but there were none left. Raila was waving them into the stronghold. Within, the bones were sealed behind stone and mud brick, a final defence.

Ain climbed to the roof, crowding in with Raila, Ade and the others, many of whom stood with bows ready or with feet upon large pieces of stone – much of it rock salt. Men and women also lined the rooves of other buildings, their own makeshift weapons ready. When the walkers came, they'd face quite a barrage. If the Sands willed it, they wouldn't need to use the hunks of stone, providing the salt did its job.

He hefted his own piece of rock salt and waited.

Wind rose, whipping up sand as the dark mass neared. Ain affixed his face wrapping and rolled his shoulders.

Raila shouted over the wind. "On my signal we fall back to the tunnels."

The swirling sand neared, yet the buildings diffused it. He could see the silent walkers striding forward – at least, most of them were. Some were stumbling. One reached out to grab at another, knees wobbling. The apparently unharmed walker shrugged the hand off and continued as the first shuddered to the salt-strewn ground.

None offered so much as a turn of the head for the homes and other buildings – even when stone hailed down, those that kept their feet had eyes for one thing only: the stronghold.

"It's working," someone cried as another pair of walkers collapsed.

Ain gripped his hunk of rock salt as the first few corpses reached the heavier concentration of salt, where their steps slowed, faltering. More and more crossed into the line of heavy salt and fell by the time they arrived at the building. One corpse reached for the barricaded door, fingers stretching.

An arrow pinned it to the ground.

It twitched and hints of green slowly started shrivelling to black.

Soon, dozens of bodies littered the space before the building. Yet more and more came. Ade and the other archers were knocking the walkers down, hunks of rock sending the corpses tumbling to the ground. When the creatures hit the salted earth with fresh wounds – or at least tears in the skin – they ceased moving quicker.

Ain heaved his own stone when one corpse drew near. The block tore a gaping hole in its shoulder, revealing the cactus beneath the skin. It did not topple, but its legs were weakening – the wounds it had taken from Wayrn's traps beyond the Cloud were obviously enough.

A few cheers rose from the rooftop when the numbers seemed to have thinned.

But the jubilation did not last.

"Look," Wayrn called. "Something's happening."

Bulky shapes, hard to see clearly in the haze, were appearing from the rear of the remaining corpses. Each seemed too broad for a single man. Ain squinted. More walkers, scores and scores of them – and the reason they appeared too broad? They were carrying their fallen brethren.

"What now?" Ain glared down at them.

No-one offered an answer; he probably wasn't heard over the wind.

But he did not need one.

The purpose of the creatures quickly grew clear. The first pair of walkers dumped the bodies they'd carried onto the salted sand. And then the next, and then another group, until half a dozen fallen corpses lay across the earth.

They were building a bridge of corpses.

24. SETO

Seto let his head slip into his hands, a groan escaping as he leant his elbows upon the polished table. He looked up after a moment. In the soft lamplight, Giovan and Lavinia's expressions were bleak. "Have you put her somewhere safe?"

Giovan nodded, looking to Lavinia, who offered more detail. "Stefano is watching over her, trying to figure out the song, trying to discover how this could have happened."

He looked up. "Your husband is being careful, I take it?"

She smiled, a brave gesture it seemed. "Of course. He knows what I'd do to him if he got himself turned to stone."

"Yes, yes. Well, let's set that matter aside for now, I suppose. Giovan, you wanted to update me?"

"I did. One of Holindo's teams found something. You remember we thought some of our Ecsoli had fled?"

"Indeed."

"I don't think that's the case anymore. Two of my

Ecsoli from the original search party were found near the harbour... they had been de-boned."

Seto straightened. "De-boned? Like fish?"

"It's unpleasant, sire. When we lifted them they flopped about. I had to carry one to the barracks," Giovan said, his jaw tightening.

"Gods, why? What new terror can this be?"

"One of the remaining Ecsoli tried to explain but it didn't make sense to me. I've arranged to have that Ecsoli woman brought here; the one without a house."

"Bethana."

"Right. Her Anaskari is the best among them; Holindo thinks she'll be able to explain it, too."

"Very well. She is waiting nearby?"

"She should be. The Lord Protector was bringing her to the council room."

Seto stood, wincing at the ache in his knees. Blasted body; how much longer did he have before he was bed-ridden? Feeble and useless, someone spoon-feeding him damnable mush? "Then let's not keep them waiting."

The ache had receded a little by the time he reached the council room, but he still took a chair rather than stand, as Danillo and Bethana of Casa Nemo were doing. He waved everyone else into the high-backed seats. "Sit, all."

He regarded Bethana. The tall woman appeared fit, unlike those Ecsoli who had let internment wear them down and her dark eyes held the same deep bitterness they did upon her defeat. "It seems some of your fellows are making good on their promises."

"Of course. They seek their freedom," she said, and Seto had to admit Holindo and Giovan's assessment of her language skills had been accurate. She bore no true accent but there was a lingering formality to her words.

"Yet you yourself did not join the search?"

"I will assist you now."

"Assuredly," Seto said. "But I'm afraid I cannot happily skim past your reluctance to help before. It is disappointing."

She smiled, resting her bound hands on the table. "Are you calling me a spy, King Oseto?"

"I am trying to discern whether you will speak truthfully when I ask about these false Ecsoli and their bone-harvesting."

"I will speak truly, and I leave it to you as to whether you believe my motives for remaining behind while others searched."

"Very well. What strange motive do you offer for refusing freedom, land, and perhaps even dignity?"

"Nothing strange; I simply do not wish to make my home in Anaskar."

Now Seto smiled. "Alas, my lady – we are not planning to send you back to the Land of the Sun."

"Nor will I ask it. Ever. There are lands beyond your desert, lands where I will not be scorned. That is my price," she said.

"She has been quite a studious prisoner," Danillo explained. "Elida, who has been teaching her Anaskari, has been talking of Holvard."

"I see." Seto stood, moving to a nearby sideboard where he poured himself a glass of fire-lemon. He drank and exhaled; a fine batch. "Very well, let us test your veracity. Help us understand and then stop what is happening here in the city and we will enable your travel to Holvard."

"I have your word on that?"

"As king."

"Swear it by Ana."

Seto did so and Bethana nodded. "The Ecsoli your people have been seeing are imposters, as you suspect," she said.

"How are you certain?" Giovan asked.

"The bone-harvesting."

"Go on," Seto said.

"In Ecsoli, it is a foul act committed only by the very worst degenerates. *Untouchables*. It is punishable by the stripping of family name, holdings, and future. More, it is often a death sentence for the entire extended family of any individual caught."

Seto set his drink down, raising an eyebrow at her. A piece of her own history? "Go on, Lady Nemo."

Her jaw remained set. "It is a desperate way to gather a tiny amount of power; the bones are used like small towers to conduct and focus the power for those without masks or armour. Not enough to threaten a city, but as a stepping stone toward something better."

"How does this prove that the Ecsoli are false?" Danillo asked after a moment of silence. "There is no record of such practices here in Anaskar. Only Ecsoli could have brought such darkness to our shores."

"Someone has taught whoever it is," Bethana said, shaking her head.

"For that you have even less proof than your other claims," Seto said.

"No. I know it because the targets have been true Ecsoli only."

Seto narrowed his eyes. "Why would that be so?"

"Because the vast majority of those who are still here, who refused to return to Ecsoli are like me – members of House Nemo. Whoever is doing this, feels no remorse attacking Nemo, we who are seen as less than human."

Another moment of silence before Seto took his seat once more, leaning close to Bethana. Her face revealed no trace of guile that he could detect, only tightly controlled anger and... self-recrimination? "All you say still points to someone from Ecsoli being behind this, you know that. What else gives you such assurance?"

"No Anaskari have been harvested."

"That we know of," Giovan interjected.

"The sightings went on for some time before you asked for Ecsoli help – they're seeking Ecsoli bones especially, they wanted you to use the Ecsoli in your search."

"Why?" Danillo asked.

She offered no answer.

Seto leant back and folded his arms. "A fine question, Danillo. And this still proves only what we suspect and not what you claim, Lady. What are you holding back?"

Her mask of stoicism slipped for just a moment, revealing doubt and anguish, and then the wall returned. She folded her arms. "I have told you all I know. What are my orders?"

"To return to your cell," Seto replied.

"Then you prove yourself a liar, fit for spreading only broken oaths."

He chuckled. "I never said forever. Stay there until you are ready to tell us what you are holding back. Giovan?"

He stood, hauling Bethana to her feet and prodding her into the hall. She said nothing and Seto waited until their footfalls faded before he spoke again. "So, it is clear an Ecsoli is behind the disturbances and now the de-boning. The real question becomes, does Bethana know who and why? Is she involved?"

"If it's part of something underhanded, it might explain why she didn't search. She wanted to keep out of sight," Lavinia said.

"Let's not rule out one of our citizens – the girl mentioned Enso, did she not?" Danillo said.

"True," Seto admitted. "The Perfume Rat – it seems he has found powerful friends. I will have him hung from the walls."

"Holindo and I will ferret them out, Seto," Danillo said.

"And I will continue to work on restoring Abrensi," Lavinia added. "If there is a Song to reverse what has been done, we will find it."

"If Stefano has no ideas, dig into whatever archive you must." He stood, resting his knuckles on the table – a convenient gesture to cover for the momentary weakness in his legs. "And let's try and draw Enso's benefactor out into the open, since we all know he isn't the one who used Fiore."

Danillo nodded. "No surprise if the two are connected."

"We'll soon know," Seto said. "Let's have Holindo or Giovan choose someone to volunteer as bait."

25. Fiore

Fiore looked to her feet, to the soft carpet of the Lord Protector's study. "I didn't do it. I'm not lying."

Lord Danillo removed his Greatmask, revealing a stern face. But his voice was soft, and he didn't seem angry. "I know, sweetheart. I'd just like to know *who* made you do it. I know you didn't learn the Song of Stone by yourself, did you?"

"No, My Lord."

"Good. But you don't know who it was?"

"I..." she swallowed. Like every time before, it was suddenly hard to speak. Green flickered across her vision and she shook her head even as she clenched her fists. "I can't say what I want to."

"That's fine." He lifted the creepy Greatmask. "I am going to use Argeon here to help me find out who is behind this. It won't hurt," he added.

"Oh." Fiore glanced to Giovan, who gave her a nod.

"He knows what he's doing, Beanpole."

The Lord Protector replaced the yellowed bone mask, casting his eyes into shadow. "You may feel a sensation as Argeon searches, but it will not cause pain," he said, his voice echoing.

She nodded, sitting still, tensing her muscles, trying not to move.

"You can relax," he said. A pale blue glow came from the mask and the sense of something enormous and old, so old that it seemed a part of the world itself, washed over her with a ghostly touch.

The green flickering flared but when it met the blue it faded a moment, before returning like a fire caught in wind – and that she felt; a heat ran across her skin and her mouth became dry.

But the blue blazed back then shrunk to a spear that shot through the green and then it seemed to travel miles and miles away, beyond the palace walls, down into the Second Tier and along the streets like an arrow. It did not stop for man, horse or building – finally splashing to a halt in the dim basement of a brothel.

"Very subtle, Enso," the Lord Protector said.

And then all the colours disappeared – taking the heat with it. A faint howl of fury, like an echo in her mind, faded away too.

The Lord Protector patted her hand, then spoke. "Holindo, do you mark my works?"

A pause.

Fi glanced around the bright room with its soft-looking armchairs and huge fireplace. Who was Holindo? And *where* was this man exactly?

"It's the Three Petals; the basement. Fence them in but don't enter until I am there. The woman has some power."

Another pause.

"Good idea. But wait as long as you can – I am on my

way."

"What's happening?" Fi asked.

The Lord Protector was already halfway to the door. "Thank you, Fiore, you did well. Please stay with Giovan for now."

"We won't need bait anymore, will we?" Giovan asked.

"No. I tracked our enemy via the hold she had over Fiore, but in doing so have alerted her to the fact we now know where she is. We have to move quickly."

"Sure you don't need one more sword? I could take her to Lavinia?"

"Hear her story first; she will be able to speak now," the Lord Protector said, and then he was gone.

Giovan sighed, but sat across from her and smiled. "See? Just like I told you. Everyone will believe you now."

"I suppose so." She fidgeted with the sleeve of her tunic. "I'm sorry you have to stay here with me. I know you want to go out and fight."

"Only to pay them back for what they did."

She nodded. "To Lord Abrensi."

"To you, Fi. They used you, and I won't forgive that. Now come on, tell me what happened?"

"Well, it started in that inn we went to," she said, and explained about the green light in the fireplace and then the voice. It was as though a weight had been lifted, now that she could finally explain. Now that she had control over her own voice again. "I thought she was kind at first, but I guess she wasn't. She told me I'd be helping everyone. And I wanted to help, I didn't know what she was doing," she said, her words starting to come faster.

"We know, remember? Now take a breath. Was there anything else?"

Fi did as he suggested. "She said her name was Vipera

and somehow she made it so I couldn't tell anyone it was her."

He nodded. "Good. Everything helps. Did she mention whether she had others with her or was she alone?"

"She didn't say."

He tapped his fingers on the table. "That's probably all you can tell us, right?"

She nodded. "I'm sorry."

"Don't be, it's fine. Let's get you to Lavinia, then. See if you can help her with the search for a song."

He led her out of the rich room, into another, then out into the halls and down a flight of steps. She followed Giovan through a series of storerooms, the musty scent mixing with fresh fruit that big men were carrying. A kitchen followed, warm and bright, bread and sweet loaves cooling on benches. She breathed deeply. As he passed one bench, Giovan grabbed a pair of the smaller breads and then they were climbing a different set of stairs, rounding a long hallway lined with fading paintings.

"Catch," he said, tossing one of the sweet loaves over his shoulder.

She leapt into the air, limbs flailing, but caught it with a grin. She took a bite, filling her cheeks. It was soft, warm and sweet – like nothing she'd ever tasted before. "Thanks, this is amazing."

"Just don't try that without me around," he said, licking his fingers. "The cooks can get a little grumpy down there." Giovan stopped before a pair of ornate doors bearing an intricately detailed feather-quill of silver. "She'll be waiting; good luck."

He started down the hall, boots clacking. "Be careful," she blurted after a moment's hesitation.

"I will, Beanpole," he called.

Fi smiled. Maybe Giovan was rough and smelt of sweat and leather and steel, so different from Father, but he was kinder than the other people in the palace, nearly all of whom seemed serious and distant.

Except Lavinia, who she'd only met once but... at least her smile was nice.

Fi pushed open the door and gaped.

Books, scrolls and shelves stretched as far as she could see – only one wall was visible before her, where a closed door bearing the stern mask-symbol of the Mascare stood. Otherwise, it was oil lamps and books, books, books. So many! And she'd thought Father Canto's single, full shelf had been a lot of books.

Just how rich were palace folk to have all of this?

"Can I help you, young lady?"

An older man in a deep green robe stood before her, hands folded before him. His fingers were ink-stained, but it didn't seem to bother him.

"Ah, I'm Fi. Fiore, and I'm here to see Lavinia."

A slight frown crossed his features. "And you're the young Storm Singer?"

"Yes."

"Lady Lavinia is this way, please follow me." He took Fi down between the shelves, winding through them in the dimness where the scent of paper and leather and dust was almost strong enough to make her sneeze. They continued until nearing a glow, which turned out to be a large square table covered in books and lamps.

Two figures sat at the table across from each other – Lavinia and the other Storm Singer, her husband, though Fi couldn't remember his name. The librarian announced her and then disappeared amongst the shelves.

Lavinia smiled. Her fiery red hair seemed to burn in the light. "Welcome to the Royal Library, Fi. Would you like to help us?"

"I want to try but I don't know if I'll be able." After all, Vipera had fooled her so easily, how would she be able to help powerful Storm Singers? Fi pushed down a wave of resentment.

"You'll do fine," the man said, his gentle voice easing her. He was a handsome fellow; even more than Lenaco from the village, and this man's blond hair was nearly as long as his wife's. "In fact, we've been wanting to try something with you, if you don't mind?"

"Like what?"

"Nothing dangerous," Lavinia assured her. "Here, join us. This is my husband, Stefano."

"We just need you to write out the words to the Song of Stone," Stefano said once she'd taken a spare seat. "Then, we're going to try singing them backwards."

"Oh." Fi frowned. "Will that work?"

He chuckled, a kind sound. "We're certainly going to find out."

26. SETO

Seto sat in a quiet tavern across from the Three Petals, tapping his foot as he stared across at the grand old building with its trellises and balconies. Potted flowers lined the glowing windows, their colours muted in the night. He waved off an offer for wine or ale, which Giovan accepted, sending the serving girl to the other soldiers.

"Surely that's long enough?" Seto demanded. "I'm not a child; they should know that."

"Lord Protector's orders, sire," Giovan said. It looked as if he was hiding a grin behind his mug.

"I see? And who is king here, Giovan? Shouldn't *I* be the one giving orders?"

"How am I to choose, with three masters?"

"Bah. You're all conspiring against me."

The sergeant leant forward. "If I may, My Lord, you need to trust Captain Holindo and Lord Danillo. You're too important to risk. We don't know everything this Vipera is capable of."

"Well, I mean to find out," Seto said, as across the

street, Holindo's orange and silver uniform stood out before the pale stone of the brothel. The royal captain signalled, and Seto was striding out the door, Giovan on his heels and the rest of the men following.

"She escaped," Holindo rasped, his expression dark. "Well before we or Lord Danillo arrived. He's chasing her now."

Ill fortune. "What of Enso?"

"Not so swift – the men we had underground took him. We're holding him inside but we're getting a bit of trouble from the Madam."

"A woman only just past her prime, dark hair? Faint Braonn accent?"

"Aye."

"Leave her to me. Giovan can organise questioning of those who work here. Tell them not to back any Weeds into a corner; just note who they are because we'll want to watch them instead."

"Ah, Weeds, sire?"

Seto shook his head at his own foolishness. Holindo would hardly be accustomed to highly specific and often unimaginative slang used around brothels. "How easy it is to slip back into the habit of my old role. If the women and men working here are 'flowers' then those who also once would have worked for me as spies, are referred to as 'weeds'. Charming, I know."

Holindo raised an eyebrow. "So... visiting dignitaries are preyed upon here?"

"And sometimes our own lords and ladies. Especially if I cannot learn anything from the Ways in the palace. But that's enough reminiscing," Seto said. "Let's go appease Deylilah and then it's time for a nice little chat with the Perfume Rat."

The brothel's lavish reception room stood lined with flowers and pale pink and turquoise draping – overall, somewhat gaudy despite the muted tones. Perhaps it was the heavy scent of jasmine.

Deylilah strode over to Seto the moment he entered. The men Holindo had left on the door strode to stop her but he raised a hand. "It is fine."

She had not aged, it seemed, in the time since he'd left his role as Lord of the Underworld... while he himself had aged enough for the both of them. Her hair was still dark and her skin mostly unlined. "Seto, I want your men out of here unless they're planning to open their purse strings. We had an agreement, did we not?"

"Of course, and it seems you broke it," he said, keeping his voice stern.

Her eyes widened in shock, a true shock if he was any judge of character. "How is that possible? I always—"

He raised a finger. "Who has The Perfume Rat been meeting in your basement?"

"A woman. She calls herself Vipera." Deylilah folded her arms. "I don't have anything to do with whatever they're doing down there. I only saw inside once, and I never looked again."

"You weren't concerned? This is your establishment."

"I couldn't choose who became the next Rat now, could I? You left and that was that."

"A rebuke, Madam?" It was true of course, but it still stung a little.

"I don't need him holding back money or sending the best girls over to the Little Palace or the Arches instead of here, it's that simple. I kept my mouth shut and looked the other way."

"Good. Then I trust you'll be doing the same now, no

matter the outcome."

She narrowed her eyes. "What does that mean?"

"Our dear friend Enso is about to find out." He looked to Holindo. "Which room?"

"Up the back and to the right, ground floor."

"Very well."

Deylilah called after him as he started down the corridor. "He won't talk, you know. He's just as scared of her as I was."

A bloodied Enso sat tied to a chair in what was obviously one of the girls' rooms, a generous bed with silken sheets and behind a screen painted with erotic scenes, was a basin with make-up and little perfume vials. The Perfume Rat blinked a swollen eye. "She isn't human. She'll kill you all," he sneered as best he could, though the blood trickling from his forehead and lip did much to diminish the bravado.

Seto signalled for Holindo to close the door. Then, without acknowledging Enso's words, he leant in and whispered to the captain. "Draw a knife and stand behind him. Close enough to let him know you are there, but make no move or sound."

Then Seto sat before the Perfume Rat and crossed his legs at the ankles, hiding the discomfort it caused.

And he waited.

Enso twisted his head in an attempt to see Holindo. "You won't intimidate me."

Seto said nothing.

"I'm not impressed by the theatrics, Seto."

Still he waited.

And waited.

Time stretched on, no-one speaking. From beyond the hallway came the muffled sound of voices, the words indistinct. A clean up seemed to be in progress, based on the scuffling and thumping, dragging sounds. Hopefully one of Holindo's seconds had ensured the basement was not part of that clean-up.

At one point, long after his own muscles had stiffened and he had shifted positions, Seto heard Deylilah's raised voice but the ruckus soon died down. In the relative hush that followed, Enso licked blood from his lips – a nervous gesture or an idle one? Perhaps the man was simply thirsty.

"You're wasting your time. I will not betray her." He was breathing a little harder now; no doubt the combined injuries and the ropes were starting to get to him. Doubtless the man had served up his share of unpleasantness, but it seemed unlikely he'd received enough that he'd withstand what Seto had planned.

"Captain, take his head and then drive that blade of yours into Enso's left eye. Slowly."

Enso blinked – but did not crack. Holindo took the man's head and lifted the blade, pausing. "How far, sire?"

"Until I say stop."

Holindo started lowering the blade. Enso thrashed, heaving his body where it was tied to the chair, but Holindo gripped him harder, unable, for the moment, to use his knife.

"She will kill me and then kill you," Enso gasped out.

Seto stood. "Not if I kill you first. Now speak, where is Vipera? What do you do here?"

Enso hissed. Seto signalled to Holindo, time to push the Rat. Enso would be able to speak just fine with only one eye.

Before Holindo could act, Enso let out a scream.

The sound of bones snapping filled the room. His cry

slid into a screech as more and more bones snapped, his limbs twisting until his body gave a mighty heave, out of the arms of a surprised Holindo, crashing to the floor.

One final snap and the Perfume Rat was still, his head lying at an odd angle.

Seto spun to the door, hand on his knife, but the hallway was empty. There was not even the hint of fleeing footsteps or a glimmer of disappearing fabric. Only scantily clad young men and women moving in and out of rooms, arms full of bedding.

"Seto!" Holindo's rasping voice stretched into a shout.

Back inside, the captain had fallen back against the bedpost – sword in a white-knuckled hand. Enso's arm was moving, his sightless eyes empty. The arm raised itself to the man's head, fingertips brushing the bloody gash, and then it stretched out to write on the floor, stopping only once for more dark blood.

And then Enso's arm fell away, and the body grew still again.

On the floor, written in the man's own blood were four words only.

Do not seek me.

27. FLIR

Flir turned the wagon east, into the sleet.

The road was a cold stone blade forging through muddy fields. All empty of crop or crow, all quiet – farmhouses standing against the cold, rooves covered in frost, smoke rising from chimneys. The air seemed to claw at her cheeks as she turned her face into the wind, looking over her shoulder.

Pevin lay in the wagon bed, covered in blankets, wedged between foodstuffs and tents. So far, he didn't appear to be worsening. A small victory.

The sound of hooves from behind drew near, and Kanis hailed her. "Someone *is* following us," he said when he reined his horse in.

"You saw them clearly this time?" Flir asked. Two weeks on the road and several times both she and Kanis had seen enough to suspect someone followed. Hints of smoke aligning with their own camping, a dark horseman several hills or turns back – a traveller who never caught up to them. Unusual, slowed as they were by the wagon.

And now, a mere day or two out from the capital,

passing through what should have been green farmlands, Kanis had sought to discover just who was trailing them. He was betting on Aren himself; Flir put her money on one of his men. Pevin, when he wasn't sleeping, would have said the same.

Kanis shook his head, flicking beads of rain as he did. "No. I thought I'd catch him, but he turned before I could get a proper look. Clumsy of the both of us – I don't think it's someone used to following unseen."

"Then we keep an eye on him."

"You don't want to a put stop to it now? I could set an ambush easily enough."

Flir glanced along the road ahead. "Not yet. It might be no-one. We'll wait for the bridge. If they cross after us, we can trap them a little easier."

"Good." Kanis cracked his knuckles. "I'll be looking forward to it."

"Aren't you feeling belligerent. What's gotten into you?"

He shrugged.

"Out with it. Is it about that damn woman and her bone in your hand?"

"No. It's Aren. I don't like him."

"That all?"

Kanis grunted. "Don't pretend you trust him just to goad me."

"I want to know what he's up to just as much as you."

"Do you think he really knows more than he lets on? About us?"

"Possibly."

"Well, I think it's a ploy. Same with the old lighthouse and the Ice-Priests."

"That wouldn't be hard to verify, if the priests are

really going missing."

"He could be using it to his advantage."

"Let's say he is. What does he want?"

Now Kanis swore. "Don't be stupid, Flir. Don't tell me you didn't feel what I felt. That kid could have taken all of me back there."

He was right, but was there more to it than greed? "But he didn't. And neither did Aren. I'm not saying I disagree, but what's the end point to this supposed long con? They save us, then put themselves at risk to cement trust... for what?"

"That's what I can't figure out. If they can take strength from dilars, why isn't Aren much more powerful? He could have been doing it for years, and people like us would be disappearing. And if he was, I would have heard of it. I haven't been away *that* long."

"He said he only came across the knowledge recently. Perhaps it takes a long time to perfect. I can't imagine he'd have had many volunteers... we should have asked him about that actually."

Kanis nodded slowly. "Or there's something at the lighthouse that he needs?"

Flir sighed. "I don't know. If you want, we can go there once we meet the Conclave and see what's going on."

"Right. One thing at a time, I suppose."

When Pevin woke he was well enough to help set up camp but he was troubled by news that Ice-Priests had been disappearing. "If it's true, this is grave news. With such a clinging winter, we could face terrible snowstorms, famine... fighting over resources, and not just those in the north. It will happen here, too, further south."

"Perhaps it is already happening," Flir said. She tossed

a log to the flames, greedy, grasping hands of orange that didn't do much to warm her. "We all saw the fields."

After a moment, Pevin said, "I would like to find out the truth, dilar. After we see the Conclave, of course."

Flir placed a hand on his shoulder. "You don't have to ask permission. And I'm curious too."

"Thank you," he said, relief clear on his face. "My younger brother is our Priest – he took the role in my stead. I would hate to think my pig-headedness had cost him his life."

"Isn't he working in your family holding?" Kanis asked.

"We are from the east... but not so far south as the lighthouse. But if he had been called down to help, as has happened in the past..."

"We'll find the truth behind Aren's claims once we're done in Enar," Flir said. "But for now, let's get some rest. I'll take first watch; we still have our friend following."

While Pevin and Kanis arranged their bedding within the tents, Flir sat with her back to the flames and stared into the darkness beyond. A troubling thought had come to the surface. Slowly, over the course of the trip, despite how much he irritated her, Flir had come to enjoy working with Kanis again. It was like old times, which was an alarm bell all of its own.

And yet, they'd achieved much together.

Even earlier, trying to figure out Aren's true motive together brought that sense of shared purpose. Something she'd missed since Notch left, and since she lost Luik. Not that Pevin wasn't a friend... but he wasn't an old friend.

Old memories were stirring with her realisation too, memories best left where they couldn't impair her judgement. Memories of Kanis, of their time together before all the trouble with the royal family. Time when he'd been as tender as he was brash...

Flir sighed. Maybe being home again was messing with her head.

After all, she couldn't fully forgive Kanis for everything he'd done, just because she was feeling confused about whether she was homesick – and worse, when she couldn't even decide *where* she was feeling homesick for.

***

The dawn was a cold one; the end of her nose had surely turned to ice and a reluctance to leave her blankets had her scowling at herself as she rose. Anaskar's climate had her getting soft. Still, how much fondness could she really have for such cruel weather?

"Any visitors?" she asked Kanis as he handed her a cup of steaming *picha*, the scent of lavender strong. The second cup he gave to Pevin, who'd already broken his tent.

"None."

"Well, let's keep an eye out anyway."

This close to the capital, the muddy road was busier. There should have been more farmers and merchants taking their wares in to Enar but with such a poor-seeming harvest it was mostly travellers in worn clothing, a single patrol of soldiers in their fur-lined armour, and one young family with large bundles of what seemed to be their entire possessions.

When Flir asked what they fled, the mother pulled her child close and shook her head, refusing to answer.

"We don't want trouble, lady," the man said as he

hurried them along.

Flir exchanged glances with Pevin and Kanis.

By the time they reached the glittering green expanse of the Venach River, the sun had broken through the clouds, falling upon a pair of wagon trains. The lead wagons were blocking one another near the mouth of the arching Venach Bridge – beyond which, eventually, waited the capital.

"Looks like we're not getting through in a hurry," Kanis said.

Men who appeared to be in charge of each wagon were shouting at one another about who had right of way. With one train heading in and the other trying to leave, and both turned enough to prevent the other's progress – not to mention anyone else's – Flir had to stop herself leaping down from her own seat and smashing the wagons to splinters.

"If we toss a few wagons over the side, that might help," she replied.

"That's a little uncharitable, dilar," Pevin said.

Kanis crossed his arms. "Sounds good to me."

One voice rose to a screech. "Last chance, mud-head. You don't move, I'll blow you and the whole bridge to the sky."

"Shut your mouth, Junish – fur-man like you could never afford *acor*. Now get your nag out of my way," the second said, hefting an axe.

Flir frowned. An argument over right of way was one thing; blowing up the only bridge over the mighty Venach was another.

Darkness flashed, catching her eye – high on the bridge's entry-column.

An elongated figure seemed to cling to the stone.

Black, leathery skin stretched over protruding bones, and despite its gauntness, it was huge. When it moved, deep purple highlights were visible beneath the sun. It crept down steadily toward the two men – and before Flir could shout a warning, it dropped onto the man claiming to own *acor*.

Blood splattered onto his wagon as his scream tore across the river. The dark creature wrapped its many legs around the man, bearing him to the flagstones with a sharp crack. The other merchant fell back, fumbling for his whip. All along the trains other men were scrambling from their wagons, even the armed guards. Splashing followed as men threw themselves into the river and pounding feet thundered across the bridge, heading toward Enar. But the thing seemed satisfied with its first victim… until a long arm or leg shot forth at a seemingly impossible angle, impaling the second caravan leader.

Flir spun to Pevin. "You can't help us with this, understood?"

"But dilar—"

"Flee if we cannot stop it," she said, cutting off his words as she leapt to the ground. Kanis was right beside her.

"What by Mishalar is it?" he asked.

"Never seen anything like it."

"Me either."

"Remember, we don't know everything it's capable of," she said as she sidestepped a gibbering man. Kanis had already thrust two guards from his path, his winged mace ready. Flir had her short sword drawn as they approached the nearest wagon, which obscured the thing on the ground.

"It's fast," Flir whispered.

Kanis gave a nod.

The creature had dragged the second man closer, looming over him almost protectively. It was an insect-like cage of legs and arms, the sinuous body catching the light and setting the purple patches shimmering. The skull was elongated too and its eyes rested low on the head, spots within the iris lightening to amethyst. Its jaw hung open over the bloodied corpse of the first man. The creature's mouth was wide enough to swallow the fellow whole, yet only gurgling sounds came forth as a grey substance spewed free, spreading across the dead body.

Like a web.

Flir ground her teeth; it turned her stomach. But despite her revulsion she could tell a sword wasn't quite right. She sheathed it, with half an eye on the nearest wagon. Kanis was breathing a little hard but he dropped to a crouch, then leapt forth. He swung his mace at the creature's hunched back.

A sharp crack split the air – as if steel had struck marble. Kanis was thrown back, cursing as his mace fell to the ground. He cradled his hand, flinching as the creature spun, the grey substance spraying as it howled.

It reared up, front legs raised.

Flir dashed to the wagon. She gripped the wooden sides and hauled the cart into a spin – flinging it into the creature. Wood exploded and the steel frame clanged to the stones. The dark creature shook its head as if dazed, more grey web flying across the bridge. Kanis scrambled back, snatching up his mace.

"We're not doing much damage here," he shouted.

"I know."

"Any ideas?"

Flir glanced over the wreckage... and there it was. Dark powder now coated the creature's legs and the bridge beneath it. *Acor*. It had to be worth trying.

"Start a fire," she called.

"What?"

"Just do it, fool! I'll draw its attention."

Kanis ran for one of the unharmed wagons in the train, having either decided to follow her orders or having seen the *acor*, had put it together. Flir tore a wheel from the next wagon and hurled it at the creature's head. It dodged easily. She ripped her sword free and backed away as it scrambled after her – good. She kept giving ground, leading it further from the bridge and across the cold earth beside the road. A dark leg speared forth and she deflected it with her blade, backhanding a second leg with her free hand.

Bone cracked but she ignored the pain. "Kanis!"

"Hold on a little longer."

The purple eyes regarded Flir from where it towered over her. Its toothless mouth was opening, lower jaw falling as more of the grey, web-like substance filled the cavity. It sucked in a breath and spat – but Flir was already diving aside.

She rolled to her feet and deflected another stabbing arm. Her sword shattered. Warm blood ran down her face and she wiped at it as she skipped further away.

"Give me some room," Kanis called.

Flir hurled herself back, pushing hard off the ground. She landed then somersaulted into a handstand, pushing herself away even further as a boom rocked the earth. A rush of hot air stung her face and hands as she crashed to the mud.

But she sprang to her feet as soon as the heat eased –

to see the creature standing, unharmed.

"Bastard."

Like before, it appeared stunned but had not fallen.

It had to have some manner of weakness, but what? The dark thing still hadn't regained its senses; the purple orbs were closed and the limbs twitched. Yet there, now that it was still, mouth agape...

"Kanis. I need more *acor.*"

"It's no use," he called from where he was circling the thing. "We didn't even hurt it."

The creature's eyes snapped open – one following Flir and one locking on Kanis. It fell into a crouch, then charged – heading for the bridge. Flir started after but it was too fast. It scrambled to the top of the column then into the very sky itself, shimmering as its legs moved in a blur.

And then it was gone.

28. FLIR

Enar's fourth-finest inn, so proclaimed by the portly owner, was warm and welcoming, with a cheery fire, comfortable seats, good service and food that looked like it should have been as grand and sumptuous as anything on a king's table.

And yet it tasted like nothing to Flir.

Only the wine cut through her dark mood, a welcome bitterness. "What was that thing?" she asked over the din of voices and the crackle of flames.

Kanis sighed. "Enough, Flir. I don't like being beaten any more than you, but I've already told you I have no idea. We've gone over every creature – mythical or otherwise – and it's just not there."

She ignored him. "And how did it escape? And why did it leave then? We weren't any closer to killing it. Was that why people were fleeing the area? Had it only just arrived – and if so, from where?"

"I have been thinking on the how, dilar," Pevin said.

"And?"

"We've already established that it was spider-like, yes?

Well, why not a web that we could not see properly?"

"I saw nothing like that, Pevin," Kanis said. "And I was *very* close."

"From my angle I thought I saw it clinging to something, once it left the bridge."

Kanis signalled for another round. "And it went off into the very sky, I suppose?"

Pevin spread his hands. "Or across the river to a point we could not see. The banks do rise quite steeply to the east of the bridge."

Flir slapped the table. Cutlery jumped, as did their plates and Kanis caught his drink. "There's an old guard post downstream," she said. "Who's to say it didn't go there?"

"Well, I don't want to know," Kanis said. "Tomorrow we meet with the Conclave and then we're leaving."

"We can't let it attack the city, Kanis," Flir said.

He grunted.

"I mean it."

"Fine. Then we warn the Conclave and let them deal with it."

"Think they can?"

"We're not the only dilar on the continent, you know."

"What does that mean?"

"The Conclave has a pair of knuckle-brains under their employ. I don't know if you remember them? Two brothers, Ledal and Depeva."

"Don't remember them." She sipped her drink, glaring at him. "But I'm not going to dump it in their lap and disappear."

"Fine. We're running low on funds; how about we charge the Conclave? How does twenty thousand gold pieces sound?"

She folded her arms. "Why not fifty then?"

"Let's focus on the Conclave itself first," Pevin said before Kanis could reply.

"Good idea." Flir put her cup down and stood. "I'm going to get some sleep."

But once she was in her room, door locked, she found she couldn't fall asleep despite the soft bed. When she dozed, the creature stalked her dreams and once – waking in the deep of night, the tavern below quiet – she could have sworn one of the thing's harder-than-steel legs was right beside her. But it was only the wall; she'd tossed her blankets aside and rolled up against the cold wood.

She sat up to collect her blankets before slumping back down. "Gods grant me rest."

But when they finally did it was all too soon that Pevin was knocking on her door. "We don't want to be late, dilar," he said.

"Late?" Pale light streamed through the window. She groaned at it.

"The Conclave, Flir," he said. "King Oseto's offer."

"Give me a moment."

She stumbled to the porcelain basin, splashed the chilly water on her face and gathered her things before meeting Pevin in the hall. "Let's go."

They found Kanis below; he was finishing a drink, which he pushed back as they approached.

"Thirsty?" Flir asked as she pushed the door open.

"Just wanted a little something to take the edge off what we discovered yesterday," Kanis said, catching up.

"Good," she said. "Turn up drunk to our meeting with the Conclave." Her breath steamed in the cold air. The streets and architecture of Enar were not so different from Whiteport – everything was bigger and it was noisier, but it was still dark stone, icicles and fire markets, people in furs and heavy beards and women carrying swords and hand axes. Nothing out of the ordinary, yet how many knew of the danger less than half a day from the walls?

Kanis chuckled. "Do we even have an audience with them yet? I didn't see a response to the request we sent. If they don't even know we've arrived—"

"Worry not," Pevin replied. "A messenger from the palace has already allotted us an audience for this morning. He arrived while you were relieving yourself."

"Right."

The main thoroughfare led up toward the palace – or the old palace. It was, as Pevin told her, now known as the Citadel. It loomed before them now, subtly different to when she'd last seen it. The great wall was gone but a deep moat of ice still surrounded it, the water long-since frozen black. The docks were concealed by the row of merchant-buildings for now. Statues and engravings of Royal Stags had been replaced by a curved circle made of granite and carven words of a simple creed *The Circle Serves All*. Very egalitarian but what did it really mean? Had life changed for people in Renovar? In the city, even? There had still been beggars on the way in, and passing one of the city's jails yesterday had seen it open for business.

Twin sets of guards, all carrying crossbows and axes, barred their way at the moat. Pevin explained who they were, revealing a wooden token marked with circles, which earned them a grunt and a wave into the palace – citadel.

At the entrance, they were met by a servant who led them down a long, dull hall. Dull, since it now lacked any of the magnificent tapestries it had once held; spun with silver and gold, they had created sparkling rivers and lakes and shining armour on the heroes of old. Here, Tandavir should have been seen charging his horse to slay the World-Eater.

Now it was bare walls and the occasional lamp.

"The Conclave will see you right away," the man said when they stopped at the large double doors of what used to be the throne room. Flir hesitated before pushing on the door; the last time she'd been inside a lot of people had died. Needlessly, for many of them, as it turned out.

Inside, the throne room had been changed; it now seemed to house smaller rooms within the large throne room. Braziers burned bright and warm, flanking the Conclave itself. Aside from the servant, who was even now closing the doors, it was only the six members, both men and women seated at the circular table.

"Welcome," one man said, a white-haired fellow who bore some familiar features. Had he been part of the original Conclave that she and Kanis had helped into power?

Those who had started out with their backs to the entry were already rising to shift their tables around, enabling them to see their visitors.

"Forgive our lack of preparedness," the white-haired fellow continued, quickly introducing himself as 'Circle-Member Wodka', then including the others, though few names registered. "We are very pleased to have you here as speakers for Anaskar. We have been debating your king's offers since he contacted us and are most pleased that he understands certain individual elements were responsible, and responsible alone, for the ill-fated attack on your city. We would love to resume regular trade as soon as possible." He smiled. "We miss Anaskari fire-lemon among other items."

Flir did not glance at Kanis, who hopefully had the presence of mind to keep calm. If the Conclave didn't recognise him – or she herself – then all the better. Especially Kanis, since he was one of the 'certain individual elements' Wodka had mentioned. "That is heartening to hear," Flir said. "I know King Oseto seeks a lasting peace between Anaskar and Renovar. He is quite firm in his desire to avoid something like the Ecsoli manipulation and invasion in the future."

Wodka inclined his head. "A graceful transition. You do, of course, refer to the proposed search for bones of ancient Sea Beasts, the source of the Anaskari Greatmasks?"

"I do, Circle-Member Wodka. Does the Conclave see cause for concern?"

He spread his hands. "Perhaps not concern."

A thin woman leant forward, her hands folded before her, nails lacquered red. "Please understand, we are not concerned about cooperation in principal. It is the specifics we have yet to wrangle. If such a repository of powerful bone *does* exist here in Renovar we could not simply hand it all over to Anaskar – to any nation, for that matter."

Flir nodded. "I believe King Oseto offered some manner of compensation – masks of your own."

Wodka continued. "Certainly. A number to be determined at a future date, to be allotted by the only nation with the knowledge to craft such items."

"True," Flir said. "And only *if* more bones exist."

The thin woman replied. "Which we must be prepared for."

"The king would not stop at the crafting and bestowing; he would offer training from the Mascare too," Pevin added. "I do not believe he would offer such powerful defence and then not help his ally use it to protect their own people. Who knows from where another attack might come?"

Wodka paused to confer with the man seated directly beside him, who whispered back, and it seemed Wodka and the thin woman were the only two who were going to speak. "Let us further discuss this new facet to the original offer. While we do so, please enjoy your time as guests. Perhaps a meal in the Citadel's famous food hall?"

"Sounds good to me," Kanis said before Flir could accept the offer.

"Very well, please allow Dinnav to guide you there. We will send for you," Wodka said as the Conclave started rearranging their tables to once more form the circle.

Outside, Dinnav led them through the empty corridors to the food hall, which was a huge, open area filled with tables and chairs. Merchant stalls ringed the room, each boasting a different cuisine: from home, Anaskar, Medah and Wiraced and even so far away as Holvard. It created quite a riot of scents, though not all were complimentary.

"The Conclave certainly loves its circles," Flir said.

"They believe it is the ultimate symbol of unity," Pevin replied, his gaze lingering on the stall boasting the 'best lamb and olive this side of the desert'.

"Who cares so long as this lot can cook? I'll find you," Kanis said as he strode toward one of the Anaskar stalls.

Flir found a table that appeared quiet enough and sat with a sigh. So much was still the same... yet so much had changed. Even the odd arrangement for eating was, if not unpleasant, certainly perturbing.

"You look gloomy," Pevin said when he returned with a steaming plate of lamb, potato and green olives.

"I think what I miss about home is going to be the things that are already gone." She shrugged. "It'll pass."

Before Pevin could respond, a shout rang across the room. Flir turned in her chair.

Kanis held a struggling man with one hand, bowl of fish and rice in the other and a wide grin on his face. The fellow kicking and struggling – all useless – was dressed in a nondescript cloak but once his hood fell back, Flir raised an eyebrow – caught somewhere between surprise and a feeling of inevitability.

Grav, the cultist.

29. NOTCH

Prince Ren was younger than Notch had expected – perhaps close to Sofia's age, or even a little younger. The man still carried himself with the assurance of one long accustomed to rule, and he was near-to smothered in silver and blue silks. He wore no weapons, though his belt carried a thin, empty scabbard – doubtless for a rapier or some other duelling blade.

While his scabbard was empty, his standing as a royal seemed to permit him to bring forbidden objects into the meeting room – for he wore an odd mask.

Similar to the face wrappings used in the desert, it covered his mouth and nose only, leaving his eyes exposed. But unlike the wrappings used by the Medah, this mask was made of bone and it replicated the lower half of a human face, jaw, and teeth. A little grotesque but less so once Notch understood its purpose.

"It will conceal the words I speak, should my snivelling siblings be listening in," Prince Ren said after introducing himself. He spoke in a rather pleasant, calm voice, and slowly enough for Notch to follow, but he clenched and unclenched his hands in his lap as he did so.

Notch looked to Alosus, who wore a slight frown. "We can hear you quite clearly, Your Highness."

He nodded. "It will only obstruct those listening with bone."

"I see. A prudent precaution."

The prince looked to Notch. "And you are from the New Land? Tell me, is it so very different to here?"

"Ah, some things are the same." Notch took a moment to consider his words. He needed it – not only to translate them into Old Anaskari but to switch focus. Questions about Marinus were hardly high up on the lad's priority. "My skill with the old tongue is poor. Can I speak to Alosus in Anaskari and have him translate?"

Prince Ren nodded and for the next hour, Notch described Anaskar from daily life to military, political and artistic endeavours, geography and climate – but slowly, through Alosus. Speaking, then waiting for Alosus to translate and in turn translate Ren's question, if it had been delivered too quickly or if the words were unfamiliar, then answering again, was more tiring than he'd have expected.

Finally, the prince seemed sated and he leant forward. "I have a boon to ask of you both."

"A boon, Your Highness?" Alosus asked.

"Yes, though I would reward you with whatever you ask, if it is within my power." He stood. "I will leave you to think upon it, upon how it might be achieved, and I will seek your answer on the morrow."

"We will give it most serious consideration," Alosus answered.

"Good. Then here it is, plainly said. When you leave, I wish for you to take me to the New World, to Anaskar."

Alosus was already bowing. "We will indeed think upon it, Prince Ren."

Notch fumbled through his own bow – the prince had turned to leave before Notch finished straightening. Once the door closed, Notch looked to Alosus. "Kind of him to give us tonight to think it over and come up with a way to smuggle him out of here."

Alosus sighed. "Truly."

"What does this mean? Where does this lad and his request fit in here?"

"I cannot say. Vinezi rarely mentioned his nephews. My feeling is that few would miss him, somehow. Tonight, we will learn more – the ball will offer a wealth of information."

Notch shook his head. "I'm not one for dancing."

Alosus grinned. "Nor I, but I suspect that I at least will be fending off more conversations than dance requests."

"Thanks."

The big man's smile faded. "Everyone will be asking to dine with you, to speak with you at a later date, in private. Accept every offer; you don't want to offend any of their fragile sensibilities. And some conversations will be fine opportunities."

"I will. But you know we're not here to win brides or trade partners."

"I do. But until we can arrange to visit the Library of Souls it's best to keep all paths open."

"A visit the Mare family must approve?"

"Yes."

"Which means we have to tell Prince Ren we will spirit him away or go to another family member."

"Perhaps both."

Notch scratched at the stubble on his cheeks. "Then

I'm going to need a razor."

"Don't worry," Alosus said. "I'm sure someone has already set the servants in motion."

"That sounds ominous."

And it was. As if summoned by Alosus' prediction, Notch had barely slumped into one of the regular-sized chairs before the room was swarming with servants, all dressed in black livery. One bore hot water, soap and razors, others carried great armfuls of clothing and soft shoes. A young man bore a tray of perfumes, but the fellow only approached when the grey-haired woman, who appeared to be the leader, deemed Notch presentable.

Which meant his regular, worn clothing – all except the bracers, which no-one remarked upon – was whisked away for cleaning and he was left in dark pants and a red tunic. Thankfully, it was not of silk but cotton and a solid belt offered at least the semblance of dressing for utility. Even his hair, which had grown nearly to his shoulders, had been pulled back and tied into a knot at the back of his head. His reflection in the standing mirror the small army had brought along was respectable enough that he might have been mistaken for a minor – if battered – nobleman, rather than a one-time captain and mercenary.

"Do I actually have to wear any of this?" Notch asked Alosus. Alosus wore a similar outfit, though his vest rested much closer to orange. It showed off the fire-like markings on his shoulders.

"Best to follow custom."

"Let me see, then," Notch said. He took the first bottle, tinted green, and removed the lid. Citrus, lime probably. He replaced it, going through several scents – each becoming increasingly floral, until he found one of cedarwood and nodded. The lad seemed to suppress a smirk, as if he'd been expecting such a choice, but offered the vial without comment.

"Dinner will be served in the Hall of Graces," the head servant explained. "You will be escorted." And with that, she rounded up her helpers and left; leaving behind only one woman.

"Please, follow me, sirs." She seemed none too pleased at her task, giving Notch a look of suspicion and openly sneering at Alosus.

They wound through the marble halls once again. Darkness poured in through the windows between lamps that held the strange crystals used outside the palace. He'd have to ask Alosus about them when he didn't have to focus on the somewhat daunting prospect of being made to dance.

The sound of lively music drew them deeper into the palace and finally to a grand hall where dancers spun across a floor of golden wood.

The Hall of Graces was lined on one side by long tables, then came the dancers swirling in an array of pinks, yellows, blues and greens and next, beneath a wall of more subdued banners, a small table where two women and one man sat watching the dancers. They were dressed in purple robes, much like the Inquisitor at the docks. While they bore no particular bone-crafted device, they seemed to be marking down their observations.

Before he could ask Alosus about them, a figure appeared before him – Lady Casselli.

"I have a seat for you, Captain. I would be honoured if you sat beside me."

Her dark hair now fell around her shoulders and she wore a lighter dress cut higher, revealing more of her legs. Bathed in the warm light, the noblewoman was even more alluring than before – yet he had not dismissed her smile from earlier.

"That would be more than pleasant," he said. "Assuming Alosus can join me? My use of the Old Tongue is not sophisticated."

"Of course," Lady Casselli said, and led them around the dancers and to the nearest table, which was surprisingly small. It held only four chairs, two of which were occupied by servants. It was quite modest compared to some of the other tables, which were much longer and stuffed with men in similar, if richer attire to Notch, their colours often softer. Most drank and spoke amongst themselves, ignoring the dancing.

Lady Casselli sat and gestured to the chair beside her, then motioned to one of the servants, who stood and rushed off. "Sit, Captain Medoro." To Alosus she said, "My servant will arrange for a suitable chair."

"Thank you, Lady," Alosus said, and stood beside Notch, appearing at ease even though he towered over the table. Yet he did not seem to be drawing much attention. As Notch looked around, he found more eyes drawn to him. Many men and women, and some children, were glancing surreptitiously over wine glasses, while some stared quite openly. Some offered faint smiles, as if to a distant, uncouth cousin. More than a few did not appear to like what they saw at all. One man wore a breastplate of steel where he sat, his head shaven and scarred. Notch nodded to the man, who blinked, then returned the gesture.

"They're *burning* with curiosity," Lady Casselli said. "Even the Ocean."

"The Ocean?" he asked.

She lifted a silver fork and waved it toward the largest

table – the royal table, judging by the silver, grey, and blue clothing. Not to mention the two figures wearing Greatmasks. Their power was palpable even from across the hall. They flanked an elderly man who wore a silver circlet; he was being fed soup by a servant, who bore the man's fussing and snarling with stoic patience.

Notch looked for Prince Ren but could not find the young man, though there were plenty of other royals at hand. Like the other tables, they tended to speak amongst themselves, ignoring the battle at the head of their table and taking no callers. Few seats were empty; the womenfolk of the Mare family did not seem inclined to dance. Many bore a similar set of features, dark eyes and sharp noses, and while they tended to be more subtle about their curiosity, he still caught them watching.

"Expect a visit between courses," she said.

"From who?"

"One of them, several. It's hard to say; they like to pretend they aren't interested. Marinus' first son or perhaps the king's niece on the harpy's side."

Notch raised an eyebrow. "One of them has wings and claws?"

Lady Casselli's laugh was a purr. "She likes to think so."

"I'm causing some unrest, it seems."

"They simply want the attention – you are the most interesting thing to happen to the court in years. A man from the new world, it is remarkable. You would be a fine trophy, something to trot out at evenings like this, and then be returned to some gilded cage until the next event," she said, and her tone had grown dark.

"And what do you want from me, My Lady?"

"Perhaps the same."

"Am I so fascinating? There's a whole land full of other Anaskari back across the sea – I'm no more than a mercenary now."

"But you are here and they are not, and once a War-Hero, always a War-Hero; that's the way of things here." She rested a hand on his own. "Besides, haven't you ever desired something different to yourself?"

"I have." He met her dark eyes. "But I am a stranger here; I cannot trust every beautiful woman who comes my way."

"Understandable." Lady Casselli removed her hand but did not seem offended by what he hoped was a suitably honeyed rebuff. Her servants returned with a large chair and Alosus was finally able to sit. Right on their heels came lines of servers carrying steaming trays.

The musicians switched to a more stately song as the dance floor emptied.

Notch straightened at the scent of meat, a lightly sautéed chicken, and had to restrain himself from tearing into it with his knife and fork when it was placed before him.

But Alosus touched his arm, nodding up to the head table.

There, the servers were concentrating most of their efforts – and while no-one made any effort to include the king, there was a moment of quiet. Heads were bowed in prayer and one of the older men, a man perhaps Notch's own age, spoke into the hush.

"By the grace of Ana but also my grandfather, we are provided this bounty. Be thankful. Savour what has been prepared on our behalf, what the Gods have left behind that we might take and grow strong."

And then the clatter of cutlery filled the room.

Notch ate with as much decorum as he could muster; every bite was better than the last, such rich flavours. Even the odd red peas, the *opas*, were a welcome spice to compliment the pepper sauce. He talked about Anaskar with his hostess as he ate, occasionally assisted by Alosus when Notch discovered he didn't have the words.

Lady Casselli hung on his every tale and it seemed not an act – she was quite interested about the 'new world'. By the time the first course ended, Notch was beginning to worry his voice wouldn't last an entire evening, but Lady Casselli stopped her next question and stood. Alosus was already rising, and Notch followed their example as a tall figure reached the table.

"You honour me, Prince Tanere," she said.

Prince Tanere was the fellow who'd made the speech and bore a more than passing resemblance to Marinus. The silver trim on his clothing had a precision to it that hinted at military to Notch's eye. The prince offered her a warm smile before taking the empty seat, gesturing that everyone should sit.

"Forgive my disinterest in small talk, Casselli, but tonight I wish to speak with our guests, for we have much to discuss."

"Our pleasure, Your Highness," Alosus said.

Notch echoed the statement.

"Wonderful to hear, Slave-Alosus and Captain Medoro of the new world. I find myself very curious about Anaskar and surrounding lands but chief among my curiosities remains a stolen Crucible. Tell me, do either of you know what that snake Vinezi did with it?"

30. NOTCH

Notch hesitated. "Please excuse my limitations with the Old Tongue, Your Highness."

Prince Tanere waved a hand.

"The Crucible died with Vinezi in the mountain temple," he said, and explained, with Alosus' help, in brief, the events. Treading carefully, he minimised his own role in the struggle, establishing himself as a bodyguard set to the sidelines for his own safety.

"I see." The man's expression had grown dark as Notch spoke. "This is a grievous blow – Ana damn Vinezi's mouldering ghost."

Yet there was the chance that a second crucible lay somewhere beneath the city. The invaders seemed to think so, since they had Dilo and Tenaci searching for it, and they'd have known Vinezi still carried his own. And if it existed, was it a bargaining chip? Or perhaps the *possibility* of handing one over might be enough to get what he needed – access to the Library of Souls.

But if such a powerful item was given to the Ecsoli, what would it take for another Vinezi to attempt to cross the sea with it to seek more bone for forging? On the other hand, did they really have a reason to try it? The whole of Ecsoli believed they possessed the final bones of the last Sea Beast anyway.

"Your Highness..." he hesitated. "I would like Alosus to translate again, if you don't mind."

"Please do so."

Notch kept his voice calm as he switched to Anaskari. "There may be a second Crucible beneath the city and some of the invaders seemed to know this – is it a bargaining chip here?"

Alosus' eyes widened almost imperceptibly – had Tanere noticed? The man was drinking from a glass and did not seem to be following too closely, in fact, he was paying Lady Casselli's breasts more attention. "Notch, if that is true leave it be for now. We can get what we want another way."

"It is so powerful?"

"Yes. Your king would benefit from it more."

"And if they already know and we try to hide such knowledge?"

"I don't think the prince knows – he would have asked after it. Those Ecsoli who invaded seemed to have kept it to themselves for now."

"Then we just have to rely on our clout as novelty items with news from afar?"

"Yes."

"So what do we tell them we've been talking about?"

"Marinus. You're not sure how much to tell."

Notch nodded slowly. That might work. He turned back to the prince. "Your Highness, I do bear some details of your father's passing... but I feel this isn't the right setting for such grim talk."

The prince leant a little closer. "No. You are doing a fine job of being diplomatic, go on, Captain."

Again, and slowly, Notch and Alosus gave a version of Marinus' death that painted him as driven if greedy, and betrayed by Vinezi. It seemed a neat way to further obscure Notch, Sofia and Seto's role in the confrontation.

Prince Tanere took a deep breath and exhaled. "And you saw his corpse with your own eyes?"

"We both did." Odd questions for a son to ask but perhaps, in the Land of the Sun, it wasn't so strange.

"This is grand news indeed." He stood. "I will call upon you later, as your testimony will be invaluable. Enjoy the rest of your meal, gentlemen." He inclined his head to Lady Casselli. "Lady."

"Your Highness."

The second course, roasted beef, was then brought in, allowing him a moment to gather his thoughts. The meat swum in a peppery-scented gravy. Heaps of golden potato lathered in butter followed, along with pumpkin and what might have been bacon – only it was also fiery. He noticed that Lady Casselli's plate was still quite full; she had not eaten much, but why?

The musicians, who were almost hidden in the far corner of the hall, started a new tune, something strident but not so fast as before. Lady Casselli sighed as she stood. "I suppose I should maintain my standing as a Lady. Please excuse me for a song."

"Of course," Notch said, unable to prevent a slight frown as she swayed onto the dance floor. He lowered his voice. "Why now? And why at all?"

"Remember I told you that Ecsoli was a competitive place – this is one way a woman competes here. As to why now, during the middle of the meal? I believe it is so the Lady can enjoy her dessert."

"What?"

"This way the dance isn't hanging over her and at the same time, she has remained a dutiful host to her guests by not immediately alighting to the dance right after our arrival."

Notch shook his head, part admiration, part disbelief. "You certainly know the way of the nobility."

"Yes. Vinezi's legacy was not all hideous, it seems."

Lady Casselli had taken a space all of her own, her dance bearing a sort of pattern but one unpredictable. There was a give and take to her movements, not unlike swordplay. As she moved, her dress spun and twirled, revealing her toned legs – he could not help but notice. Yet there was more to admire in her skill than her figure alone. Even when she smiled over at him, he found himself transfixed, unable to respond.

When he did manage to glance away, it was clear that other men felt the same – Tanere among them.

After a time, one of the Inquisitors had risen to continue watching. The others were still writing, marking down their judgements, perhaps.

"What are the Inquisitors doing?" Notch asked.

"They are noting down who has performed to what standard. Whoever is deemed the 'best' tonight is generally rewarded with gold, silks or sometimes slaves."

"Oh."

Alosus' jaw was set.

Notch leant closer to the man. "I will do all I can to help you find them."

"Thank you, Notch."

Lady Casselli was returning, a light sheen of sweat across her brow. She drank from her lemon-water and sighed.

"You are a fine dancer, My Lady," Alosus said.

"I agree," Notch added. "I'm sure the Inquisitors would be pleased."

"Perhaps. But now that I've danced, I find it was as much for me as them." She resumed her questions, but now they were more focused on his life. Through the next course and a dessert of light sweetbread and vibrant fruits, Notch spoke of the Glass War and more recent events, downplaying his role but not removing himself. It was probably best if he remained seen as at least somewhat heroic and Alosus did not attempt to stop him.

Later, when the flautist let the final notes fade into the hall but before the dance floor emptied, Alosus gave him a nod – which was a welcome cue. Another word and his throat would have collapsed.

"Your hospitality has been exemplary, Lady Casselli," Alosus said as he stood. "But we are regrettably weary after a long journey."

"I would hate to keep either of you from your rest," she said. Her eyes lingered on Notch. "Do call on me again, either of you, if you need assistance."

"We will," Notch said.

"Good. And I trust I will see you again, Medoro of the New Land."

"I hope soon," he replied, following Alosus from the room.

Waiting beside the crystal lamps at the entryway were a small group of servants, dressed in black as the others. In the shadows, they would have been near invisible – easy for the nobles to overlook, perhaps.

One servant took Notch and Alosus to their quarters, explaining that their weapons and clothing were safely within. Finally, the lad handed over a piece of parchment sealed with the purple of the Inquisitors, which Notch did not open at once. Inside, lamps were already lit and cool water and coffee had been set out on a tray in a sitting room – two bedchambers adjoining the room.

"What is this?" Notch asked as he broke the seal.

"A meeting card," Alosus said, glancing at it. "Within will be Houses and times, evenly spread across the day of course, such is the fastidiousness of those who wear the purple." He was stretched across a huge divan, eyes closed.

The parchment bore symbols with times, but no names. One symbol, the wave – the Royal symbol, appeared several times. Others only appeared once, horse, lion, bear and falcon. A twinge of pain at the sight of the falcon; distant relatives of Sofia, no doubt.

"How can I know which royal is which?" he asked. "There are four silver waves here."

"You cannot; doubtless one is Prince Ren. But I will be with you."

Notch tossed the parchment onto the sideboard, slumping into the smaller chair opposite. "So who is our best chance? Tanere? Will he be indebted to us, if we testify for him?"

"Possibly. But do not discount Lady Casselli."

"Truly? I understand she is quite... interested in me but is she so powerful? I mean, she dined with servants before we arrived and she was first to meet us. Like she'd been given a tedious chore to take care of while the Mare had their fun."

"Look at the same event from a different perspective, Notch. She alone met us in the palace – you are quite the curiosity and it was she who did so. And here, dining alone is not a sign of one without alliances, if that was how it seemed."

"No?"

"No – she *is* able to dine alone, meaning free to dine with whoever she chooses. That is a sign of her strength in the palace."

Notch threw a leg over the chair's arm. It was soft enough that his calf barely reached the wood beneath the fabric. "But she's not seen as a threat?"

"A certain amount – but not all – of that strength comes from Tanere."

"And the rest?"

"She is head of the Carver's Guild and many believe her to be the finest carver alive."

Notch nodded slowly. "Then I will definitely see her again. Tomorrow. I need to get to the Library and you need to find that slaver. What is the symbol of her family?"

"A fox."

"Ah." He'd seen the symbol of a fox on the list – last in order, early evening at a guess. "Then by tomorrow's end I want to be standing before the Library of Souls."

"If luck is with us, you might just get that wish."

"And if not, we're going to make our own luck, Alosus."

31. AIN

Ain folded his arms as he stared at the green stronghold.

The walkers were gone, or at least, their fleshy shells were now no more than scattered piles on the ground. What began as a bridge of bodies had quickly spread and then evolved into an impenetrable wall of melded cactus. It had swallowed the building, the creatures sealing off the prison. So far, all attempts to cut through had resulted in weapons being caught fast.

Salt seared the plants but did not break them down, as if together, they were stronger. Either that, or whatever force had driven them in the first place was using some manner of counter-measure.

Which spoke of great power indeed.

And while only the very occasional creak of stone could be heard, it was probably only a matter of time before the building succumbed.

To combat this, Raila was arranging an attempt to burn the plants but Ain did not hold much hope. And more, he was growing increasingly concerned for Majid and Jedda. How did their party fare? Weeks with no word, and now a force far beyond what it seemed anyone at the Cloud could counter.

Ain left Raila and the others to try their oil and flame, seeking out Wayrn, who he found sifting through scrolls in the building he had been given to use as envoy. Or perhaps home; the man had been at the Cloud for over a season now, his Medah was even more accomplished and he was growing tanned, where at first, his fair Broann skin had tended to burn.

"Still searching for that mystery language?" Ain asked.

Wayrn shook his head with a sad smile as he turned from his desk, which was littered with scrolls, quills and ink pots. "Not today. I fear it may still elude me yet. Perhaps if I could compare the language beneath Anaskar with what you have here once more... but there are more pressing things afoot, of course." He collected a pair of scrolls, unrolled one a little and nodded before handing it to Ain.

"What is this?"

"Perhaps a precedent to what happened out there," he said.

Ain read the text, an old, flowing script. "'There was a time when our Pathfinders were also warriors, for two generations all clans, Snake, Cloud, Wanderer and Mazu were united in driving back the green Plague-Men'." Ain paused. "All clans united, how old is this?"

"It is an account of an elder which was transcribed perhaps five generations ago, maybe more, from an even older document."

"And this was in Raila's library?"

"Yes."

"What is it?"

Wayrn grinned. "It's called *Stories of the Sand*. It's a

collection of children's tales."

"Sands, truly?"

"Read on; it gets more interesting."

Ain did so. The Plague-Men were said to have been born from the northern sands. They would creep closer and closer to camps, blending with true cacti, until they could puncture skin with their needles, inducing endless sleep, whereupon the plant feasted on its victim. "'In the end, only the fabled Stones of Shali could turn them back with their ancient thunder.' I have never heard of the Stones of Shali."

"Who might have?" Wayrn asked. "It's the first clue I've found but if it is nothing but a story, I would like to be able to rule it out as soon as possible so I can keep searching."

Ain snapped his fingers. "Usrahed. He's the oldest man in the Cloud, his father used to be a Scroll Keeper. I'll take you to him now."

Outside, the wind had died down, allowing voices filled with frustration to reach him, even as he gave the stronghold wide berth. He took Wayrn between the white clay of the houses, slipping through an olive garden and finally coming to a small home that lay across from one of the wells – Usrahed hated to walk too far for his water.

"Let's hope he's awake," Ain said before he knocked on the door.

No response. Ain knocked again, a little louder this time – and now a voice echoed from within. "Who calls?"

"It's Pathfinder Ain, Usrahed. We need your advice."

Glass clinked and a moment later, the door opened. Usrahed squinted against the light, his bushy eyebrows wild, but his wrinkled face still broke into a smile. "Ain, so it is. Come inside." He tottered his way back to a pile of cushions, lifting a bottle of spiced-wine and a glass as he did. "Who is your foreign friend?"

"Wayrn is the envoy from Anaskar, a messenger of peace and something of a scholar."

"Ah." The old man nodded. "I've heard them mention you. Well, sit and let me bestow my wisdom. What is it you need advice on? Because if it's women, I thought you were already married, young Pathfinder."

"It's not women," Ain said. "It's about the legend of green Plague-Men, do you know it?"

He frowned over his drink a moment. "Hmmm."

"What about the Stones of Shali?" Wayrn asked.

"Shali? Now her I remember," he said. "She was the Goddess Among the Dunes; back when the clans worshipped various gods. Her full name was 'Shali-Marineka' and it was an old, old word for the way the night sky turned the dunes pale. It was said the curve of the dunes at night was her hip and waist where she slept in the sands."

"Poetic," Wayrn said.

"So it was then," Usrahed replied.

"And her Stones, what were they?" Ain asked.

He tapped a finger against the rim of his glass a moment. "I think... yes, I remember that part too. Father used to tell this one when I was a lad." He closed his eyes. "The stories said that Stones of Shali were two pieces. One of onyx and the other jasper; supposedly the shards were broken fragments from great swords wielded by the two Sky Gods, who would fight over the world. When their blades met, pieces broke off and it sent a mighty thunder echoing around the world, splitting apart the very mountains and the earth to the north. The legend used to be told to children as a way of explaining thunder, that thunder today was the faintest echoes of that first clash."

"And Shali collected the shards?" Ain guessed.

"She did. She gave them to a great hero, who used them to try and unite the clans. It is said he perished in the Great Maw."

"Great Maw?" Wayrn asked.

"A crater in the desert. It is a cursed place," Ain said.

Usrahed snorted. "No curse out there but the curse man takes with him, Ain. If the Stones do exist, they're said to be at the bottom."

"What chances they still lie below?"

"Ever heard of anyone climbing down to check?"

He shook his head. No-one went there, despite the relative closeness to the Cloud.

"How far is it?" Wayrn asked.

"Half a day there and back; we might be able to rule it out quickly." Ain shrugged. "Or even find the stones themselves, if they exist."

"I say we try it."

Ain nodded. He thanked Usrahed and the old man waved them off with a blessing of sorts, returning to his drink.

Raila was more supportive of the idea than Ain had been expecting; she was pacing before the stronghold, hands on her hips. "I remember those legends... myths, perhaps. But nothing else has worked; you might as well try it. Take a small party, Ain, but remember your job isn't to take foolish risks. The Cloud needs you."

"I understand," he said. Yet he hesitated to get things underway himself, even as Wayrn hurried off to gather provisions.

"Ain?"

"I fear for Jedda and Majid."

Raila's expression darkened from frustration to something much more sombre. "As do I. And maybe it is only that fear that makes me feel it has been far too long."

"Then let me search for them before I chase the legend of the Stones."

She regarded him a moment, then shook her head. "It is obviously too dangerous. It is very likely that more of those things will be coming. What if you run afoul of them beyond the Cloud? How will you protect your clan if you are days or weeks distant? What if you are captured or killed by whoever is out there, directing these things?"

"Jedda and the others are probably in danger now and have been for weeks."

"And so might they already be lost to us, Ain." Raila softened her tone and a touch of pity appeared in her eyes. "You may have to confront that possibility."

He shook his head. "I refuse."

"You are too important to the Cloud."

Ain took a deep breath. "Then is not visiting the Great Maw too great a risk also?"

"You could return by nightfall."

"So could the walking corpses," he countered.

Raila gestured to the wall of unnatural cactus that had covered the stronghold, and which, so far, had proved impervious to everything that had been tried. "What if that grows, Ain? What if it envelops more homes? The wells, the oasis itself? True, the walkers may also return, but none of those possibilities means you can do nothing at all, which is what you seem to be suggesting."

"Elder, I—"

"Listen to yourself. You cannot search for Jedda and Majid, and so you refuse to investigate something that may help us? You have not sounded quite so childish since you were a child."

Ain looked away, heat flushing his cheeks. "Forgive me, Elder."

"I will."

He met her steely gaze. "And I will search for the Stones of Shali; I simply fear it is... I don't know. A slim hope. Isn't the whole idea far-fetched? We're searching for charms mentioned in children's stories and abandoned religions."

"How much more believable is the notion of a man who can feel the paths of those who have gone before? Or the magic within bones of long-dead sea monsters? Or darklings? Yet all are true, Ain."

She was right, of course – about everything; yet he could not turn away from a lingering hope, the hope that somehow, Majid and Jedda were still alive out there somewhere. That they needed him. "Thank you, Elder," he said. "I will do my best for the Cloud."

32. SETO

Bones littered the damp basement in broken piles, as though a child had thrown a tantrum before fleeing – in this case, into the aqueducts below. For now, Seto had pulled his men out for their own protection, but soon enough someone would be heading after Vipera. Unless Danillo had already caught her, but the man was yet to return.

Seto bent to lift one of the pieces, a femur, carved with vaguely familiar runes. He glanced up at Holindo. "I'll need these taken back to the palace, immediately."

"Yes, sire."

Hopefully Bethana would be able to tell him something of the runes' meaning or purpose, though he would need to question her once more first. One thing was clear, even without Enso's death, whoever Vipera was, she was powerful. Ecsoli too, as evidenced by her Compelling. Yet how much of her power came from whatever form the scattered bones had originally taken? And how much did she already possess?

Seto kept one piece in hand as he strode from

Deylilah's establishment into the cool night air, joined by his guard, who in turn surrounded his carriage on its way back to the palace. Once within, he sent servants to check with Lor in the aviary for any messages, and to bring Bethana to his private kitchen.

"I feel the need to do something, even if it is only to prepare a meal," he said, when he caught a glimpse of confusion on Giovan's face.

Attached to his rooms, it was a modest space with stove and oven, basin and benches. It did, however, boast a generous pantry, which he rummaged through while he waited, selecting salt, pepper, and from the icebox, the day's catch – swordfish.

By the time Bethana was shown into the room, her hands still bound, her feet able to manage only a shuffling walk, he already had the fish frying. Giovan motioned for one of the guards to stay in the room and for the other to remain nearby. Prudent, but again, not necessary – it was as if Flir, or Holindo even, had taught Giovan how to mother his king.

"Why am I here now?" Bethana asked.

He chopped zucchini as he spoke. "I have changed my mind."

"About what exactly?" Her tone was wary.

"How useful you are to me."

Bethana's lips tightened. "You need me; you have admitted as much before."

"But I do not need someone who cannot be honest. You lied about who was behind the de-boning." He pointed his knife at her. "One more chance, Bethana."

"I don't know who it is."

"Perhaps. But you are sure it is Ecsoli. And more, you are certain it is one of your own."

She looked away.

"This *is* your chance to reach that new life in Holvard."

Bethana lowered her voice. "You are right; I believe it can only be Ecsoli. I did not want to accept the possibility."

"Why?"

"Because I hand-picked whoever it was." She cursed in the old tongue. "It was one of my own, no other Ecsoli would 'de-bone', as you have termed it."

"And you are sure of that fact because such de-boning is the very crime those of your command committed in order to be relegated to House Nemo."

"Yes."

He flipped the fish and it sizzled in the pan. "Now that is the honesty I expect."

"How did you know?" she asked.

He moved to the bag he had placed on a nearby bench and retrieved the femur, handing it over. Her eyes widened; she traced the names with her finger.

"What does it say?" Giovan asked.

"It is an epitaph and a name – my name," Bethana said. She dropped the bone.

"There are others," Seto said. "Many bear your name but also the names of others from your House."

"Whoever it is..." She shook her head. "I went to the prisons myself, over months I selected them all. We travelled the very world together, fought together. I still can hardly believe any would do this to their own companions."

"Yet someone has." Seto lifted the pan from the heat. "You must have suspicions, doubts."

"Even if I do, my guess will likely fly wide of the mark. Who survived the invasion? Who fled? Who snuck back onto the ships for Ecsoli? There are too many possibilities."

Seto began serving onto two plates, the scent of the fish rising to meet him as he did. He added the zucchini, then sprinkled salt and pepper quite liberally before sliding one plate toward Bethana. With his free hand, Seto motioned for Giovan to unbind her. The man did so with a slight frown, but did not comment. Bethana took a mouthful, her expression one of surprise.

After taking a bite himself, Seto shrugged. "I have done better; I have overlooked the lemon. In any event, there are more bones. They were being used as towers to amplify power as you said, all are marked with runes for names. Yet many runes I cannot fathom."

"I am no Carver but I will try," she said.

"Good."

After the meal, he led Bethana and their escort to one of several studies included in his quarters, where men were still laying out bones. There was enough for two dozen skeletons, though not a single skull had remained in the basement, and some pieces were fully carved into other shapes, rather than simply being carven. It was clear that Vipera had been de-boning for some time, and that it was possible not all corpses had been Ecsoli.

Seto lit additional lamps while Bethana strode around the large mahogany table that sat in the centre of the room. She touched some bones, only looking at others, her expression dark. At times, she muttered to herself beneath her breath.

"Does it not seem someone from House Nemo with carving experience is a likely candidate?" he asked after a time.

"Yes. Only none of us had that training. We were all trained to become Os-Bellator," she said. When he raised an eyebrow, she added, "Bones of War."

"Then someone in a past life?"

"No."

"Perhaps a woman? One called Vipera?"

Bethana frowned. "No-one in the House used that name. Is that who it is?"

"I believe so." He regarded her again. "Are you certain no woman under your command had carving experience?"

Bethana was firm. "No. I once asked, for I wanted to create something, but no-one came forward. And some of these runes look ancient, even to me."

"Then Vipera has help," Seto said.

"I believe so."

"But from who?" Giovan asked. "Who among those Ecsoli who invaded, would know runes old enough to seem ancient even to Bethana here?"

A chill slipt between Seto's shoulder blades.

Do not seek me.

The four words written in Enso's blood. And the Perfume Rat's own words before his death: *she will kill me and then kill you.* The 'she' the man had referred to was not the one who called herself Vipera – it was Vipera's master.

And she could be no-one else.

Chelona.

33. SETO

Seto waited as Danillo examined the bones one at a time, Argeon glowing a soft blue as the Lord Protector circled the table. The study had long-since emptied of all others, leaving a new quiet, save for the occasional clunk of bone, and a whirlwind of doubts and fears in Seto's mind.

When Danillo finally stopped it was to seek one of the leather-backed chairs, a piece of bone in hand. "This is all becoming more dangerous even than I first thought," he said. "And I have to wonder why this young woman took the skulls? How much more potent a magic has she carried away with her?"

"Indeed. What do they tell you?" Seto asked, gesturing to the bones on the table with his chin.

"That whoever carved them knows facets to the art long lost here in Anaskar – things that even Argeon is slow to recall."

"But he can understand?"

"In time, I think he will more fully. Most are what we surmised; to bolster power. Many are curses on the Nemo, and were left perhaps as messages. There is considerable vitriol there."

"Then Vipera was certainly part of House Nemo."

"I believe so." He lifted the piece he held. "Here is the one that Argeon has explained to me – the runes here are for 'sun' and 'dryness' or 'drought'."

"Drought? To what end? Protection?"

"Or causing?"

"But why cause a drought? If it was being used as a weapon, the effects would hardly be immediate."

"Perhaps it is one part of a larger scheme? I will know more in time, Argeon is at work. There is one of my ancestors that I will soon have access to that can tell us more."

"That's something," Seto said.

"Yet still the most troublesome question – who has given this Ecsoli such knowledge and power? No simple masks worn by regular Ecsoli would know what Argeon is now uncovering. It would have to be an ancient mask, yet Argeon senses none like he himself and it perplexes him. There is a vast power, that much even I have sensed, someone or something lurks behind Vipera."

"I see." Seto moved to another chair with a sigh. It was time to share what he suspected. But if he did, could he reveal the whole of his actions? For he was to blame for everything that Chelona had done and would do, there was no denying such a fact. "Do you know where she is?"

Danillo tossed the bone back onto the table. "She hides herself somehow, still. I nearly had her in the Lower Tier but the trail closed."

"Danillo, I have a theory that I hesitate to share but which I think we all must face."

The man leant forward in his chair. "Go on, Seto."

Seto exhaled. How much to reveal? "We were never able to discover where Chelona's spirit settled, if it did at all, after she left the mask." Of course, the idea that she merely 'left the mask' was still a necessary half-truth for now, and the circumstances around how – and around Seto's deceit, were best left unexplored. Yet he often wondered, did Danillo think upon it often? For the Lord Protector had to realise, if Chelona could 'leave' the mask, could not his own daughter be freed from Argeon somehow? Perhaps the man had come to the logical conclusion – based on the misinformation Seto had given – that a spirit without a body was not a life.

"A troubling thought."

And it was hardly the whole truth yet Seto was well-accustomed to the guilt by now, he was too much of a coward to reveal everything about events in Cera Tower. "Agreed. She could easily be behind this."

Danillo exhaled heavily. "To what end?"

"Impossible to say but do we need to know *why* in order to suspect and to plan for the possibility?"

"No, but I do fear there are little effective steps we can take in order to prepare, beyond a sense of heightened readiness, without knowing her motives."

"We have you."

"Take some comfort, in that," he said. "But remember also what happens to the ship when caught between storm and reef."

"We will find a way to protect Anaskar from such a fate," Seto said. "The first order of which will be to find Vipera."

Danillo nodded. "Give me until dawn to learn more about her altars and to rest. Then we will find a way to strike back."

"Take the time you need," Seto said as he stood. "I will check on Lavinia's progress."

"You must rest sooner or later, too, Your Majesty."

"So I must," he said as he left the study, heading down the short corridor and then exiting his chambers by the Ways; it would be quicker. The dark passages between rooms were lit only in places, but he knew his way well enough to reach the corridor near the Storm Singer's quarters swiftly enough.

He brushed webs from his hair as he exited from beneath a tapestry, letting the section of wall slide shut behind him, and then he was nodding to the guard on his way in to Lavinia's rooms. They were sparsely furnished, and most surfaces bore instruments, lutes, lyres and silver bells. Despite the late hour, humming drifted from beyond the door to the dining area. A soothing sound, yet it came with an underlying tension. Seto hesitated, hand on the door – what if the song were dangerous?

When it ended, he knocked before entering.

Lavinia, Stefano and Fiore were all smiling where they sat around Lavinia's small table. Her children were obviously sleeping, since they were no-where to be seen, but an adjoining door lay half-open.

"Your Majesty," Lavinia said. "Is something wrong?"

"Perhaps. We have learnt more about Vipera and it seems there is someone directing her." That would have to suffice for the present; it wouldn't do to burden Fiore with the knowledge of more adversity. Though when the time came, and it would be soon, she would probably handle it well enough, considering her overall demeanour so far.

"Troubling news," Stefano said. Like Lavinia, his voice was rich and pleasant to the ear.

"Yes. But lighten my night. What has you all smiling?"

Lavinia put an arm on Fiore's shoulder. "Fi is trying to teach us a Song of Seeking, she wrote it herself to help her little brother find his pet ferret. We have finally learned the first few words; it's in her own language."

Seto raised an eyebrow. "Oh? Impressive, Fiore."

"Thank you, sire," she said with a little smile. "It's really useful but it only seems to work if I know who or what I'm looking for. It's never led me to treasure, or anything."

He chuckled. "I may have to call upon you the next time I lose my patience."

"Deal," she said.

"What of Abrensi?" he asked.

"Still no progress." Lavinia said with a sigh. "We tried singing the Song of Stone backward, both the whole song and the word order itself, along with two dozen other chants but nothing works yet."

"We won't give up," Stefano added.

"Good. What of Abrensi's own library? Or any other archive?"

"We've tried that too, Seto," Lavinia said, giving him a look. "Let us worry about this. You get some rest."

He shook his head, but he found himself smiling. "There must truly be some conspiracy here in the palace – are you all competing for the honour of nursemaid to the king?"

"Yes. Now go seek your rest so that I might win," Lavinia said.

He raised his hands in mock-defeat. "Very well, until tomorrow."

By the time Seto returned to his chambers, dismissed his servants, drank a tall glass of water – despite the way it would wake him too soon – and collapsed into bed, he could barely turn his head and force his eyes open to check the balcony window. Was it open? No, he'd closed it earlier.

The haze of sleep fell over him and his thoughts drifted.

Fiore was full of surprises.

A Song of Seeking.

Written by the girl in a language she created. Impressive. Very practical, too. A shame it only worked for things she already knew. Which meant there was no way to use it to find lost Sea Beast bones then – something even Argeon could not do thus far. Nor had it been possible for Metti or Danillo to seek out Vipera earlier, since neither had met or even interacted with the woman.

Seto sat upright, drowsiness banished.

Things or people she already knew.

Fiore had already interacted with Vipera, via the green lights.

"She can find Vipera."

34. FIORE

Fi hummed her song softly as she followed the Lord Protector and Bethana along the moon-lit street. The slap of waves against the harbour was barely audible beneath the shouting, singing and music from the taverns and inns – so much louder than back home. And the words to the songs! If Father Canto heard them he'd likely set fire to the whole street in a pious rage.

Or at least, say he would.

The clink of steel on steel echoed from behind. It was Giovan and his men, only five of the Royal Guard, since King Seto had insisted that Lord Danillo take *some* at least. His words had been pretty heated, yet he hadn't shouted. *If you all insist on coddling me like some wretched child, then you will certainly not undertake your little snake-hunt without additional eyes. Take Giovan and some of his men.*

And the Lord Protector had bowed and done as he was told, Giovan pulling her after the red-robed man, while Lavinia stayed back to speak with the king, whose sour expression hadn't been too different from those made when her little brother would throw a tantrum.

"Anything new, Fiore?" the Lord Protector asked.

"Not yet. We're still going the right way." She resumed her song, still humming to herself as they walked. Somehow, finding Vipera hadn't been as tough as she'd been expecting. Like when looking for Sedda's ferret, she simply thought of the green wisps of light and the sound of Vipera's voice as she imagined it, and a little echoing hum appeared.

So far the echo had led her all the way from the palace, down through the tiers and now to the harbour – where the echo was strongest, and it grew even clearer when they started across the enormous wooden planks that made up the docks. There were so many ships, and all so huge, that she lost her place in the song several times.

Some of the dark shapes were just giants – three masts, so much sailcloth! And some bore pretty stained-glass cabin windows, warm light glowing within. At one boat, with a giant naked woman on the front, she saw a man smoking a pipe. When he caught sight of the little group, led by the Lord Protector, the fellow turned and slipped away.

Maybe he had the right idea. Her heart was beating fast and she didn't know whether it was a deep anger, excitement or worry. Probably all of them. Who knew what would happen? She might get to see some real magic from the Greatmask.

On the other hand, she might only see more death and pain.

Hopefully it would all be for Vipera – the woman was evil; she hurt and killed people. And she'd used Fi as part of it.

King Seto and Lord Danillo had not concealed their purpose. When they found her, they were going to "put a stop to her". Fi had heard that before. And she knew who was responsible – *her* song would lead them to Vipera.

Fi frowned as the echo grew clearer. It wasn't a good feeling, really. The song wasn't supposed to hurt people, it was supposed to help. But the woman had killed a lot of Ecsoli and who knew how many others. There was no forgetting that; Fi had seen Bethana's face when they set out.

She remembered Lord Abrensi's face too.

And the way it felt to have accidently done that to him, to have been used.

"We're running short on timber, Fiore," the Lord Protector said as the boats began to thin out near the end of the wharf, where posts stood wrapped in rope. "Is she in one of these ships?"

Fi shook her head. "Not that close. More like..." She pointed across the dark water. "Out there." No boats, big or small, were visible on the water. Just ripples of moonlight. Barely even a hint of a breeze either and the ships nearby were quiet, not so much as a creak coming from any of them.

Giovan stared across the harbour. "Can she hide on the water?"

"Let us find out," the Lord Protector said. Argeon began to glow, the soft blue casting shadows. He was quiet a moment, then he nodded. "There is a ship out there, she's concealing it somehow, but I have it."

"Can you break the spell?" Bethana asked.

"I believe so but if I do, she will know. She may flee again."

"She probably already knows we are here and she hasn't fled yet," the tall woman replied.

He shook his head. "Argeon is taking steps to shield

us. We need a boat; she is alone out there."

"You're sure?" Giovan said.

"Yes. Come, we will borrow a boat from nearby," he said.

Giovan glanced down at Fi with a grin. "Looks like you're rowing, Beanpole."

She stuck her tongue out at him before hurrying after the Lord Protector, who was already untying a much smaller boat than the big ones around them, yet it looked like it would easily fit everyone.

"Won't they mind?" she asked the Lord Protector.

"It will be returned," he said.

"The real question is, will it be returned in one piece?" Bethana said.

Lord Danillo ignored her, motioning for everyone to get in. Fi hesitated, her hand outstretched for the rail, half-leaning, half-falling to grip it, then stepping in carefully. The boat rocked beneath her, a little sharp when the others followed, but she found something to cling to toward the back – a barrel. Good, something solid. Something that didn't seem to move all by itself. Not like the boat... or the deep, dark, endless water. What if she fell in? How fast would she sink? Ana, what was down there? Fi swallowed a tiny groan as the boat started toward the open water.

She clenched her teeth. Forget all that, stay calm – back to the song.

Fi resumed her humming, holding onto the pattern of words until her fear receded enough that she could focus on the echo once more.

Despite his little joke, Giovan rowed first and then another man while Fi gave information to Lord Danillo. By the third rower – Bethana – they were very close, even though there was nothing visible.

"We'll hit her ship if we don't slow down now," she told Lord Danillo.

He signalled to Bethana, who moved her oars around and started rowing the other way, slowing their progress. "How do we board her?" Giovan asked, keeping his voice low.

Lord Danillo rose. "I will reveal her ship. Once I do, I want you after me – just make sure someone stays with Fiore." The mask turned to face her. "Use the Song of Sleep if you need to."

She nodded.

Giovan leant in close to talk to one of his men, then waved the fellow onward. He gripped the boat as they clambered forward, then paused.

"Shield your eyes," Danillo instructed.

Fi covered her eyes with her hands.

Blue light flashed, so powerful that she caught glimpses of it at the edges of her hands. She pulled them away in time to see the Lord Protector and one of the guards halfway up a rope ladder that hung from a bigger boat.

Bethana and the other soldiers were close behind and Giovan was watching them, hands on his hips. He sighed when they disappeared from view, lost beyond the rail, with only the dark sails above.

"Thank you for staying with me," she said.

He nodded with a smile, but motioned for quiet. Fi crept forward to listen.

A strange silence filled the night.

She swallowed. Shouldn't there have been footsteps, crashing, shouts or something? Instead, there was only the water lapping against the sides of each boat.

It stretched on.

"Something is wrong," Giovan said. "Stay close." He drew a knife and held it between his teeth. Then he moved carefully toward the ladder and started climbing. Fi did as she was told, the rope thick and coarse beneath her hands.

Giovan climbed over the rail first.

She hurried the last few steps, pulling herself onto the wooden floor.

And there was movement but no sound.

A guard lay on the floor, face twisted in pain, one of his fellows dragging him away from the two struggling figures; the Lord Protector, mask blazing blue, and a woman in her own mask – this one of silver, a mask that perfectly moulded to her fine features. She was beautiful, slender, her frame braced against whatever onslaught the Greatmask Argeon sent her way.

When she shifted, falling back, her silver robe slid open to reveal dark body-wrappings. Was she meant to be some sort of assassin? Fi glared at the woman from where she crouched. Giovan waved for Fi to flee, his mouth open but no sounds coming out. Nearby, Bethana was shouting at the woman – who had to be Vipera – but held no weapon.

Blue flashed again and Vipera stumbled.

A blur of red followed as Lord Danillo flashed forward, swinging his arm. His blow knocked her to the ground. He stood over her, hand raised, fingers splayed. She struggled, but it seemed his hand kept her in place.

Vipera beat her fist against the wood, her rage silent.

And then the rasp of heavy breathing filled the air.

"Who is your master?" Danillo's voice was firm, commanding, in a different way to the way Father's had been, or Lord Abrensi or Lavinia. It did not encourage agreement; it demanded obedience. It promised pain.

"Who is yours?" Vipera replied. Her voice was soft and somehow soothing.

"I think we both know the answer to that."

"Then you know mine – and I gain nothing by speaking to you."

"You might gain your life."

"It is already ruined and what's left *is* hers," Vipera replied. "And I do not begrudge her that final piece."

"Then tell Chelona that I and Argeon stand in her way."

"So you think," Vipera replied, but now her voice did not seem so confident. "We hold more cards than you imagine."

"What do you do here in the harbour?"

"You will learn soon enough."

"And your fellow members of House Nemo? Why betray them?" he asked next.

Vipera hissed at him.

"Why?" Danillo repeated the word and the sense of power was immense; somehow, he was forcing Vipera to respond.

And though the woman tossed her head, the mask now splintered but still beautiful where it caught the moonlight, she did not seem able to resist. "A curse upon you! It was *they* who betrayed me, fool." Her mask jerked up to gaze directly at Bethana. "And Lady Nemo is here. How fitting that you might see the final nail driven home."

"Alani? Is that you?" Bethana asked. There was shock and something else in her voice – hurt.

"Of course it's me, bitch!"

Bethana fell back half a step at the venom in Vipera's voice. "What are you saying? We never betrayed you?

How can you think that?"

"Must everything be spelled out for you, Lady? You left me in the city to burn!"

"What?"

"No-one came for me – not a single one of you," Vipera screamed, her chest heaving now as she thrashed against Lord Danillo's hold. Yet he was too strong.

Bethana's voice was choked with tears. "Alani... We didn't know. I didn't realise –"

"You didn't care enough to search," Vipera snapped. She composed herself somewhat. "But that doesn't matter now. I have someone who does care. And perhaps my revenge is incomplete, but it will be finished soon. Watch for me, Bethana. I will find you."

Vipera lay back, her body relaxing into the wood.

And then her clothing seemed to empty all by itself, leaving only her mask atop the robe and black wrappings.

And I will see you again, too, Fiore.

Fi flinched.

"Where did she go?" one of the soldiers asked, his sword held ready.

Lord Danillo shook his head. "I cannot trace her – she is clearly receiving help from her mistress."

"And did so with this boat," Giovan added. "It was hidden *and* there was some sort of silence forced upon us once we were here."

"Part of her plan, no doubt. She obviously wanted time here on the water without being interrupted."

"For what?"

Lord Danillo motioned to a dark hole in the floor. "Perhaps an answer lies below decks." To one of the other men, the guard who wasn't bandaging up one of the other's arms, he said, "Watch over her."

Fi nearly asked permission to follow anyway, only to realise the Lord Protector meant Bethana, who was leaning against a rail, an empty expression on her face. Fi crept after Giovan as he followed Lord Danillo down a steep ladder.

Below the top floor – or what had Lord Danillo called it? A deck – she found them standing around a strange creation.

A single glowing lantern had been arranged to rest above a steel rack with wheels. The lantern cast light upon a row of skulls. Each had holes cut out of their backs and then someone had lined them up so that the light passed through the eye-sockets.

That was disturbing enough, but it was the large glass bottom that had her inching back toward the nearest wall. Giovan was kneeling by it while Lord Danillo lifted one of the skulls.

"It's water-tight, My Lord," Giovan said. Then he chuckled. "Which is probably no surprise."

"Look at this," Lord Danillo said. He lifted the skull. "Good, clean work here. Someone who knows Carving." Fi shrank even further into the shadows. Why would Vipera do such a thing? And to people from her own family? A queasiness rose up in her stomach.

"How are they connected then?" Giovan asked.

The Lord Protector replaced the skull, leaving his hand atop it a moment. He rocked the rack; it slid smoothly where it spanned the glass bottom. "Perhaps if I line it up..." he slid the rack with its row of skulls further, until the skulls rested directly beneath the lantern.

Light beamed down from the sets of eyes, spearing deep into the water below.

Fi gasped.

Giovan spun, and Lord Danillo's mask snapped around to face her. "I'm sorry," she said, stepping into the light. "It's only me."

"Fiore, it is not wise to surprise us," Lord Danillo said.

She lowered her eyes. "I didn't realise I could do that, My Lord."

He was silent a moment, and then laughter echoed from the mask. "Well said. Come, you might as well see properly."

She knelt near – not too near – the edge of the glass, which seemed awfully thick at least, and peered beneath the water to the very depths of the harbour. The beams of light, twin sets somehow strengthened by the skulls, revealed the wreck of a ship. Most of it was still covered in shadow, but the biggest mast and parts of the deck were clear. Big holes covered the ship.

"She's looking for treasure?" Fi asked. "That doesn't seem right."

"Perhaps it is only half-right," Lord Danillo said. "There might be very valuable – and dangerous – material down there."

"*Acor*?" Giovan said. It sounded like a guess to Fi, but Lord Danillo nodded.

"Can we be sure?" Giovan said. "What if it's something else down there? I mean, how long has she been out here searching with her stolen skulls, did it really take her so long to find one wreck?" He gestured to the rack and then some shelves, they too lined with skulls. "There are many more skulls here than the number of Ecsoli that went missing."

"All true," the Lord Protector said. "In fact –" He stopped, and spun for the ladder.

"What is it?" Giovan cried.

"She's returned."
"Where?"
"The palace!"

35. NOTCH

Notch left the final meeting that had been scheduled before his dinner arrangements with Lady Casselli in an odd mix of frustration and exhaustion; one emotion gave him an energy that he tried to burn off by striding along the marble floors, with Alosus nearly pounding along after him. The other feeling – the emptiness of exhaustion, had his mind foggy; it took him several corridors to realise Alosus was asking him to slow down.

He did so with a sigh. "Sorry. I'm getting fed up and I'm tired. And I'm feeling foolish too."

"Foolish?" Alosus frowned. "You handled yourself quite well with the various lords and ladies, save for the minor embarrassment with Balios. You weren't to know his father died in a brothel."

Notch had to laugh. "No, not that. I mean last night, when I vowed we'd be standing before the Library of Souls by now."

"You aren't so far from that. Lady Casselli will arrange it, I'm sure. If not, things went well with Prince Ren. We should not rule out Tanere either."

"Maybe you're right and maybe we can smuggle Ren out. I should be thankful; I'm a lot closer than you to your goal, it seems." He paused. "Can I ask you something, Alosus?"

"Of course."

"How do you stay so calm? I mean, your wife and child..."

"Because I know the slave trade, Notch. Slaves – especially Tonitora – are prized possessions. Very, very valuable. When Yolanda and Mane were re-sold it would have been to a noble or wealthy family. Even if they are halfway across the nation, they are alive."

Notch nodded slowly. "That I understand... but you must have doubts. Impatience to find them at least?"

"I do. But those doubts and fears are simply deep within, where they have stayed since Vinezi separated us."

"Well, I hope you know I'm impatient on your behalf too. I mean what I say. I will help you. For as long as it takes, I will help you. For all you've done for me, I owe you at least that."

"You have already pledged as much, Notch."

"I thought I should say it again."

Alosus put a large hand on Notch's shoulder. "Then thank you."

In their rooms Notch collapsed into the nearest chair and closed his eyes. A thousand names tumbled through his mind; this lord, this lady, married to this one, pursuing that one, offers of allegiance, bribes for trade concessions – couched in the most flowery language of course – snide comments about other Houses and the full range of human response to the king's ailing health, from sympathy to outright glee and disdain.

How many of them would he recall tomorrow?

"Notch, we must prepare for the evening meal," Alosus said.

"Right." Notch pushed himself from the chair with a groan of effort, then found the nearest basin. He splashed water on his face and took a stray lock of hair, pulling it back into the tail. The shadow of a new beard was coming in, but he couldn't force himself to shave. Lady Casselli would have to make do with an unshaven dinner guest. He did, however, re-apply the cedarwood perfume again. They'd expect it of course, and while the scent wasn't offensive it was hardly necessary. What need did a soldier have of such foppish trappings?

Before he left, he checked on the additional wrappings he'd taken to using in order to conceal the bracers. It would have been easier to simply lock them in his rooms, since they didn't seem to have any purpose and he could not figure them out, but that was too great a risk. They were safer on his arms.

Lady Casselli met them in another expensive gown – this one of a fierce yellow that contrasted wonderfully with her tanned skin. "Please, gentlemen, join me in the dining room – our meals are nearly ready. I imagine you are both famished after a day of talk."

"Very much so, Lady," Notch said as Alosus rumbled his own thanks.

The dining area was typical of the palace rooms he'd seen – spacious, lined with paintings, rosewood chairs and marble-topped tables set with crystal ware and silver cutlery, and lit by the strange crystal domes that Alosus had explained were powered by stored sunlight. More magic courtesy of the bone charms that seemed so much more woven into Ecsoli life than in Anaskar.

No wonder they'd been running out of bone.

Casselli's crystals were set with pink quartz and cast the room in a softer light, offering a faint tint to everything.

A servant stepped forward, a tray of drinks in his hands. Mostly wine, but one mug appeared to offer ale. "Sit, please," Casselli said.

Notch chose a seat and Lady Casselli arranged herself beside him, with Alosus on her other side, taking the larger, Tonitora-sized chair. "I am looking forward to more stories about your home, Medoro," she said. "But after we eat, of course."

The first course of swordfish quickly blurred into a second and then the third course, not long after which a servant appeared. "Forgive the interruption, but Inquisitor Quintun wishes to speak with Tonitora Alosus."

"Is something wrong?" Notch asked.

"He did not say, sir."

Alosus stood. "It will no doubt be about my status; it is nothing to fear."

"Why at this time?" Notch asked. "I don't like this, Alosus."

He smiled. "It is their way; to appear when least expected."

Lady Casselli placed a hand on his arm. "In Ecsoli, when a slave's master dies he or she usually becomes possession of a family member. With Vinezi Mare dead, Alosus must be re-assigned, possibly to Prince Tanere or one of his uncles."

"Worry not," Alosus said, laying some emphasis on the words. "There is some advantage to this and it is not unexpected, as we discussed."

"I still don't trust them." Lady Casselli remained silent as Notch stood. "Let me come with you."

"It is not permitted. But we will speak after." He switched to modern Anaskari. "Remain on guard here, Notch – be careful what you agree to while I am gone."

"I will," Notch replied. "And you be wary yourself."

Alosus thanked their hostess and followed the servant from the room. Notch only sat when the big man was gone. He took another drink, setting the mug down a little harder than he'd intended.

"A brooding look suits you, Captain," Lady Casselli said. She glanced to the remaining servants, who started clearing away the plates.

"You are generous, My Lady."

She shifted closer and he caught the cool scent of mint leaves. Something predatory had slipped back into her gaze.

"Tell me, Lady Casselli – are we free to converse here?"

"Free?"

"From prying ears."

"Ah." She smiled, then patted the table. "Beneath the marble is a charm to stop our words leaving my rooms. Do not fear; speak what is on your mind."

"In all my time here, few have asked my purpose."

"Go on."

"I am seeking answers that Alosus believes only the Library of Souls can give. I want permission to ask a question."

She raised an eyebrow. "Few outside the royal family are given such an honour."

"You seem well-connected, My Lady."

"I am." She trailed her fingertips across the back of his hand and up his arm, a tingling sensation left in her wake. "I suspect we are in a position to help each other, much as I'd hoped."

He looked her in the eye. "I am a stranger here, what can I do to help someone of your standing?"

She stood, taking his hand and pulling him to his feet, leading him from the room and down a dimly-lit hallway. "First, tell me why you travelled across the seas to ask a question of the Oracle?"

He hesitated, despite the way his pulse was beginning to quicken. It was one thing to speak of his search with Alosus, in Anaskari, when no-one would know. And even though he had meant to ask Casselli tonight, or at least ask someone of influence soon, it did not seem prudent to say it aloud when there was a chance someone in the palace might seek to use his quest against him somehow.

"The charm's reach covers us now," she said, glancing over her shoulder, "and will do so in my bedchamber also."

Notch stared after her. He had to take a chance; he owed it to Sofia. "I want to ask them about reversing the Sacrifice. Is such a thing given the same name here, in Ecsoli?"

Casselli stopped, turning to face him – some of the warmth gone from her voice. "It is – and that is quite the request; not something you would make for just anyone, I wager. They must have been dear to you, Medoro."

Notch clenched his jaw. "She was like the daughter I never had."

"Ah." Her tone had regained its warmth. "That is a quest I can support." She continued into the room at the end of the hall, where only a pair of candles glowed yellow – but it was enough to see the large canopy over the bed, the rose silk sheets. She swung the door shut behind him, then stepped close, slipping her arms beneath his tunic to run her hands across his torso.

He shivered in response.

"We can speak of my side of the bargain after," she said, softly.

He was already breathing hard. Gods, how long had it been? He was on fire, surely? And her hands were a welcome ice, roaming across his skin. Yet Alosus' warning echoed. *Be careful what you agree to.*

Notch turned and took her by the shoulders, pulling her body against his own and pressing his lips to hers. "I would know now, My Lady."

"Would you?"

"Yes."

She cradled his face with both hands. "Very well. I want a new, better Paradisum. One free of the endless, vicious cycle of one-upmanship."

"With you at its head?"

"Not at all." She kissed him again and he returned it; drawing back when her teeth grazed his lip. "I would lead from the shadows, Captain. And you can help me simply by being my escort."

"Escort?"

"To throw my enemies off the scent," she said, then pushed him toward the bed. "Enough talk, Medoro of the New World."

36. FLIR

Grav sat slumped in a chair across from them, mouth drooping into a miserable frown, his hair dishevelled. Kanis was still grinning at the man, chewing his fish as he did. Fool was no doubt taking Grav's appearance as proof that Aren was following them for some sinister purpose.

And maybe it would turn out to be just that.

Flir folded her arms. "Talk."

"I came here to ask if you would reconsider helping us, dilar," he said.

"Let me be more specific: tell me why you followed us in secret?"

He swallowed. "I didn't want to be so underhanded about it, truly. I know it was disrespectful to you and Mishalar... but Aren thought it best. He said he couldn't afford to waste any time, if I was to convince you he wanted you to be able to leave from Enar and head right to the Lighthouse."

Dinnav approached the table, his circle-patterned robe swirling. "Apologies for interrupting but the Conclave will see you now."

Flir stood. "Don't let him go anywhere," she told Kanis and Pevin.

"We won't."

She followed the servant back to the meeting room, where Wodka alone waited.

"Thank you for returning so swiftly," he said. "Let me first assure you that I speak for the whole Conclave for the moment."

"And I am authorised to speak for King Oseto."

"The Conclave has decided to approve of the exchange – in principal, and of course, everything depends on what you discover. Any other specific details about quantities and training will be held aside at this early stage."

"Then you're willing to let us search?"

"More, we will provision you and open the archives to guide you in wherever you choose to begin your search."

Flir inclined her head. "Thank you. That is most welcome." Wodka turned to Dinnav, but Flir spoke before he could issue an instruction. "I would like to warn the Conclave also, of a deadly creature that attacked us on the Venach Bridge."

"Oh?" His expression became one of concern. "Not a Chilava?"

"No. Something I have never seen before." Flir described the encounter. "I'm not sure how it might be stopped or even if it will return, but additional patrols or warnings wouldn't hurt."

"Indeed. Thank you, Flir." He stood, gesturing to the servant. "Please ask Dinnav for anything you need in your search."

"Follow me, madame," Dinnav said. "Your companions will be sent for."

He led her to a room lit by a cosy fireplace, half a dozen chairs set around a long table which had been stacked with uneven piles of books and scrolls. "You'll notice each group is ordered by region."

"Region?"

"Yes. Myths, legends and 'monster sightings' from various locations around Renovar."

Flir had to laugh. "You're very efficient."

"Thank you. It's a matter of pride." He sketched a bow and left.

Flir took a seat before the nearest pile, grabbed the first book and placed her feet up on the table, leaning back until the chair creaked. The cover suggested it dealt with inland, west of Enar. She stretched for another pile – this one was better, the coast at least. She skimmed the pages. Mermaids, sea serpents and monstrous ice turtles but no Sea Beasts, it seemed.

The door opened and Kanis entered, Grav and Pevin trailing. "What are these for?" Kanis asked.

"Conclave wants us to search," Flir said. "So I'm looking for reports or legends that might help."

Pevin was already handling scrolls from one of the other piles. "These look like local histories."

"Well, see if any of them talk about a Sea Beast or sea god or something similar," Flir said. "Everyone, take a pile."

The scuffle of chairs being moved followed, then the regular swish of pages being turned, and after no small amount of time, Kanis' grumbling. "We aren't even halfway through this bunch," he said at one point. "Has anyone found anything?"

Flir slapped her book closed. "Not in the far east."

"I have something," Grav said. "It's just one mention;

a frozen lake in the north – the Blackthorn Mountains."

Kanis tossed his book onto the table. "Where the frost-wights are supposed to live? Sounds like a dead end."

"Ignore him," Flir said. "What does it say?"

"Ah, it's an ice-fisherman's legend; it says that on a blue moon, a great monster would rise up and break the ice, swallowing any fishermen caught there. They called it the *pal-envaic*."

"The deep fear," Flir said.

"I'm not convinced," Kanis replied.

Flir shrugged. It was slim.

Pevin patted several books from his pile. "There are recorded sightings from the south east." He paused. "By the Lighthouse keepers."

Grav straightened but Flir held up a hand. "Before you tell me we could search for the missing Ice-Priests at the same time, I'm aware of that, Grav. Pevin, what else?"

He reopened the book with the green cover. "Well, it's said the lighthouse spotted fountains of water shooting into the air much, much larger than any whale... several keepers over the course of... two, no three centuries worth of records. Sightings both day and night, no real pattern... and," he reached for several scrolls, wincing as he stretched, his ribs no doubt still tender, "these include accounts from villages only a little further north and I'm sure if I kept looking, there would be others."

"That's sounding a little better," Kanis said.

Flir nodded. "If we do go there first, it wouldn't be hard to speak with locals, to see if it still happens."

Grav was beaming. "We would help as best we could, also, dilar."

"Pevin?" Flir asked.

"It seems it is worth investigating," he admitted. "And again, to be utterly selfish once more, I do worry about my little brother."

Kanis pushed his chair back. "I think that settles it."

"I agree," Flir said. "But I don't want anyone getting their hopes up. There's a very simple and possible explanation for the sightings off the lighthouse, you know."

"Such as?" he asked.

Pevin slowed the straightening of his pile of books. "Oh."

"What?" Kanis asked.

"The Anaskari Sea God," Pevin replied.

"Exactly," Flir said. "I'm not saying we won't investigate the sightings, but I fear we might only be ruling them out."

"How can we do that?" Kanis asked. "It's not like you can compare dates and times when the Beast was seen in the harbour at Anaskar with what we have here."

Flir shrugged. "As I said; we can't afford to ignore that many sightings. If there's nothing to it, we look elsewhere."

"Well, it's better than sitting around here," Kanis said. "Ready when you are, I suppose."

"We just need to make one little stop first," Flir added.

Kanis frowned. "I hope you don't mean—"

"I do mean that, Kanis. I mentioned it to the Conclave, but I just can't leave that creature out there roaming around devouring people."

"Because we were so effective the last time we tried to stop it."

"Well, this time will be different."

37. FLIR

Upstream from the old guard post, Flir crouched across from a large opening in the river bank. It had been half-concealed by a makeshift... nest, and the morning sun did not penetrate far into the darkness. But recently overturned earth surrounding the hole was a good sign that *something* had made its home there not too long ago.

"Are you sure?" Kanis asked. There was no hint of the usual flippancy in his voice.

"This is where the tracks led."

"No, I mean, are you sure about this? You left Pevin and that weasel Grav behind, doesn't that suggest you think this won't end well?"

"Nothing's ending here, Kanis – except maybe that thing."

He gripped her shoulder. True concern darkened his eyes. "How? And no more bravado this time. How are you planning to stop it? The damn thing nearly had us both; I still don't know why it took off."

She lifted a thrice-lantern from her pack. "I asked Dinnav to include one of these."

Ashley Capes

"Well then, the creature is finished. You have a light," he said as he folded his arms.

"It's a thrice-lantern, it's brighter than most. Didn't you see how it reacted to the explosion?"

"The *acor* didn't even scratch it."

"No, but I think the flash of light stunned it. I think we can do the same, and then get in close. Try to find a weak spot."

Kanis scratched at his cheek. "It's not much, Flir."

"You let me know when you come up with a better plan." She lit the lantern, squinting against the light; it really was harsher than a regular lamp, even in the daylight. "Just make sure you do it before I get inside."

He swore and followed her, mace held ready. Flir gripped a dagger in her free hand, slowing as she approached the rent in the earth. Possessing immense strength and miraculous healing did not make her indestructible.

This... thing was an unknown, and that wasn't something she was used to. "If I can distract it with the light, you have to get close."

"I will."

"Right." She lifted the lantern and stepped into the nest.

The light showed a bend in the earth, nothing more.

She started forward, straining her ears, and soon came to a place where the woven walls stretched around a deep, wide depression of sandy soil; doubtless where the creature slept. Not a single scrap of light filtered through the roof or walls as river mud and the grey web from its mouth had been used to shore up any gaps in the reeds. There were no bones – human or animal – no blood, no trace of the creature itself, even.

"This is impressive in its own way," Kanis whispered. "With the roof and the bends in the entry, so little light would reach this point. What is this thing?"

Something flashed in the sandy pit as she approached and Flir knelt, sifting through the sand. Coins and twisted pieces of steel. One piece may have once been a belt knife. She held up a palm full of coins; most of which were the new, triangular currency. "Look at this."

Kanis moved closer and his eyes widened when he saw what she held. "How did... no, forget I asked. I think we should leave, there's nothing here we can use. What if it comes back while we're in here?"

She dropped the coins. "Then we stick to the plan. Or break our way out – think you're still a match for these walls?"

"Good point." He ran a hand through his hair.

"But you're probably right about there being nothing useful here."

"Then we should leave. The Conclave already has your theory about bright light, which is probably accurate, so we can get back to what we came home for."

Flir flicked the sandy earth. Was it the right thing to do? Plainly Kanis had decided. But when it came to conflicting loyalties, how by the Gods did he make the decision so quickly? Perhaps he simply didn't care. And Seto's quest *was* important – vital in many ways – but did that mean it couldn't wait for a time while she hunted down a deadly monster that threatened her countrymen? All the years in Anaskar... it had been enough to forget a lot, even some of the bitterness that she felt for her old home.

But it was not possible to simply turn away.

"Flir?"

"I'm thinking."

"Let the Conclave worry about this; you have a duty to Seto."

Still she hesitated. Was he right? More likely he was just telling her what he thought would get him out of the nest as soon as possible. Mishalar, it was probably both. "Fine. But I haven't finished with this thing." The sight of the belligerent merchant being covered in the grey webbing flashed in her mind.

"Good," Kanis said. "Tell me all about it – outside."

They exited the nest and headed back along the river, rejoining Pevin and Grav at the road, where they mounted up and started southeast. "But just because the nest was empty, don't assume it's gone," Flir said as she finished explaining what had happened.

As before, the chill in the air seemed to keep most travellers indoors. When they stopped at a roadside inn that nightfall, all anyone could talk about was the bad weather and the poor harvest. No-one had even seen such a creature. And nor did they see sign of it the next day or evening, when camped in a stand of trees set off the highway.

"I guess it's sticking close to the river," Kanis said with a shrug, when Flir woke him for his watch one night.

Not long after dawn the following day, Flir caught a glimpse of rising smoke from Ithinov, and soon after they crested a small hill to look down upon the village. It was no more than two dozen homes with a single, two-storey inn, and an earthen square ringed by a few merchant stalls. A statue and a well waited in the centre of the square but there was little else of note.

It was what reared up beyond the village, a little ways out of town, that drew the eye.

The First Lighthouse.

Looming above the coastline, it was a towering creation of black granite, easily as tall and broad as one of the towers in Anaskar. But it stood in a state of disrepair – there was no glass in the windows that wound their way up to the crumbling roof, the ancient terracotta tiles patchy over its frame.

As a girl, Flir had climbed the steps to the top only once, and even then the room had been falling apart. Creaking floorboards and pigeons roosted above, the droppings staining the walls and floor. The massive lantern had been missing, only shards of the crystal housing remained.

"Ithinov seems even smaller than the last time I bypassed it," Kanis said.

Grav pointed west of the city to the rocky hills. "The tunnels are there, less than half a day from the village."

"Let's get settled here and then start on them. I want to take advantage of the daylight."

"Because you think the creature prefers the night?" Kanis asked. "Do you think it followed us?"

"Perhaps it does like the darkness, though it was daylight when we saw it last."

"Ah, I'll find Aren so he can accompany us," Grav said.

Flir tapped her heels against her horse's flanks and led them down the hill and into the village. They passed no-one on the way to the inn, though smoke rose from two chimneys and she caught glimpses of movement between chinks in curtains.

The interior of the inn seemed even quieter since it was empty, but the owner welcomed them with a smile from where he stood before a polished bar. "Travellers, please rest here, if you would. I will send the boy to tend to your horses."

"No need," Flir said. "We'll be setting out again soon, but we'd like to take rooms."

His smiled flickered in doubt at her first words, then returned when he heard her request for rooms. "Wonderful. Let me find your keys. Two would be enough, I assume?"

"Four would be better," Kanis said.

The innkeeper nodded slowly, as if considering Kanis' request. It seemed unlikely he'd have a shortage of rooms. "Ah. Very well. Four rooms, I apologise."

"No trouble. How much?" Flir asked, removing her purse. It bore a welcome weight, now that the Conclave was paying their way.

Again, the innkeeper paused. Then he chuckled. "Why don't we settle up when you return – plenty of time for such matters then."

"You're sure?"

"Of course." He handed over four keys. "Just do come back; we have a wonderful trout dish."

"Very kind, old boy," Kanis said, and took a key from Flir, starting up the stairs.

Flir followed, and by the time they'd prepared and started off for the hills, Grav was getting anxious, since the innkeeper explained that Aren had not checked in.

"When I asked, he also claimed to be expecting the Ice-Priests back soon."

Flir glanced at him as they crossed the square. "That's odd."

"Ask her about it," Kanis said, pointing.

A young woman was drawing water from the well; it seemed she was having trouble working the rope. Yet she did not appear frustrated, a smile of determination perhaps, on her face. "Can we help you?" Flir asked.

"Oh, thank you," she said, stepping back, releasing the rope as she did.

The bucket started to plummet back down – Flir caught it and pulled it up, handing the woman her water. "There you go."

"Thank you," she said. "You must be travelling?"

"Yes," Flir replied. "We'd be grateful for any information you might be able to share with us."

A slight frown marred her features. "Share with you?"

"About the Ice-Priests; we've heard they've been disappearing around here."

Her smile returned. "Oh, no. They'll be back at any time now. I think perhaps they were lost. Well, thanks for the help."

"Wait, I'd still like to ask..." Flir trailed off as the woman scurried toward the nearest building, fumbling with the door a moment before entering.

"Strange folk here," Pevin observed.

A man started across the square from a nearby smithy, greeting them but not stopping.

"He seemed normal enough," Kanis said.

Flir shook her head. "Maybe they're just a bit backward." She didn't think it would be very easy to gather information from them, if they were all so... oddly slow of thought. "Let's finish what we came to do."

She resumed their march through Ithinov, passing a house with a man standing at the window. His face was oddly familiar, but she could not place him. He was dressed as a sailor; had she seen him in Whiteport? Anaskar? He gave a nod as they passed.

A little ways out of town, before they were due to take the western trail at the upcoming crossroads, they met an older man with wild, red hair. He carried a bow and sword at his belt and his cloak was of white animal fur.

Flir hailed him. "Greetings. Do you travel this road often by chance?"

He appraised her with what seemed to be a mixture of curiosity and distrust on his face. "I do at that. Why do you ask, young lady? Come to see the Lighthouse, eh?"

"We've just come from Ithinov and we plan on staying there tonight actually. I wonder, do you know it well?"

"I do."

"Then would you know if the people there are... well?"

Now he smiled. "If you're staying there, you must mean the Boles the innkeeper and his daughter, right? They're both a little funny, I suppose. Kind souls though."

Flir relaxed a little at his words. "Ah. Would you also have heard about people disappearing around here?"

"Sorry, been away for some time. I'll ask around when I get to Boles'." He started moving again, calling over his shoulder. "You'll find me in the common room tonight if you want to talk some more."

"That set your mind at ease any, Pevin?" she asked as they resumed their own trek.

"Somewhat. A very quiet town, still."

"True. They might just be a secretive bunch that doesn't want attention."

Kanis snorted. "So they ask for help with the priests and then lie about it when help comes?"

"Perhaps they're in denial," Grav said. "I hope you all still believe me; the Priests and other folk really have been disappearing. Aren has proof; he's already visited Ithinov before. He spoke to the mayor."

"Well, that's who we'll be speaking to when we return," Flir said.

The morning wore on and the ground grew rockier with it, moss climbing across the bigger stones. The sun crept out from between the clouds only once, then it hid itself away again, sending the temperature plummeting.

Grav gestured to an open part of a nearby hill; it looked to have been cleaved by some monstrous blade at one point in the past. "There. It's not far now. At the base there is an opening but it's been sealed."

"Then let's see what..." Flir trailed off, stopping in the middle of the trail as a chill that had nothing to do with the cold fell over her. The man in the window, back in the village...

"What is it, dilar?" Pevin asked.

"Now I recognise him!"

"Who?"

"The sailor in the window," she said. Yet he was no sailor – he was a merchant. And more, he was dead. She'd seen him die herself, mere days ago, on the bridge, at the hands of the spider creature.

"What damn sailor, Flir?" Kanis asked.

She spun onto their backtrail. "Something is very wrong in Ithinov."

38. FLIR

It was noon by the time they made it back to the village. Everything appeared as before. All quiet, all calm. More so, since there were now no people moving about in the streets. The doors to the inn stood open, inviting, yet it gave Flir a shiver.

But she did not head for it yet, instead she turned on the homes near the edge of town. "I have to see."

"He might just have a brother, you know," Kanis said.

"Heard that once before," Flir replied as she knocked on the first door. No answer. She hit a little harder, and still nothing. "Is anyone home?" she called as she leaned toward a window. The curtains were drawn.

He was in there, he had to be. She folded her arms then unfolded them. "Hello?"

Pevin stepped beside her. "Dilar, perhaps—"

Flir leapt forward, thumping the door with the heel of her hand. It shattered, crashing into an empty kitchen.

"Dilar." Pevin's tone was disapproving.

"I'll replace it if I need to." She moved inside slowly, but no-one appeared to check on the intrusion. When she reached the bedroom, she found a sleeping figure – not the false sailor, but an old woman. Was it the wrong house?

But a more concerning question took its place – why hadn't the woman woken?

"Forgive the intrusion," Flir said. She approached. "Can you hear me, ma'am?"

No answer, just the steady rise and fall of her chest.

Flir bent over the woman, shaking her gently by the shoulder. Still the old lady did not stir, did not wake. Flir shook the woman again, a little harder – nothing. "Something is wrong here," she said to the others as they joined her. "I can't wake her but she's breathing just fine."

"Try a blade," Kanis said.

"What?"

"Prick her finger."

"I gave her a good shake; there's something wrong, that should be clear by now."

He shrugged. "Then we try another house."

But it was the same in the next home; a balding man would not wake though he was breathing easily. His neighbour too, didn't even twitch – Flir tried a house on the other end of the street while the others searched, meeting at the well.

"They're all asleep. It must be magic," Grav said. He licked his lips, a nervous gesture. "And there are certainly less people than last I was here."

"Could be a drug," Kanis added.

"Let's check the inn then," Flir said. She started toward it, the sinking feeling she'd been battling coming on strong once more. The village of Ithinov was no longer a village, that much was clear.

"Boles?" Flir called as she stepped inside.

The innkeeper did not answer.

"Check our belongings, Kanis. Take Grav," she said. "Pevin, we're visiting the kitchen."

Kanis started up the stairs, a pale-faced Grav in tow; the man was nearly stepping on Kanis' heels. Flir took Pevin around the bar and pushed her way into the kitchen. Beyond the swinging door rested a warm room, fire burning in a large stove and at the end of a long bench, piles of food covered in cloth. A back door, which presumably led to the stables, lay ajar. "Might as well check on the horses," she said, heading toward it.

"Dilar?"

Pevin had not followed; he was staring at the bench.

"What?"

"Is that the innkeeper?" He pointed to what she'd taken for food, part of a hessian bag visible at the end. She frowned at it. There was a certain bulkiness... "Mishalar." The hessian bag was hair – the man's head was visible beneath the cloth.

"Boles?"

He made no answer. She strode to him and yanked the cloth free. The innkeeper lay – face down – on the bench, still in his apron, breathing freely.

The back door swung open, revealing the red-haired traveller.

His eyes were wide, and his wild hair sat in even greater disarray than before. He held his bow, arrow ready. "They're all asleep," he announced. "I've even been to some of the outlying farms..."

"We know," Flir said. "Was anyone awake when you got here?"

He shook his head. "And I don't plan on staying; you lot should leave too."

The thunder of hooves grew close, voices calling to one another. Flir dashed back to the common room and leant between windows, glancing through the dusty pane. Soldiers were filing into the village. At least a dozen, all well-armed – but it was the leader that caught her attention.

Tall, a little older than the others, but familiar. She squinted; the man's features were vaguely frog-like. "Bastard." Govenor Mildavir led his men toward the inn, his complaints about the village clearly audible.

Kanis appeared on the landing. "Flir, this is getting ridiculous. The maid is sleeping on the wooden floor, right beside the bed..." he trailed off when Flir motioned him for silence. She jerked a thumb over her shoulder, then held up her hands, all ten fingers showing, then repeated the gesture with only two fingers.

He nodded and fell into a crouch, motioning Grav back.

Pevin peered over the bar, his expression one of concern. There was no time to hide. Flir swore beneath her breath – they'd simply have to force their way out.

"And this time I want proper wine in there. And some decent blankets; the caves are atrociously cold," Mildavir was saying as he approached the door.

"I don't know if she'd like us changing anything, My Lord," replied a second voice.

"Bah, she's not interested in that. Innkeeper, you have guests," Mildavir hollered as he entered.

Flir leapt upon the man, locking him into a choke-hold and dragging him from the door. He hissed and spat but she kept her grip firm, enough for him to breathe but little else as he tried to pry her arms free.

The next soldier into the inn drew his sword after a

moment of shock; he was soon joined by several others.

"That's far enough," Flir said.

The lead soldier, a grizzled-looking fellow with captain's stripes pinned to his chest pointed with his blade. "You're one of those freaks, aren't you? Half of Whiteport is looking for you. Let the governor free and we'll go easy on you."

"Actually, you're all going to turn around, get back on your horses and leave. Then I'll dump this sorry sack of refuse in the square – and *I'll* go easy on *you* and your men."

The captain lowered his blade, glancing to the top of the stairs, noting Kanis, then the bar, and finally out through the window into the street where he gave the barest of nods, so slight that she wouldn't have seen it if she wasn't already watching.

Flir dragged Mildavir further into the centre of the room, just as glass shattered.

A blade whipped down into the chair nearest where she'd stood a moment ago – a soldier leaning into the common room. His eyes were wide with terror and blood was already running to the floor. The fool had torn open his own side on the jagged remnants of the window as he leant in to strike.

"Joris!" One of the men outside cried. Joris was groaning but Flir kept her eyes on the captain.

"He won't last long if you don't do something," she said. "Now isn't the time to—"

The kitchen door swung open and a smiling Boles walked out. His nose was still a little squashed from his odd sleeping position, but he certainly seemed unperturbed about it. "Welcome, guests," he said as he approached the captain. He barely glanced at Flir, his eyes offering no recognition. "Please rest here, if you would. I will send the girl to tend to your horses."

Flir fought down another shiver. The innkeeper had said near the exact same thing upon meeting them – that, somehow, was just as disturbing as his complete lack of concern over the stand-off occurring in the middle of his inn.

"Don't be a fool," the captain shouted.

"Sorry to trouble you," Boles continued, still approaching the soldier. "If you like, we can discuss the fee tomorrow. Why don't you rest? I can find you some keys... I'd say about a dozen rooms, one each, right?" Now his smile seemed a touch proud. As if he'd learnt from his last customers.

The captain glared at the man, then reached out and hauled Boles closer, setting a knife to the man's throat. "Now, keep still and I won't have to cut your fool throat." To Flir, he said, "This one dies first if you don't let the governor go."

Flir eased some pressure on Mildavir, who'd stopped tearing ineffectually at her arms. "Your men seem awfully keen to slaughter innocent villagers, Governor."

"Kill him," Mildavir spat.

"No." Flir cut off his air again, but the Captain had already drawn his knife across Boles' throat. Blood sprayed forth, running down the man's apron.

Boles blinked. "Please stay calm, everyone. There's room aplenty for you all. We can clear out the stables." His voice had taken on a rasping quality and blood still ran from the wound that should have killed him. "It will be warm enough. We have hay."

The captain's face drained of all colour and Flir felt her arms slacken. Mildavir slumped to the floor, dead or unconscious, she didn't know.

The innkeeper was still smiling. He turned to look back at the soldier holding him, tearing the wound a little further. His voice was distorted. "I can carry your belongings myself, Captain."

The soldier fell back, and Boles stumbled free. He spread his arms, as if still determined to welcome everyone. "Have I mentioned that we have a wonderful trout dish?"

"Kill that thing," the captain growled. His fellow soldiers lifted their crossbows – or at least, two of them did – the third was heaving the contents of his stomach onto the floor. Strings snapped, and two bolts sped across the space, knocking Boles back into the bar, where he slumped to the floor.

"Kanis!" Flir snatched up a chair and hurled it at one of the crossbowmen. It smashed into his temple and he fell. A knife appeared in the other's chest; Kanis' aim was still true.

More glass crashed.

Flir spun, backhanding the first man into the room. Bone cracked, and he flew into the wall, crashing through the wood. The next soldier hesitated, by then Flir had already launched a kick. It whipped his legs out from under him and he crashed to the floor, striking his head.

Another crossbow bolt twanged. Pain exploded in her ribs. She swore, hurling another chair at the man. Kanis had reached the ground floor now; he'd already dropped the Captain and now he burst into the street.

Someone grunted – the sound coming from behind.

Searing pain sliced into her shoulder, she spun, wrenching the blade from the grip of her assailant. Mildavir. The man's face was red with fury. Another bowstring snapped, and the fury changed to shock as he fell to his knees, then slumped forward.

A feathered shaft protruded from his back.

The traveller stood atop the bar, bow in hand. He was breathing hard and his mouth was agape. "How can you still be standing, girl?"

"I'm not a girl," she said. "But thanks." She raised her voice as she started toward the door, stepping over the bodies with some trouble, considering the bolt in her lower ribs. "Kanis, don't kill them all. The governor's dead and we need answers."

39. NIA

The messenger collapsed from his horse, stumbling to the loam at Nia's feet, so short of breath that he could not even speak. His mount too, was breathing hard, her flanks white and heaving.

"Water!" Nia called and a boy hurried to a waiting barrel. "And someone tend to the horse."

A small crowd had gathered beneath the branches, worried faces but no talk as yet – it was just as Danillo had warned; the fear was starting to take hold. People were afraid that the Ulag might return but they didn't believe it enough to say it out loud. Why would they? It was impossible, and yet the threat lingered in the form of horrible tales passed down through the generations.

And now, the return of Pannoc in such a state was enough to unsettle them even more.

Nia held the man's head in her lap, accepting the flask someone handed over. She helped Pannoc drink, then hushed him when he tried to speak again, choking. "Catch your breath."

When he did, he looked up at her and his eyes were

wide – and not from exhaustion. "An army approaches. From the south."

Nia tensed. "Who?"

"I cannot say," he said after taking another drink. He shook his head. "But they move steadily, dark shapes all of them. They carry axes and their chant is no language any of us recognised."

"It's the Ulag, returned," one voice cried.

Nia glared at the man. "That's not possible."

"But what about that corpse one of the grove-girls found?" This from a tall woman hovering to the back of the crowd.

Nia helped Pannoc to his feet before raising her hands to quell the rush of questions. "The Ulag have not returned. But whoever this is will be met and turned away. How many, Pannoc?"

"Perhaps two thousand."

Nia frowned. Steep odds. She could muster maybe five hundred warriors with such short notice... but their bows would cut down whoever threatened the grove. "Go, tell my father what is afoot. Tell him to move the Autumn Grove, in case we cannot stop them."

Pannoc set off at a stumbling jog while someone else took his mount, her sides were still heaving too. Nia looked to those gathered. "Spread the call – I need every able-bodied warrior, each with their own quiver. Full. Meet me south of the Old Spring."

Nia dashed along the shady paths, calling everyone to arms, dodging green-clad men and women as she did, bearing down on the fletcher. Ceveris was resting before his workshop, soft smoke curling from the chimney.

"Ceveris, I need every arrow you have and more. Hostile force to the south," she shouted as she neared.

He jumped to his feet. "On your word."

She flashed by, his voice echoing as he called for his assistant. Someone was spreading the shrill bird call for alarm. Good. At her own quarters Nia snatched up her bow and both quivers before mounting her steed and heading south, to the edge of the Bloodwood where warriors were already gathering.

It did not take long for the bulk of them to arrive and she walked among her people, speaking to those who seemed most anxious, placing a hand on the shoulders of others as she passed, until Pannoc arrived, bringing with him a last score of warriors.

"A swift mobilisation but a shame we are so few," the messenger said, looking over their force.

"So soon after the darkness with Efran, and even if we had the time, I doubt we could pull together two thousand from the whole forest. So many are young," she said.

"The Oyn-Dir is working to move the grove once more. He asked me to tell you to be on your guard. He believes something is amiss in the Wilds."

"Not just the army you saw?"

"He could not be sure. He said he was still being 'blocked' somehow and maybe it had to do with the altar, maybe not."

Troubling, but one thing at a time. "Thank you, Pannoc." She sighed as she glanced across the gathered men and women – even, to her eye, some almost too green to be along. Yet everyone had to have a first battle sometime. One young man was wrapping his forearms with leather to protect himself from the snap of his bowstring.

"They will fight to the last, My Lady," Pannoc said.

"I know that, truly. I simply don't have any inspiring words to offer and I know they will need it, with all the talk of the Ulag."

He blinked. "Because you are finding it difficult to hold out any hope?"

"No. Because I don't particularly care for speaking before crowds," she said with a smile. "Tell me, Pannoc. Do you believe it is the Ulag?"

His lips tightened. "The chant was more convincing to me than the axes. And they bore the look more of the dead than any living warrior."

She nodded. Whatever waited in the Wilds, she would stop it. Her people would stop it. Nia tapped her horse's flanks and trotted out, stopping before her small army. Each face looked to her, expectant, some with traces of shock lingering. "I know how sudden this all is," she said, lifting her voice. "And I have heard some of you ask me, should we have moved, or hidden once more? You know my father can, and is now, moving the grove to protect your loved ones who remained. But that is no guarantee – for no guarantees exist in life. If we fall, the army out there, if it really is Ulag, will not turn from the wood. They will search and seek until they collapse, or my father tires and they find our homes." She paused to take a breath, then raised her voice once more. "Unless we stop them now, stop them out there before they even set foot in our forest! And we will! Our arrows will fly true! Our blades bite deep."

A cheer rose like a wave.

She turned her horse and started along the old road into Wilds, Pannoc close by and behind him, Ceveris. The morning wore on and she held her reins only loosely, letting Sparrow follow the trail as she stared ahead, as if she could pierce the distance between her force and the supposed Ulag.

But it was not too long before noon when figures appeared on the trail ahead – clothed in green. They were cresting a small rise, tree line stretching off to one side and tall grasses to the other. They were not so far from the mound where the rose altar rested.

"It's Dira and Klandt," Pannoc said. "The others I sent to warn you, Lady Nia – they should be out of harm's way at least." He signalled to the approaching pair, whose expressions transformed from worry to relief.

As her warriors slowed and the drum of hooves eased, a droning, deep chant reached her. An ugly sound, discordant – and it seemed purposefully so. The chant was part of their weapon, the fear it brought. "How close are they?"

"Beyond the rise," Dira said, her jaw set.

"Let's take what little high ground there is," Nia decided, then turned back to face the rest of her warriors. "Arrows ready!"

Nia led them to the crest.

Below, an army of darkness was approaching. They covered the road, the grass, the weeds – nothing slowed their steady advance. Sunlight glinted on their axes, their chant echoed from gaping mouths. Nia couldn't stop a shiver. Even decrepit-seeming, even appearing dead, they moved steadily if not swiftly, and a menace preceded them. It was not just the chant, but the history, the myths about them and their bloodlust that they carried.

But alive or dead, they had to be killed.

Whispering rose amongst her ranks.

"Raise arms," she shouted. "Take strain. Hold until I say."

The creatures drew nearer, the front ranks within range. A little more, a little closer – there was steel to taste. Nia dropped her arm as she shouted. "Loose!"

Hundreds of bowstrings snapped, and arrows flew overhead in a long arc to rain down upon the Ulag.

And not a single arrow found its mark.

Each shaft simply passed through the bodies below.

"Again," Nia cried.

The second volley flew straight and true – but struck nothing. No creature faltered, the chant did not lessen. And they walked on. Evenly. Steadily. No matter the terrain.

"Are they ghosts?" Cerevis asked. He'd lowered his bow. Whispering had grown to muttering behind her.

Before Nia could offer an answer, the whole array of Ulag shimmered and then disappeared, as though wiped from the Wilds by an unseen gust of wind. The droning chant seemed to linger after the shades were gone, and then it too faded.

Cries of surprise echoed and Nia shook her head. Had the Ulag been true ghosts? Or some illusion, created by whoever made the rose-bone altar? But if they were ghosts, ghosts that decided to disappear *before* engaging her force, before inflicting anything more than the beginnings of fear – what purpose could they possibly have?

No, it had to be an illusion, surely. The Ulag *needed* to be seen. They did not disappear until her entire force had witnessed their approach. "Someone is behind this; a true ghost would have a better purpose."

Pannoc snapped his fingers. "Your father's warning."

"Well, he was right. Something is awry here, but what? Aside from the missing army?" She folded her arms.

"There was no point to the whole exercise, if whoever was behind it was going to have us come all the way into the Wilds simply to watch some Ulag shades disappear..."

The moment she finished the words, Nia heard them properly.

All the way into the Wilds.

She swore. "It's a ruse. A ruse to get us to leave the grove." She wheeled her horse and charged through her warriors, waving at them. "Back to the forest!"

Once free of the press of bodies, she kicked Sparrow into a canter and then a gallop. Wind streamed through her hair and the thunder of pounding hooves behind her followed. The Wilds flashed by as she rode. Whenever she had to slow her mount she ground her teeth at the delay, but she wasn't going to kill Sparrow to return. Father would have moved the grove from the south already; everything would be fine.

There was every chance she was wrong, anyway.

Yet when she reached the wood and then the grove, hours later, her horse exhausted as she, there was a silence to the homes and paths. Why hadn't Father moved the grove? She leapt from Sparrow to call and run into the houses, but no-one answered until she found herself drifting to the edge, where Autumn Grove met the amber of the Sap Grove.

Or should have.

People were crowded around hewn earth, earth that had once been covered by the Sap Grove. The trees with their amber veins were gone, leaving a gaping hole in the forest, where the sun poured in, glinting on abandoned chunks of amber, shattered branches and crushed leaves.

And bodies – at least a dozen grove-tenders, their heated knives cold now, their buckets gone.

"What happened?" Nia asked the nearest person.

The woman turned, tears streaking down her cheeks. It was Hild, one of the Herbalists. "Lady Nia. It was terrible. They tore the trees forth and dragged them away. No-one could stop them."

"Who did this?"

"I don't know who they were," she said. "They took the sap too, from the crates."

"Hild, what did they look like? Can you tell me that much?"

She wiped at her nose. "They wore white robes and hoods, My Lady. I think they were Anaskari but I can't be sure. How could they do this to the forest? To the trees? It was as though I felt every scream deep in my chest as each one was torn from the earth."

"Are you telling me they did this with their hands?"

"Oh, no. Sorry – it was with bones. Most of them were wearing breastplates made of bone."

Like the Ecsoli invaders she'd heard so much about? Dark news. "Is my father safe?"

"Yes, he's in his rooms, I believe."

Nia thanked Hild and started toward the tree line. Had the Ecsoli returned and taken to wearing white instead of blue? Was something else afoot in Anaskar? Or did she need to look closer to home – to Gedarow's Sap Born friends? Unlikely that they'd have access to Ecsoli bones of power, however. And Hild had thought they were Anaskari. Either way, the Lord Protector needed to be told.

Perhaps Father would have some ideas too.

And she needed his wisdom, for she could not even begin to guess why Ecsoli warriors would steal the sap and the very trees from the earth, if it wasn't to create more Sap-Born? Nor could she imagine what alternatives existed. But there was no way that other uses for the sap would be welcome ones.

40. AIN

The Great Maw spread before them beneath the bright sun, a dark abyss with no bottom.

Or so it seemed from where Ain stood at its edge.

The depths were impossible to fathom, light did not penetrate far enough. It illuminated the sheer sides of the crater only – pale stone streaked with orange. In places, it seemed a crack in the earth's crust would reveal a way down, but he had yet to follow any of the faint paths to check. At the very limits of his vision, there seemed to be odd patterns on the walls, but it may have been no more than a trick of the light.

"This may not be enough." Wayrn dumped a pack at his feet with a grunt; half the size of him, it was bursting with rope.

"There are some faint trails here." Ain knelt, placing his hands against the stony ground, the heat filling his palm. All the paths were faint; few people ever travelled to the Maw. Some of those who had visited had their paths come to an end here, in a sparkling mess over the blackness. Stronger were the echo of hooves and boots from their back trail, where people travelling from the Cloud to the west bypassed the Maw. Where Ain knelt now, the paths remained faint, like gentle heart-beats, just the occasional thump, almost too soft to detect.

He closed his eyes.

Somewhere... across the Maw, was there a path heading down? It was so faint! "We need to get closer to the other side."

"Right." Wayrn hauled the rope onto his shoulder and Ain collected their water.

The thump of the possible trail grew slightly stronger when they reached one of the deeper cracks in the earth. Once they unloaded, Ain again crouched and placed a hand on the desert floor. There *was* a path, but it didn't seem reliable – had only a handful of travellers ever used it? Four people? Three? Less? Just how far did it reach? What if it ended halfway down, a dead end? He sighed. "There's a trail but I cannot say how deep it goes, someone has climbed here but so very few."

"That's good enough for me," Wayrn said. "I'll prepare the stakes."

He nodded. "Let me try again."

Once more he closed his eyes and focused on the faint rhythm of the path, someone *had* been here. Boots, hands slapping against rock to grip protrusions, climbed down, but the path grew so faint too swiftly... if only he could somehow reinvigorate it, make it stronger. Short of having a few score people climb down before him, that was hardly likely.

Unless...

What if he sent a pulse along it, like when driving off the darklings? Sands, it was worth a try. Ain gripped the trail; like holding smoke, his fingers closed over nothing.

Yet when he instead tried to cradle the path, it was easier to get a sense of its length and direction. It meant he wouldn't be able to snap it like a piece of rope, but the pulse would still have to come from him somehow.

And the only thing likely to travel along something so faint, something like smoke, would have to be air, surely? Would it even work? It had to be worth attempting. He took a deep breath and exhaled – gently, slowly – and the ripples it created travelled along the path, shuddering down, down, deeper than before. There was even the sense that it travelled further. Success! He took another breath and exhaled again, a little harder... and the path disintegrated.

Ain cursed.

The path had completely vanished – it was as if no-one had ever set foot within the Maw.

"Sands." Ain rose. "I lost it."

Wayrn looked up from where he was tying coils of rope together. "Did you sense anything more?"

"Just that it goes deeper than I first thought. It might be what we need."

"Then we try it," Wayrn said, testing the strength of the knots.

"Are they strong enough to hold?" Ain asked after watching Wayrn a moment.

"Absolutely," he said.

"We're carrying a bit of extra weight, with the water and rope, aren't we?"

Wayrn nodded. "Not enough to make a difference." He grinned. "Unless you're planning to take it all down there with you?"

Ain laughed. It eased some of the tension. He put on the gloves Wayrn handed him and then accepted a hammer and pouch of steel spikes. "Keep them handy," he said. "We might have to tie off and start again. Hard to know what the face of the crater will be like between here and the bottom."

And with that, Ain's tension returned.

But there was no choice. He had to try. The Cloud was under threat. Silaj and Jali were under threat. And the sooner he put a stop to the Plague-Men, the sooner he could convince Raila to let him search for Jedda and Majid.

"Ready?" he asked Wayrn.

The man beat the heavy steel stakes he'd wedged into the earth a few more times, then a reserve stake, and hooked the hammer to his belt. Next, he looped several coils of rope around his torso. "Ready. Let me lead – just follow and we'll reach the bottom in no time."

Wayrn gripped the rope first, then braced himself on the edge of the crater, stepping down as he leant back, soon standing against the cliff face. "Give me a couple of body lengths," he said, then started down in earnest, moving with his usual grace and confidence.

"Sands protect me," Ain said before he followed.

The first passage of the climb did not trouble him. The rock face was sheer but easy enough to navigate. He only lost his footing once, but kept himself steady. Fragments of rock fell beneath him, one glancing off Wayrn. The man looked up, concern on his face but it changed to relief when he saw Ain.

"Sorry."

"No problem," Wayrn said. "Just take an extra moment to check each foothold down here, it gets a little worse."

When Ain reached more uneven footing, he slowed. His hands were already starting to ache, but he clenched his jaw and kept moving – one foot at a time, testing the weight, holding firm when movement from below shifted the rope. He soon fell into a rhythm. It was slow-going and sweat poured from his face, streaming down his back, but when he looked up, the top of the Maw was high above.

"How much rope do we have?" he called down to Wayrn.

"A goodly amount but I can't get a feel for how much further we have to go."

"What if we run out?" Ain asked.

"We use the pegs, one at a time."

"That sounds like it will take forever," Ain said.

"Better than falling the rest of the way to the bottom."

"Hard to argue with that."

They climbed down, further into the shadows where footholds were harder to discern, until Wayrn called up. "There's an opening here!"

"Like a cave?"

"Yes... with bolts driven into the walls too." He paused. "Hold tight, I'm going inside."

Ain braced himself against the wobbling from Wayrn's movements, then resumed his descent when Wayrn called up again. At the opening, Wayrn pulled Ain into a dark tunnel, one that was tall enough to stand comfortably within. Ain flexed his hands, shaking out the tightness. "What is this?"

"I think I know. Let me check." Wayrn seemed to be fumbling in his pack – he withdrew a lantern, which he lit and raised to the walls, its warm glow revealing the unmistakeable hint of tool marks.

"Someone dug this."

"I believe so. And look here," Wayrn said, shifting the

lantern to the floor and extending it over the edge. Heavy bolts of steel had been driven into the crater below the opening. "I believe there was once a platform here. If it circled the crater or zigzagged, we may have missed the other bolts."

"This speaks of something organised... yet the path was faint, barely used."

Wayrn shrugged. "But it was created for someone to use. I wonder too, was the platform destroyed? Or did the wood simply wear away over time?"

Ain ran a hand over one of the bolts. "And if they were destroyed it can only be for two reasons. To protect something valuable... or to prevent people risking their lives by coming here."

"I'd agree with that but add a third option."

"Something worse?"

"Yes. Perhaps it was done to prevent something or someone returning to the surface."

"Wonderful," Ain said. "But we have to find out." He took the lamp and started down the passage. It led to a curving set of steps, eventually spiralling sharply. He started counting and it wasn't until five hundred that the floor evened out again.

The sensation of moving air brushed against his face when he started forward again, and their footfalls echoed. It seemed a vast opening. Darkness lay across everything beyond a few feet but high above rested a circle of light – the opening of the Maw. "We made it," he said.

Wayrn joined him in looking up. "I wish we had a second light."

Ain started across the largely even floor, pausing when he caught a glimpse of something at the edge of their light. He veered toward it; human bones spread across the floor. One of those who had leapt down to their death?

Ahead, a dark shape rose up from the floor. When he reached it, Ain lifted the light as high as he could. A wall of neat brickwork, twice his own height. Nearby, a narrow opening waited. "There has to be something here," he said. "Why else build this at the bottom of the Great Maw?"

"Let's see what's inside, then."

The aperture eventually led to a smaller open area lined with tiered seating; they'd entered an auditorium. The seating rose up at least a storey high, but it stood empty. And it was the centre of the performance space that Ain approached at a half-run, Wayrn close behind.

A large, circular pattern of stones lay in the ground; it seemed to be in the image of an altar struck by sunlight on one side – only the pattern was incomplete. Two stones were missing. "It's a travel-stone," he said.

"Like the one you used on Mount Celnos?" Wayrn asked.

Ain knelt and slid one stone across to an empty space, then returned it. "Yes. Only this one is already arranged, as if it would take you to this very location."

"Two pieces missing, two Stones of Shali."

Ain tapped one side of the altar – the side cast in shadow. "These stones seem to be onyx, obsidian and simple dark river stones perhaps." He slid his hand to the sheath of sunlight. "And here, jasper, quartz and more plain white stones of no particular value."

"And so the two missing pieces are Shali's Stones, presumably."

"Maybe... but where are they now?"

Wayrn wiped at the thick layer of dust. "It does not

seem that anyone has been here for quite a long time. If someone took the stones, why aren't they using them? Surely word would have reached *someone*. Rumours if nothing else."

"Assuming this travel-stone truly did hold Shali's Stones."

"It appears likely, doesn't it? Or possible, at the least."

"It does." He stared into the dark beyond the limit of the lantern. "But what's our next step?"

"Finish our search," Wayrn said. "This place might have more secrets to give up yet."

41. AIN

Ain finished his circuit of half the crater's bottom, navigating the space well enough. His eyes had long-since adjusted to the dim light and the one hand he let trail along the wall revealed no openings. He did find several more piles of bones, mostly human but some animal, before rejoining Wayrn and the lantern at their entry point. "Anything?" Ain asked.

"Yes, but I don't know what to make of it," he said. "When you see it, I think you'll agree that it seems someone was trying to carve a piece for the travel-stone."

Ain quickened his step after Wayrn, who soon slowed, head turning.

"Have you lost it?"

"No, it's around here somewhere... there." Wayrn angled away from the crater wall to a clump of bones. Unlike the others, this one was not in pieces, but rather a full skeleton in the barest remnants of clothing. A crumbling chisel remained gripped in its hand and nearby, a shard of dark rock shaped like a missing piece from the travel-stone, tool marks rough beneath his hands when

Ain lifted it.

"I think you're right."

Wayrn gestured to the smaller clump that represented the fellow's pack. "No white stone here, however."

"But that might be all we need," Ain said. Was it worth trying the stone? The dead man before them had deemed it a worthwhile pursuit to spend his last moments on. Was he the one whose path Ain had accidently dissolved?

"Assuming it works, and that the travel-stone takes us somewhere useful."

He tapped the stone against his palm. "True."

"Well, if you want to try we have something white. It might not be stone, but it can be carved." Wayrn gestured to the bones of the fallen man.

Ain exhaled as he lifted a forearm, finger and knuckle bones falling free. It was not so long in the past that he'd been forced to use someone's bones in a manner lacking reverence. Yet the day in Anaskar's Sea Shrine with its Great Bell seemed half an age ago now. "He'll have to forgive us, but I think you are right."

He took the chisel and led Wayrn back to the travel-stone, where the man aligned the dark fragment with the gap. It fit; not perfectly but well enough. "You're up next," Wayrn said.

Ain put the chisel against the piece of bone and took the pommel of his belt knife for a hammer, breaking the bone, which was quite brittle. Then he started carving a smaller piece, working his way down toward something that would fit in the remaining empty space in the pattern. It took some time, but when he was finally ready, his hands covered in bone dust, Ain held the piece over the white section.

"Still too broad."

"Just shave off a little more," Wayrn said.

Ain paused after he set the chisel to the rectangular piece of bone.

"What's wrong?" Wayrn asked.

"If this works, what are we opening?"

Wayrn spread his hands. "Something no-one has seen in a long time. Something that may help us."

"Or take us so far from the Cloud that we cannot help it."

"True. But only if the travel-stone linked to this one somehow closes once we arrive. Is that likely?"

Ain shook his head. "I don't know. I've used so few."

"We have to continue down this path, we've already taken a risk in coming here. We have to believe that Elder Raila and the others can protect the Cloud without us for a while." He placed a hand on the travel-stone. "The longer we wait here or if we turn back now, without knowing what lies beyond this... haven't we wasted everyone's time?"

"You are right. But I still fear."

"Only a lesser man would not worry for his wife and child," Wayrn said, his tone softening.

Ain gave a smile in response. "Then let's see what lies beyond."

He took the chisel and shaved the long edge down a little more, then set the piece of bone in place, a soft 'click' following.

Then he stood and waited for the light... only none came, not even a whisper of the faintest glow. Ain frowned, ducking back down to make sure both pieces were firmly arranged. "Perhaps they must be certain stones? Perhaps the Shali Stones themselves?"

Wayrn pursed his lips, studying the pattern. "What if

we switch the tiles?"

"For something else? If we climb back up, we could find some pale stone around the edges of the Maw."

"No, these two. Place the dark stone in the beam of light and the bone in the shadow."

Ain removed the stone. "You think this will work?"

"Just a guess, really."

He completed the switch, letting the bone clink into position. As his hand left the piece, light began to stir beneath the travel-stone. Ain rose, shielding his eyes against the growing light – which quickly reached a blazing peak.

Ain turned his back on the light. Wayrn was collecting their packs. "Do you have everything?"

"I think so."

"Right. Into the light we go."

42. SETO

Seto woke to darkness, the scent of steel close.

Very close.

He did not move his head; instead, he spoke. "You are a poor assassin if you are here to kill me and have taken the trouble to wake me first. Can you not at least have been professional?"

"Do you think so?" A woman's voice answered from the dark and a warm breeze moved the curtains enough to let moonlight reveal her form – slender, young probably. Her first kill perhaps? He caught no hint of a Broann accent either... something closer to home. Ecsoli, more likely.

"Yes."

Still she made no move to deal the killing blow, instead keeping the chill of steel against his throat. "Perhaps my orders are not to kill."

"A messenger, then?"

"My mistress is losing her patience. It seems you already ignored one warning."

Seto's heart skipped a beat. "Tell me, messenger, has

she been enjoying Mila's body?"

A moment of silence, followed by a hiss. "Listen well, King Seto. Chelona may feel somewhat indebted to you and your House but that has limits, and you have exceeded them by sending Argeon to the harbour. There *is* a price."

"Such as?"

The steel was removed, and the young woman slipped back to the balcony as he rose to a half-sitting position. "Your throne."

"What?"

"I believe you heard me, Your Majesty," she said with a snicker. "A few days hence, a successor will come. You will cede your throne to him."

"No-one will accept this," he said.

"They will accept it or die by her hand."

"Argeon will stop her."

"Perhaps so, but ask yourself, at what cost? Such a struggle would be devastating to Anaskar – she would ensure that. And then you will have to ask yourself, King Oseto, after Mila, how many more would you sacrifice to cling to your throne?"

43. NOTCH

Dawn was burning a hole on the horizon when Notch returned to his own rooms, finding himself wide awake after doing his best to match Casselli's passion. She was a demanding and intoxicating lover yet somehow he'd been able to keep enough of his wits to wonder about her claim for wanting a different Paradisum, to wonder exactly what he'd agreed to. Could he use her as she used him and still reach the Oracle?

But Casselli had revealed nothing more during the night and even the sight of his silver bracers did not seem to interest her... which was odd, since she was self-confessed in her desire for power. He'd dozed a little afterwards and even now, could not shake lingering images from a dream – where lions had been tearing into a fresh kill. Were they supposed to represent Casselli as predator? Or did it have something to do with the bracers? They remained enigmatic but somewhat ornamental still. Had the white witch been toying with him? Were they nothing more than trinkets?

It seemed possible but by the same token, Notch

couldn't deny the sense that her warning had been an earnest one.

He found the chambers he shared with Alosus empty. "Alosus?" The Tonitora's huge bed did not look to have been slept in, perhaps no surprise. Notch spun for the stand where his father's sword rested – the grand sickle was missing.

Notch strode toward the door; he had to find an Inquisitor. Or a servant, anyone who could give him answers. "Damn these bastards." He thundered down the marble corridors until he came across a young servant, who he cornered long enough to explain what he wanted. Or, more likely, 'demand' was closer to his demeanour.

By the time he was standing before the ornate door, lions crossing the silver inlay, to the Palace Inquisitor's chambers, he had calmed enough to explain to the purple-robed woman who answered what he needed.

"Ah, you must be Captain Medoro, War-Hero from Anaskar," she said. The woman seemed quite alert for such an early time of day.

"Yes. As I said, ma'am. I wish to speak to my friend."

She waved him inside. "I am Inquisitor Phiran. Please set your weapon aside then follow me; I will have to consult the records."

The entryway was lined with weapon racks, all empty save for one that held a huge bastard sword that was obviously used by a Tonitora. Notch added his father's blade to the bone grip and caught up to the woman, who was halfway down a hall, already unlocking a door to what looked like a cell. The other doors he'd passed bore no windows.

Inquisitor Phiran's room was ordered, parchment, ink and shelves aligned evenly with each other. Only the skeletal hand seemed out of place, yet she did not ask him to use it – instead she gripped it and closed her eyes, her lips moving soundlessly.

He sat on the chair opposite and waited, fighting the urge to tap his foot.

When Inquisitor Phiran opened her eyes and released the hand, she took a moment to answer. "I imagine you have not had a chance to learn all the nuances of our way of life here, but I assume you are familiar with the indenture system in Ecsoli?"

"I understand slavery, My Lady," he replied.

"Yes, well. It seems Alosus has requested to compete for his freedom and that request has been accepted."

Notch sat straighter. "What does that mean? Who accepted his request – the Inquisitors?"

"His master; Prince Tanere. And what it means is that your friend will be performing in the Arena this evening."

"Performing? I'm certainly not familiar with that. Are you saying he has to fight for his freedom?"

"Essentially, yes. It is an old custom, but one which is still, on occasion, permitted. His Highness is quite generous, you see."

Notch wasn't so sure about that. "What happens in the Arena?"

"Traditionally the slave is pitted against a monster of some sort. It could be any number of beasts – Alosus will make it into a very small group of ex-slaves, should he succeed." She gripped the hand again quickly. "You are actually permitted to see him, another rarity. No doubt due to your standing as honoured guest."

"Where is he?"

"Preparing beneath the Arena."

"Who can guide me there?"

She sighed. "I will send for someone."

***

The streets of Paradisum were not dissimilar to Anaskar, if he ignored the sun-powered crystals, the clean stones and the swarms of Greatmasks and bone armour, or the formal echoes of the Old Tongue, but Notch found it impossible to take them in properly – save for a song he kept hearing. It seemed that every corner he passed, seated in the comfort of a palace carriage, the same melody was playing. It was triumphant, rather than the playful, even bawdy material he expected from street performers.

He tapped his fingers on the windowsill. What was Alosus thinking? The stakes were too high, surely. If he failed it would be his death – and if he could not defeat whatever beast they set upon him, yet somehow survived, he would be put to death anyway, as a useless or dishonoured slave, according to Notch's escort. Success meant freedom, yes – but was Prince Tanere so short of slaves that he could not simply let one slave free to search for his family, which would doubtless earn the man two more slaves? Surely the Prince could afford to buy Alosus' family from whoever now owned them?

Of course, there was every chance Notch was giving the Ecsoli Prince far too much credit. "I hope you know what you're doing, Alosus."

There was another possibility, though it was harder to see beyond it to any benefits for the Prince – what if he *wanted* Alosus to win freedom? A wild thought, and unlikely, but something about the possibility seemed...

well, possible somehow.

When the carriage crunched to a halt, a not insignificant distance from the palace, and Notch exited, he was confronted by a small stone building sitting in the middle of a soft lawn, a building which did not even seem to have a door. The sun pounded down upon him and he found himself squinting.

"Over here," his escort said as he climbed down from the driver's seat.

Notch circled the carriage, boots crunching on the gravel, and found the fellow standing before a row of evenly-spaced redwood trees. Mighty trees, their trunks were colossal but there was more than ample room to pass between each. Taking another step closer, it became clear the trees had been planted in a circle. The space in between was a mix of sandy earth and flowering weeds.

"This is the Arena?" he asked.

"Yes." He smiled. "It may seem insecure but each trunk was woven with a bone of warding. No-one may pass between without permission."

"Then slaves fight for freedom in there?" It was broad enough, certainly, but it simply seemed so... unlike the Ecsoli. Where were the rows and rows of seating for all to enjoy the spectacle? Space for the Inquisitors to judge the clothing of the spectators, or some other foolishness. "It just seems very... isolated."

"Only the royal family may witness the formal Challenges."

"Ah." *There* was the Ecsoli attitude he'd been expecting. "Where is Alosus?"

"Below. It is not far," the man said as he started along a path that circled the Arena. As the Ecsoli promised, it did not take long to reach a set of steps that led underground, where two blue-robes stood guard before a wide cell. The guards had been gambling with silver and gold pins, but they stood to challenge the servant.

"Whether he's from the new world or not, he's not permitted," one jailer said.

Notch's escort smiled. "Feel free to take it up with Prince Tanere, if you wish."

The guard swore but stood aside, waving Notch to the column-like bars.

Alosus was performing a series of stretches on the stone floor. The cell also included bars and rings for training, everything Tonitora-sized. He stopped working when Notch approached. "This isn't what I was expecting when you said there were advantages to being taken by the Inquisitors," Notch said, speaking Anaskari.

"You must trust me, Notch. When I am free, it will be easier for the both of us. I wasn't sure it would come to this... but I must take the chance now that it has been offered. I didn't wish to worry you."

"Too late," he said. "Can you defeat whatever beast they have in store for you?"

"Yes," he said, and his even tone once again made it hard to read the man. Was he quietly confident or hiding his fear?

"And what about the prince – do you trust him? What if you succeed and he refuses to free you."

"He cannot," Alosus said.

"No?"

"In all recorded history no master has denied a winner their freedom, though perhaps only a few dozen have been offered the chance in the first place."

"Isn't that suspicious itself? Why is he offering it to his uncle's former slave?"

Now Alosus frowned. "That I wonder about also. Be sure that it will play to his advantage. What of Lady Casselli?"

"It seems she's seeking a lover to distract her enemies in a ploy for the throne, though I'm sure there's more to it. But she will help."

"Notch... this is dangerous territory. You accepted?"

"I must reach the Library."

The big man glanced away, then shrugged. "I can hardly judge you for taking your own risk, as I stand within this cell, can I?"

Notch smiled, though it was fleeting. "How many slaves have survived the Arena?"

"Three."

"Three, in how many years of history in the Land of the Sun?"

"Notch, you do not have to worry."

Notch ran a hand through his hair. "But I do. I can't help you here."

Alosus reached through the bars, gripping Notch by both shoulders. "Ask Tanere or Casselli to bring you to watch. You will see."

"I don't like it; but you know I will."

"Good," he said with a smile. "So has Lady Casselli offered a visit to the Library of Souls?"

"She has promised to arrange it for noon; she is speaking with Tanere." He lowered his voice. "Do you know who her enemies may be?"

"Any or all, Notch. As before, do not trust those around you. It seems, at least, that you remain useful to the people here and so speak to the Oracle and we will leave before you cease being of use to them."

"That is long enough, Captain Medoro," Tanere's

servant said. "It is not permitted to spend too much time with the *manes-spator* before the contest." *Manes-spator* – the ghosts that walk?

"Thank you," Notch told the man. He nodded to Alosus as he was led from the holding cell, troubled thoughts plaguing him all the way back to the palace proper where he had barely reached his rooms before another servant was arriving with the noon meal, which he ate quickly.

One of Lady Casselli's pages arrived soon after, speaking with some urgency. "We mustn't keep My Lady waiting, Captain."

"Certainly not," he said, hooking his scabbard on once more then sliding his father's blade out to check the edge. *Even if you don't know your enemy, that's no excuse not to be prepared,* the old man's voice echoed in his head.

The path to the Library of Souls was no more convoluted than any other location in the sprawling palace, but after the twentieth turn Notch was certain he'd not find his way back. Even on different floors, so much was the same. Marble, tapestry, ornaments. Sometimes windows and plants, but other than that, he was utterly dependant on his young guide.

When the page finally stopped, it was to pause before a steel door with no handle or opening. Instead, the lad raised a twisted charm and set it against a panel of bone. The door swung open.

A tall figure waited on the other side. Prince Tanere.

"Captain Medoro to petition the Library of Souls," the boy announced, his voice breaking as he spoke. Was he nervous at seeing the Prince or nervous about approaching the Library of Souls?

"Very well, off you go." Tanere waved the boy away

then gestured for Notch to approach. The Prince started pulling on a soft rope, opening a black curtain. A giant skull was revealed, pure white and so long that it could only have been one thing; a whale. Or perhaps even a young Sea God. It rested on bolts driven into the wall – the bone dominated the entire room, the long, pointed ridge-like jaws were smooth with the impression of a head and deep eye-sockets rested near the top.

"Is this an infant Sea God, Your Highness?" he asked softly.

Tanere smiled. "No, it is only a whale – yet it has collected the accumulated wealth of knowledge over centuries and centuries of royalty now. If your question has an answer, the Oracle will hold it."

"And all I do is ask?"

"Once I awaken it, yes." He lifted a carven box from the floor beneath the skull and drew forth a bone pendant big enough to fit in both his palms, then stretched up to place it in the socket. "In accordance with the rules our forefathers have established, it will only answer one question." He paused, regarding Notch with a serious gaze. "You are being afforded an honour few ever received, Captain. And certainly no foreign man before you. Many have opposed this but I have vouched for you myself since you are, after a fashion, of the Ecsoli bloodline."

"Thank you, Highness," Notch said. Hard to gauge the truth of the words. Opposition to him visiting the Oracle seemed likely... but was the prince claiming to have vouched for Notch only to ingratiate himself further? A more plausible possibility was that Tanere was simply acting on his own.

Either way, he would want Notch to feel indebted.

"Do not touch the Oracle and do not waste your question. I will be waiting outside," he said, drawing forth a key as he passed.

Behind Notch, the door swung shut with a muted boom, but he only focused on the whale skull. A faint yellow glow was filling the room. The sense of a vast, vast number of awarenesses were awakening and then focusing on him. It was like a crowded city had swept down to stare upon him. His skin prickled. A faint hum soon joined the light. Notch looked to the eye; did it need him to speak aloud?

If you wish it. The voice echoed in his mind, like several dozen people speaking at once – men, women, children of slightly differing tones. *We will hear you no matter. Ask your question, Seeker of Knowledge – we see both yesteryear and today.*

"I am not from this land. My question is about what we call the Sacrifice and I do not know if people of Ecsoli understand it the same as I do."

The voice did not answer right away but the hum intensified a moment and a tingling crossed his skin. *We believe we understand the process. Ask.*

Notch hesitated. Had it 'read' him to understand the Sacrifice? In the end, it didn't matter. What mattered was that he phrased the question correctly, since there was no way to know just how strict the Library of Souls would be about the single question limit. "Do you know of a way or of someone in all the lands that can tell, show or help me reverse the Sacrifice and bring Sofia back?"

Another silence and this time the humming eased.

He found himself holding his breath. Was the skull going quiet because it did not have an answer? It had to know! Sofia deserved life, after all she'd been made to give up. "Please," he whispered. The Library couldn't fail – couldn't fail. Not after crossings the seas, battling monsters, not after becoming embroiled with witches and beautiful, dangerous women and dangerous men too. Not after turning his back on his friends who even now might need him...

We have an answer. The voice returned with suddenness. "Yes?"

While such knowledge has not been shared with us there is one who might serve your needs. Said to be the greatest Maker of Masks, seek him in the Northern Mountains beyond Ovaneus. He is called Qu-Sitka.

"Thank you." Notch knelt before the skull, hope bursting within him.

44. FLIR

Flir had arranged for the two surviving soldiers, both bound, to be held in one of the upstairs rooms under the watchful eye and blade of Pevin and Grav. Though it was unlikely the still-trembling men would be very useful.

"What do you make of it?" she asked Kanis where they knelt before the now motionless body of Boles. The man's face was frozen in the same smile, which was no longer pleasant by any stretch, even before the dried blood. The unnatural quiet of the village had returned, even more grating after the chaos of the struggle.

"It seems different to the darklings. I don't know."

"Did you notice the way he was speaking? He was repeating the things he said to us, almost word for word."

"No... but I saw him stroll out into that mess without any idea what was happening. Like someone who wasn't quite all there."

She nodded. "If he was actually alive at any time over the course of today, I don't think he was in control of his body. Or thoughts."

"Who's controlling him? And how and why?"

"That's what we need to find out, because I think the whole village might be like Boles here."

Kanis glanced back into the street, to the still-empty square. "I truly hope not."

"Let's try the soldiers, see what Mildavir was up to here. He mentioned the caves," she said, rising with a wince and heading for the stairs. It was one thing to heal quickly and another to find herself being shot almost constantly.

"Think this is connected?"

"Why not?"

Pevin admitted them, his own eyes a little haunted, and Flir took a seat on the bed across from where the men knelt on the hardwood floor, hands bound behind their backs. Kanis leant against the doorjamb.

"Grav, you might want to wait outside," Flir said.

"Yes, dilar." He left quickly.

Flir leant forward a little. One of the soldiers was Joris, who'd been bandaged up but was sweating heavily. The other, a younger lad wearing his first beard, was in much better shape. "What is Mildavir doing out here? What is in the caves?"

The young one swallowed, glancing at Joris, who winced. "Don't say anything, Lindr."

Flir sighed. "You have to know we're going to see for ourselves soon enough."

Lindr squeezed his eyes shut. "She'd kill us."

"We'll kill you," Kanis said.

"Please, I cannot die," Lindr said. "I-I have to return to Whiteport. My mother, she's—"

"Enough," Flir snapped. "You have a choice, which is more than your friends and your commander received. Speak, or I will drive my fist through Joris' face and then yours – and that is no idle threat, you know what I am."

He shuddered. "Yes. Dilar."

"Very well. Tell us what you know, and I will let you return to Whiteport."

Lindr glanced at Joris, whose eyes were half-closed; the man had obviously not heard the last exchange. New blood was seeping from the bandages at his side. "The governor... he was working for a woman. I only saw her once."

"Can you describe her?"

"I just saw her mouth really. She wore a white robe with a hood and she didn't speak to us. Just Governor Mildavir. She seemed almost as young as me but her voice... I can't describe it properly..."

"Try."

"It seemed older somehow."

Flir looked to Pevin and Kanis, neither of who seemed to recognise the description of the woman. "Was she Renovar?"

"No. Maybe Anaskari. That's all I really know. The governor called her 'mistress'."

"And your purpose here?" she asked.

He slumped down onto his haunches, staring at the floor. "I thought joining his personal guard would be a good thing for my career."

"She means the caves, Lindr," Pevin said, his tone gentle.

Lindr nodded, not bothering to lift his head. "She's doing something to the Ice-Priests... I don't know, experimenting on them or something. I heard screams once, in the rooms below."

Flir looked to Pevin. His jaw was clenched. "What about Mildavir and you, Lindr?" she asked.

"Word was getting out; we were supposed to stop that."

"By forcing everyone here to lie about it?" Flir asked.

He still could not lift his head and he lowered his voice. "No. We were going to make a show of investigating. There are robes from the priests in our packs. We were going to impersonate some of them, let people in the area start to believe everything was fine."

Pevin stood and crossed to the window.

"Then you don't know what's happening in Ithinov?"

He lifted his head and now his eyes were wide. "Do you mean... that man, the innkeeper?"

Grav opened the door. "Someone approaches, dilar."

Flir stood. "We'll talk again Lindr. Pevin?"

"I will watch him."

In the hall, Grav was still trembling but seemed a little more together. "I hear something below."

"Go inside," Flir said as she and Kanis approached the stair, starting down and peering into the common room – there, movement at the bar.

"That had better not be Boles again," Kanis whispered.

Flir ignored him, descending another few steps, revealing the whole of the bar, and stopped when she saw who it was. "Ekolay."

The traveller was pouring himself a drink, the amber whiskey filling the glass to the brim. He still wore his white cloak but had lain his bow, quiver and long dagger beside him.

"What did you find?" she asked.

"Nothing I thought I'd ever see, and nothing I can explain," he said, then lifted the drink and downed half the glass.

"That bad?" Kanis asked.

Ekolay nodded. "Don't worry; I'll save you some of

Boles' finest."

"Where?" Flir asked.

"Behind the blacksmith, there's a... nest. I missed the opening the first time. When you see them, be careful. Whatever lives there could come back."

"It's that thing again," Kanis said.

Flir nodded as Ekolay took another drink. "Ekolay, what's in there? Is that where the rest of the villagers are?"

"And some people I don't recognise," he said. "Maybe don't touch them."

"Stay here," she told Kanis. "In case someone else turns up."

He caught her arm. "Not a chance."

"Fine. Ekolay, would you protect the others?"

"From man or woman, yes."

"Good." Flir charged up the stairs and retrieved her lamp, grimacing at the still-fresh wound in her ribs. Nearly healed but she probably wasn't quite ready for things like running and jumping. Before she left, she stuck her head into Pevin's room and explained. "Ekolay is downstairs."

"Mishalar watch over you, dilar," he said.

Back in the street she glared through the blacksmith's quiet doorway, to a cold anvil. No hint of movement within the shadowy room. Where was the smith? Inside, she found him, slumped between workbenches, head on his chest, seemingly asleep.

"So where's the entry?" Kanis said. "I don't see that thing fitting in here."

"No." She wove between the half-finished pieces and pushed through the rear door to a generous courtyard.

Perhaps it had once been beautiful, but it was another nest now. Spun with the same grey web, it was augmented with dead trees, earth and paving stones, those which had doubtless once covered the ground. Empty pots lay scattered around, the corpses of a few remaining bushes were bent and broken, frost-blackened buds closed.

Flir circled yet there was no opening. "How did Ekolay get inside?"

"Let's just break our way in," Kanis said.

"Wait." Up close, she saw the gouges made by feet and hands. "It must be up top."

"Do we really have to hide the fact that we've been inside?"

She shrugged.

"Right." Kanis drew an arm back and punched a hole in the side of the nest. He withdrew his fist then struck again, tearing a few hunks free, until a rough opening had been made. "See, much easier."

Flir stepped within, finding a similar scene to the last nest – only now there was a tunnel sloping down beneath the smithy. "Listen for it coming home," she said as she readied the lantern.

"No argument here."

The tunnel wound down and around before opening into a vast chamber lined with shadowy shapes. Flir's feet crunched on something; a dead torch, the faint scent of ash lingering. She circled the room slowly, Kanis beside her. Dozens of people lined the walls. All were suspended in the webbing, only their empty faces remained free, features revealing no pain, no terror either, just a simple muteness. A line of glimmering webbing had been spun from each head to a central column at the roof – which in turn ran down to hover over a stone pool, something that looked to have once belonged to a fountain.

"What is this?" she said as she approached.

She lifted the light over the pool. Something dripped to the surface, a rippling spreading somewhat slowly, as if through oily water.

"The strands extract something from the bodies," Kanis guessed. "But what?"

In the hush that followed his question, a rustling crossed the cave.

"Hear that?" Flir started toward the sound. While not robust, it was persistent. It came from directly to the right of the entrance.

She stopped before a struggling figure; it bore no thread and the pale face was contorted in desperation. "This one's alive," Flir said.

She lifted the lantern.

Aren.

45. FLIR

Flir tore at the grey muck, Kanis working on the other side, until Aren fell forward. She dragged him the rest of the way free, setting him on the ground. The man's eyes were closed now, and his chest barely moved, as if the effort of gaining their attention had spent the last of his energy.

"I'm going to lend him some of my strength," she said.

"Now? We should move him – what if the thing comes back?"

"Aren won't last that long. Protect me," Flir said as she gripped Aren's hands and drew in deep breaths. Slowing her own racing pulse wasn't easy, the odd scent of something sickly sweet and the scrape of Kanis' boots on the earth as he paced were persistent distractions. "I need to concentrate," she said. "Just listen for something."

He stopped pacing but did not answer. She was able to focus on Aren's thin pulse and calm herself, then she began to chant until the words became mere sounds. Warmth built, sliding down her arms to her hands. She tensed, ready for what would come next.

Pain rocked her.

Flir's eyes flew open – Aren was dragging her strength once more, like a drowning man snatching at straws. She released him, breaking the link. He gasped for air, his whole body shuddering. What she'd given was negligible truly, but to Aren, on the edge of death, it was more than enough.

"Where am I?" he rasped. "I took a room at the inn and..." he paused to catch his breath.

"Talk later," Flir said as she lifted him; the fellow groaning. She nodded to Kanis, who'd taken up the lantern. "Let's check on the inn."

They climbed up and out of the nest, passing through the still-empty smithy and into the street where the afternoon light was fading. The only source of sound came from the inn – the scrape and thud of furniture being moved.

Ekolay was righting an overturned table when Flir entered; it looked as though he'd already set half the room back in order, the shattered furniture stacked in a corner. "Can you find any medicine? Aren is alive," she said.

He blinked, then started for the kitchen.

Flir took Aren upstairs, calling for Pevin at the landing. The door opened, and he peered out, eyes widening as he threw the door wide to admit them. Flir placed Aren on the bed and stood back. Grav barrelled across the room, collapsing at his master's side with a glad cry.

"Show a little dignity, will you?" Kanis muttered.

Flir said nothing, but it was hard not to agree.

"Where was, I mean, how did this happen? Is he going to wake? Thank you, thank you both, dilars," Grav said, words tumbling forth.

"Pick one question, Grav," Pevin told him, not unkindly.

"Yes, of course. Will he recover?"

"I think so," Flir said. "The more pressing question, I feel – is will we? That thing is still out there."

"Can we fortify the inn?" Pevin asked.

"We can try," Flir said with a nod. "Ekolay is bringing whatever medicine he can find; administer it if he wakes, Grav."

"Of course, dilar."

Downstairs, Flir checked on their horses then organised Pevin and Kanis with the tools she found in the stable, which they used to board up the windows in every room, after which, they prepared a makeshift palisade for the entry within the inn, using tables, chairs and even the bar itself, which she and Kanis tore free.

"Wouldn't it be better to just take the wagon, dump Aren in it and get out of this place?" Kanis asked over the regular pounding of Pevin's hammer.

"Do you think he'd survive the ride?"

"I don't know if that matters," Kanis replied. "Just because he was caught unawares here, doesn't mean I trust him any more than I did before."

"So you think he was working with Mildavir in the caves?"

"If he wakes, I plan to find out."

Aren had woken by the time they finished securing the place as best as they could – the man stirred during their evening meal, which they ate in the kitchen. Pevin, who'd taken a turn watching over the cultist, called down from the landing.

He looked better, though his pale skin bore a dark blue tint, giving him the appearance of illness or great cold, yet the room was warm enough, a brazier having been dragged up the stairs earlier.

The cult leader was drinking from the still-steaming cup of soup that Ekolay had sent up not long before Pevin called for them.

"How do you feel, Master?" Grav asked.

"Weary. And empty, like I've had something taken from me – but I know it not to be true. The creature affixed no tentacle to me." He smiled at Flir and Kanis. "No doubt I have you both to thank for my life."

"Don't get used to it," Kanis said.

"Can you tell us what happened?" Flir asked.

"As best I can recall." He set the cup aside. "I sent Tikev to Tiramof and set out alone, for speed. When I arrived in Ithinov it was quiet, but someone directed me to the inn. I knew where it was of course, I'd stayed at Boles' before. But this time he seemed... different. Still cheerful but I don't know. Like he wasn't quite himself; I tried to joke with him but he didn't understand. It should have been my first clue." Aren took another drink as he shook his head.

"Did he offer the room cheap?" Flir asked.

"He did. And again, I just thought he was being kind. I took my room, settled in to sleep and woke in that place." He took a deep breath. "I watched the creature regurgitate that gunk over one of the villagers, then hoist the man up to the wall where it attached one of those things to the fellow."

"Can you guess at why?" she asked.

"I fear it may have been trying to learn."

"What?" Flir frowned and Pevin's eyes had widened.

"I was there for what felt like days and even though the time is blended together in my mind, from what I recall

I'm growing more certain that it drank from the pool periodically. In between such actions it would control the movements of a marionette, and it seemed to ponder and then return above. When it came back, if it wasn't with more travellers, it was to take villagers up. When it returned, it was to drink and work with the marionette once more."

"Making adjustments based on how things went above," Pevin said, his voice horrified.

"We saw no puppet," Kanis said.

"Perhaps it carries it?"

It would have explained everyone's odd behaviour – if they were being controlled by the creature. Flir stood. "Where is it now?"

Aren shook his head. "I don't trust my memory. It seems that it left days ago. Or maybe only yesterday? But I feel that it is not nearby."

"What makes you say that?" Kanis asked.

"A sensation. Or a fear perhaps; I fear I would know if it approached."

Kanis snorted. "Wonderful."

"I do not claim to be able to explain it, dilar," he said.

Flir paced the room as best she could. "Wherever it is, we need to decide something. Staying here indefinitely seems pointless. As soon as Aren is ready, I think we should head for the caves. This might be our best chance."

"I will be ready by dawn," Aren said.

"Any objections?"

No-one spoke, and Pevin straightened – he was understandably still worried about his brother – so Flir nodded. "Good. We post a watch in pairs – and tomorrow we find out what Mildavir's mistress is doing to the Ice-Priests."

46. FLIR

Flir found herself pacing once more – this time before the dark rockface, the noon wearing on and the temperature falling as Kanis pummelled the stone door, swinging mighty overhand blows, fists linked.

Yet nothing worked – not for him and not for her.

And after a long, tense night spent waiting for the creature to return, either on watch or tossing and turning in her bed, Flir wanted something to kick – something she could actually break. Pevin, Grav and Aren were scouting the trail, seeking another way into the caves. Ekolay had bade them luck and left for Enar from the inn; Flir could hardly blame him.

"This is pointless." Kanis gave the stone wall another kick.

"Well said," Flir replied.

"I hope you've got a new suggestion to go with your clever comment."

"Of course I don't," she snapped. "Short of digging our way through from the side, I think we're going to have to rely on the others since we didn't bring any tools."

Kanis looked set to retort but instead, he snapped his fingers. "Maybe we do have tools after all – back at the smithy."

"It'd be another half a day there *and* back," Flir said. "Putting us back here well after nightfall. We'll be even more vulnerable."

"The creature?"

"Exactly. I'm sure it prefers night; you've seen the nests."

"It seemed to cause plenty of problems for us in broad daylight before."

"Well, imagine how much worse things will be in the dark – we wouldn't even see it, Kanis."

"You've got a point," he said after a moment's thought.

"Well, here they come." Flir pointed to the trail beyond the door. Pevin was striding with some purpose, Grav hanging back a little with the slower Aren. "Let's see what they've discovered."

"There's some sort of window set into the hills themselves," Pevin said. "It looks like they've been cleared recently. Perhaps a month ago at most – but the windows are ancient, they bear a similar spoked design to the third Mishalar Temple in Enar."

Two hundred years at least. "Let's take a look," Flir said.

Pevin led them back up trail, leaving it for a winding path lined with weeds and crossed by cracks and broken ground. They climbed as the sun started a slow fall, reaching three large, evenly-spaced windows. As Pevin had said, spoked like a wheel, parts of the glass near-buried in mildew and mould – save for where it had been scrubbed clean.

"Not much to see below; it's not lit very well," he said

as he gestured within, then folded his arms, one foot set to tapping. Flir put a hand on his shoulder. "If he's in there, we'll get him out."

He nodded and she knew from his expression, that she didn't need to add anything about the dozens of dark alternatives. She knelt to peer down through the first window. Dim light revealed little but the stony floor and the edge of what might have been a cot. Flir looked up to the others. "I don't think we can quietly remove these windows, nor stop debris falling inside, for that matter."

"Meaning?" Grav asked, his eyes a little wide. Flir was beginning to think of the look as his regular face, so far out of depth was the poor fellow.

"Meaning surprise is our best way forward," she said. "Follow us when you can, it isn't much of a drop. Kanis?"

He shifted to the next window and lifted his leg. "Ready when you say."

Flir lifted her arm. "Now," she said, then drove her fist into the centre of the spoke. The entire window shattered, bursting down into the room. The frame clanged on stone, echoed immediately by Kanis' window.

She leapt into the room, landing easily. "Throw me the lantern."

Kanis thumped down as a silhouette loomed above, it raised an arm to give her a moment to note the lantern before they released. She caught it and opened the hatch, lifting it as she turned.

A wide chamber revealed men and women in plain smocks rising from cots, most shielding their eyes from the light but enough starting to shout and demand answers that Flir frowned at them. If the fools were any louder, they'd wake the dead. Admittedly, being torn from sleep by smashing glass was hardly pleasant but if the clamour alerted their mistress...

"Please," Flir shouted. "We are here to help you. Be calm."

Kanis was echoing her words and as Pevin dropped down the gathered people began to quiet, their questions of alarm changed to curiosity. One young man stepped forward. Dark circles sat beneath his eyes and his arms were bandaged. "Who are you?"

"Can you really save us?" A younger woman said. She, too, appeared as weary as the others. Now that they had come closer, Flir saw around a dozen. Hardly an army, but surely enough Ice-Priests missing to have become a concern sooner?

Of course, Mildavir had been stopping word getting out.

Flir started to answer but a new voice interrupted. "No. They cannot." An older woman with streaks of grey in her brown hair entered the light, turning to face the gathered people. "You know that; only the sorceress can break the link."

"What link?" Flir asked the woman.

"What does it matter? Just flee, whoever you are," she said, her eyes flat with near-despair. "Your good intentions are appreciated but you will only be killed, or worse, enslaved, if you stay here too long."

Kanis folded his arms. "We're no regular fools, lady."

"Oh? Is that so?"

"He's half right," Flir said. "We are not regular. Kanis and I are dilar. We can help." She introduced herself, Pevin and pointed up to Grav and Aren.

Now excited murmurs grew and the man who'd first spoken took the hand of the young woman. "You are? Maybe with your help we finally can escape this place."

"Even if that is true about them being dilar, they will fail," the older woman said.

"Have a little hope for once, Simina," someone shouted.

Simina's jaw was clenched. "It would be false hope. Even dilar cannot break the link between our bones and that thing."

"What thing?" Flir asked.

The young man came forward. "I am Tsaro, let me show you." The Ice-Priests made way for him as he led them to the rear of the chamber, beyond the third window's reach to where Flir's light revealed thin bones coiled around a steel pole, rising up to a gaping set of jaws.

"A snake?"

"Yes," Tsaro said. "It is what keeps us here. She showed us how it works – she forced Ekhar to run, offering him his freedom if he could escape."

"What happened?"

"He'd barely taken ten steps through the door before he simply collapsed, dead."

Flir exchanged a glance with Kanis. "Has anyone tried to destroy it?"

"Impervious to anything we can manage," Simina said.

Kanis hefted his mace. "Want me to try?"

"No!" She leapt in front of the snake. "When we strike it we all feel the same pain." She shook her head at Tsaro. "What were you thinking?"

"I only meant to show them – but maybe we can ambush her, now that they're here?"

Simina did not appear convinced.

"What can you tell us of her?" Pevin asked. Flir hadn't even realised he'd not followed. Had he been searching for his brother?

"She is a fell sorceress, far more powerful than anything or anyone I have ever encountered," Simina replied.

"Does she wear a bone mask?" Flir asked.

"No. But her age is hard to determine. She wears a robe of white and we never know when she will appear – she does not seem to need doors. When she does arrive, some thug usually has water and food." She glanced at the snake. "When they were cutting into us or hypnotising us to learn the Way of the Ice, they checked on us more often."

"Cutting you?" Kanis asked. "Why?"

"To discover if she can replicate the way we manage the ice."

Tsaro swallowed. "If she can't, she plans to take us with her."

"Where?" Flir asked.

"Into the northern mountains. She says there is something there, trapped beneath a frozen lake that she needs. We will have to help her free it."

Pevin's voice was wary. "A lake beneath Blackthorn Mountain?"

"Yes," Simina said. "Why? Do you know what she seeks?"

"We do," Flir said. "Bones."

The older woman frowned. "Bones, but why would she –"

A booming buried her next words. It came from the opposite end of the cave, insistent and growing in force. Many of the Ice-Priests began to cower away, some going so far as to crouch behind the snake that kept them prisoner.

"Is this the sorceress?" Kanis asked, shouting over the

sound, a frown on his face.

Simina, who had moved toward the booming, along with Tsaro, shook her head. "No, she comes without warning."

"This is something else," Tsaro said, his eyes wide.

Flir looked to Kanis and the others, their faces full of concern. There was one very real possibility, though she had no proof to offer, nothing but a new fear. The creature. Whether it had tracked them somehow or whether it had merely stumbled upon the Ice-Priests' prison, did not matter for now.

What mattered was protecting the priests – somehow she had to stop the creature.

47. NOTCH

Notch found himself seated on a raised wooden bench beside Lady Casselli, staring down at the Arena from beyond the ring of trees. The sandy area was broad enough for a pitched battle. From their vantage point there would be few moments where Alosus would be out of sight, yet they were still positioned beyond the safety of whatever invisible barrier the bone magic had created.

"It's old magic, all this safeguarding," Casselli said when he asked about it, "but considering what your friend is going up against I do not mind the inconvenience." She was glancing around at the other audience members, who'd filled the seating quite swiftly. The vast majority of which were made up of the royal family, which meant at least one hundred people. Others were guests – Notch had been allowed to attend, due to his status. He still drew his share of stares, both of mistrust and of naked interest.

Lady Casselli herself had quickly arranged to accompany him, wanting him to begin work as escort right away – though she seemed to have spent as much time looking for Prince Tanere as anyone else.

Doubtless he was the very conspirator Notch was meant to be distracting the Ecsoli from – though any who'd seen the Lady and Prince together had to have noticed the way the man stared at her. For Casselli's part, she didn't return his attention. "He pursues all women," she said when Notch asked, not appearing perturbed that he'd guessed who she had aligned herself with. And perhaps it wasn't a difficult thing to guess in any event. "The court will have little reason to see his interest as anything more than his usual need to bed a woman, as long as you are here, Notch. If I had no lover of my own, then there might be more eyebrows raised if the Prince and I were seen together."

"Is that truly enough?" he asked. And more concerning, was it enough to turn unwanted attention his way? He did not need some Ecsoli noble mistaking him for an adversary. There was every chance he'd already taken that path.

She shrugged. "For some, immersed as they are in their own scheming. For others, it will take more but do not worry. We are preparing for that."

A cry from the Arena prevented Notch from asking his next question, as Alosus was escorted between the trees and across the sand, where he stood waiting, his grand sickle in hand. He wore no armour but had added a huge bow and quiver to his weaponry.

"Just what is he going up against? No-one will tell me," Notch said.

"It is called a roak. They live on a peninsular far to the east; it is very difficult to bring them here." There was an excitement to her voice that detracted from her beauty, though she had, like all the ladies present, taken great care with her appearance once more. Was it at the prospect of seeing the roak? Or was it the fight and the promise of death?

"He is my friend, Lady Casselli."

"Oh, I know – try not to fear. He has a chance."

"How so?"

She shrugged. "I simply get a feeling about him."

"I hope it is true," he said. "Can you describe the roak?"

"Somewhat like a stag. Only it stands upon two feet and it has antlers running down its arms, not just its head, like the fins of a fish I suppose."

A horn sounded. Prince Tanere stood directly across from them, easily visible on his higher podium, arms raised so that the sleeves of his deep blue robe slid down. A pair of Inquisitors flanked him, their attention focused on the crowd, it seemed. What would they judge the court on today?

"Family and honoured guests," he said. The prince had not shouted, yet his voice was clear despite the distance. "In preparing for today's Challenge I did a little reading of the records and it appears that this is the first challenge in nearly a score of years, so it is with some pleasure I present Alosus – the Gigansi who will fight for his freedom today."

A cheer rose. The men, women and children nearby were all smiling as they broke into joyous chatter. Alosus did not react. The people quietened only when Tanere resumed his self-congratulatory speech. "I trust you have all been diligent in keeping pace with the gossip of our beloved palace and therefore know well that Alosus was my late uncle Vinezi's slave." He paused for booing and hissing. "And before his cowardly flight across the Eternal Sea, he sold Alosus' wife and son to another –

at a price that is frankly, an insult, considering he was practically donating royal property."

Notch folded his arms.

"But I trust it will make today's struggle even more riveting to know that he fights not only for his freedom, but for his very family. And such is my magnanimous nature that I have allowed him to do so today, and given you all a chance to enjoy something out of the ordinary, something many of you younger ones may have never even seen." This part of the speech seemed aimed at the Inquisitors, who were taking notes as they watched.

"My blessing upon your fight, Alosus," the prince said before taking his seat.

Almost immediately a roar began to build. People all around the arena were shouting – whether in support or not, was too hard to say. Alosus rolled his shoulders and stamped his feet, his gaze fixed on something Notch could not quite make out, something concealed by the mighty redwood trunks and stands of royals.

Yet there *was* something approaching – and when he saw its first few jerky steps across the sand, Notch realised it was being Compelled. And more, such treatment had already enraged it; the creature's nostrils flared, and its dark eyes seemed to burn.

As Lady Casselli had said, the roak was not unlike a deer – yet it towered on two hooves, its shaggy fur streaked with mud and blood. Its torso changed, becoming vaguely man-shaped but the dark head was more elongated than a normal deer and its wicked antlers were silvery; their sharp points caught the light. Similar, if significantly smaller, were the horns that started from the elbow and grew longer until those bursting from the backs of the roak's hands protruded several feet.

And where Alosus was half again as tall as Notch, not to mention broad and solid as a tree himself, the roak was bigger again. It did not dwarf Alosus by any means, but the fight did not seem fair.

Alosus was already fitting an arrow to his bow when the Ecsoli released the roak.

It charged – so fast that Alosus only had time for one shot.

The arrow flashed across the Arena and lodged in the roak's upper chest, but it did not even slow, lowering its antlers as it closed with Alosus.

He dropped the bow and crossed his arms, bracing himself against the impact. The roak tossed Alosus to the side with its blow, then spun in the sand, snorting and pawing at the earth.

"Alosus!" Notch shouted. His cry had been swallowed by the roaring crowd. He was on his feet, reaching for the sword that he had not been allowed to bring, when Casselli touched his arm.

"Do not despair. Gigansi are not so fragile," she shouted over the din.

Alosus had reached one knee and was already lifting his sickle. The man's arms bore only a few scratches – thin trails of red.

"Incredible."

The roak charged again but this time it slowed to slash at Alosus with the horns upon its arms. Alosus ducked one blow and swung his sickle but the roak caught the weapon with the antlers on its other arm, jamming the weapon. It tried to jerk the blade from Alosus' grip, but the big man pulled back and they were caught in a struggle until the thing slashed once more with its free hand.

The blow tore into Alosus' side and he fell with a roar of his own.

Blood spilled across the sand.

Alosus rolled away, his weapon gone. The roak did not chase him, instead, it swooped down to jam its face into the bloody sand, chewing and swallowing every drop. Alosus had retrieved his bow and quiver, fitting another arrow to the string. When he raised his arms, more blood slid down his side. The gash was deep; but any other man would have had his ribs shorn in two.

The bowstring snapped. A second arrow punched through thick fur – this one into the side of the roak's neck. It growled as it reared up, shaking its head furiously. Alosus reached for another arrow, but fell to one knee. Again, the crowd hollered for blood; the nearest child spat as he cried out, eyes alight. The beast turned to charge again, lowering its horns.

Alosus was breathing hard and he did not make any effort to flee – instead he swung his fists in a mighty blow, just as the antlers reached him.

Bone shattered.

One set of horns broke but the other pierced Alosus' shoulder, slamming him onto his back. The roak lashed out with an arm, pinning Alosus by driving a talon into his thigh. Alosus' bellow was like thunder, but he gripped the roak by the throat and squeezed. Both combatants were breathing hard and the shouting from the crowd washed over everything.

Notch found himself on the ground, beating against the invisible barrier between trunks but no-one paid him any heed.

Yet a shift in the struggle was taking place.

Alosus' eyes had lost their whites and the pupils were

expanding, an ember-like glow replacing them. And despite his various wounds, his lack of a weapon and the growling beast he held by the throat, Alosus actually seemed to be gaining strength.

The gathered royals and guests had started to quieten. And then the roak started to pull *away* from Alosus.

But he kept a tight grip on its throat. The beast began to shudder and Alosus' eyes flared; still it could not break free. The trembling continued and suddenly it collapsed atop of Alosus, legs struggling weakly.

The scent of singed hair spread from the combatants and Notch frowned. The Arena was silent until a voice split the hush.

"No!"

The mighty cry had burst from the roak.

Notch fell back.

"No!"

It cried out again, its voice rough and desperate – and then it continued to repeat the word, bleating it over and over until it fell finally still, leaving the Arena in a horrified silence.

And then the cheering began.

48. NOTCH

Notch stood at the rear of a dim room in the healers' wing, the woody scents of herbs and the sharper sting from the other medicines assaulting him. He rubbed his temples to ease the ache. The wave of shouting, screaming voices had been bad enough but the desperation in the roak's cry of terror was just as piercing in his memory.

It had been a shock to learn it could speak, and perhaps just as strong a surprise to witness whatever Alosus had done to it.

Even now, Alosus was nearly wreathed in bandages, stretched across a huge bed while healers in black robes examined him, their bone masks glowing a faint red. Notch would have checked on Alosus but Prince Tanere and Lady Casselli and a familiar Inquisitor – the man from the dock who'd permitted them entry into the city – blocked him, they were whispering to each other. Notch found he couldn't even force himself to try and eavesdrop.

Finally, the Inquisitor scurried off and Tanere and Casselli turned to him. Both appeared enormously pleased.

"Will he recover?" Notch asked.

"Assuredly," Tanere said. "Which is even more wonderful, since I will continue to benefit from this Gigansi."

"You're not going back on your word?" Notch demanded, straightening, then adding a hasty, "Your Highness."

Tanere frowned. "Certainly not. I will forgive you your manner now, Captain Medoro, since as an outsider, you fail to understand what this means for me and my bid for the throne."

"Forgive my words," Notch said.

"I understand; you want to protect him while he cannot speak for himself."

"Yes," Notch said, glancing again at Alosus. "I assume you're referring to the Inquisitors when you speak of benefiting?"

"In part – I have certainly exceeded what is expected, even of a prince," he said. "But more importantly, I have discovered a line of Gigansi long-since thought to have died out."

"Then you didn't know Alosus could... draw the life from things?"

"Technically, it was the heat. He can draw the heat from a living thing," Lady Casselli added. "Though it achieved the same result."

"Yes. And when he recovers, I will have him swear allegiance to me and then we can finally do something about the rogue Gigansi."

Notch frowned. "I don't understand."

Tanere laughed and started for the exit. "You will soon enough, Captain. Feel free to stay with him tonight, but remember your testimony is required tomorrow and I expect you to be both alert and presentable."

"I will be ready," he said and then the prince was gone.

Lady Casselli lingered, her gaze on Alosus, whose chest rose and fell in an easy rhythm. "With this windfall and your witness report, we may not need anything else to achieve our goal."

"What did he mean by swear allegiance, My Lady? And rogue Tonitora?"

She stepped close, so that their bodies were almost touching. "And you will be the final delicious touch, throwing them even further off the scent, they won't even see it coming. In fact, the sooner you and I formalise things the more credence it will lend to our act."

"My Lady?"

She smiled as she leant in to kiss him, a brief grazing of her lips across his. Her breath carried the cool scent of mint and she spoke softly. "A Union. I do not know if you still call it that in your land, but our joining will go no small distance toward allaying fears that the Prince and I are conspiring."

He opened his mouth to reply but she raised a hand. "Remember your promise; I upheld my end of the bargain and I will still grant you leave to seek this Qu-Sitka but not before we have the throne. Understood?" A hardness had crept into her voice.

Notch struggled to conceal a sinking feeling. What had been a stunning victory for Alosus was quickly becoming yet another step toward someone else's goal. Casselli and Tanere had their claws in far deeper than even Notch had suspected, and it was clear that to try and disentangle himself or Alosus now would not end well at all.

Worse, tangling himself with the both of them would

make it that much harder to help Alosus.

Chelnos be damned. "Yes, My Lady."

"Good." She started toward the exit herself, glancing over her shoulder once she reached the doorway. "And as to your other question, your friend will have to swear to become vassal to the king – just like all other princes of the lesser lands and peoples."

"Princes?"

"Don't be so shocked, Medoro," she said with a smile. "It makes you look foolish and you should understand without me spelling it out, surely? Alosus is born of the line of Gigansi Kings."

Epilogue

There had been too much disruption in the harbour lately.

Strange lights from the surface, lights that pushed deep down toward the bottom, light that seared his skin when it surprised him and the others. They quickly learnt to stay away from the boat and its intrusive light, swimming swiftly for shelter – or simply away, as it searched the harbour.

What did it want? The lights spent significant time near the wrecks of the ships, things that had always made him curious, and sad – it tugged at something buried in his memory too. But the boat above, which had been searching for many tides, didn't always focus on the ships. It roamed the entire bay; that was the problem. It was hard to know just where or when it would appear, his fellow Sea-People couldn't settle the way they once had.

Sanarc and Bel were already leaving – taking everyone to find a new place.

But that was not the answer.

He had to stay, not just because the fish were plentiful

or because the harbour was safe – but because each night, when he broke the surface to stare up at the golden lights of the city, sometimes he felt on the verge of remembering something. Something important – something urgent. Faces and names. A woman with almost child-like features. A man with unshaven cheeks.

But there was another reason not to leave – the lights seemed to have stopped, even if the boat remained overhead.

He swam deeper, heading toward the wreckage. It was one of the bigger ships, but a little different to the others. It had been some time since he'd pulled himself through the narrow openings to cabins and below the decks, having searched it before and found everything of use but this time... maybe he could find out what the boat was searching for?

He kicked a little deeper, heading fore – and found that the ship had slid further into a crevice recently. If it had settled in a slightly different position there was a chance he'd be able to reach new rooms. He gripped the wood and pulled himself around a hunk of mast and came to just what he'd wanted; a new opening. It would be a tight fit, but he'd manage.

This far from the surface and the distant moon, half-concealed by the wreckage of the decks there was little light, but his eyes were well-accustomed to seeing in the darkness. He found a mess, a great steel oven laying on its side, utensils, pots and pans everywhere, bottles and jars of ingredients.

And all of it achingly familiar.

As if he should have known his way around such a place... and yet, how could that be? Fish-folk did not travel aboard ships. But it put him in the mind of the faces he sometimes glimpsed when he stared at the city, and another face. An old man with sunken eyes and a fierce glare.

And there, blade dull in the shadowy room, a heavy-looking, almost square blade.

A cleaver.

Used to hacking through hunks of meat and bone.

He reached for it, gripping the handle and it felt *right* somehow.

He blinked.

He remembered now! He had a name and a past, he hadn't always lived beneath the ocean. Once, he'd been a chef and before that a soldier. And his friends! Seto, the old man. Notch and Flir. Gods, he remembered!

Remembered the Sea Beast, the attack and all the *acor*, explosions and fire everywhere, he remembered it all.

Luik.

That was his name.

THE AMBER ISLE SAMPLE
(#1 of the Book of Never)

Chapter 1

The drunk blocked most of the firelight in Petana's only inn.

He staggered over to Never's table. The man's breath preceded him and it was not pleasant – in fact, nothing about the slob was. Some manner of bug leapt in his lank hair and his teeth were green stumps. Red-rimmed eyes squinted down at Never. A rather sharp-looking butcher's cleaver hung from the man's belt.

So much for getting a good night's sleep somewhere warm.

"You're sitting in my seat, stranger," the drunk said.

Never lowered his cup. "Good to know."

The man blinked and a frown formed. He placed his knuckles on the scuffed table; Never glanced away. Half the patrons of the Petana inn were on their feet. Talk of war in the south, of how one of the village cows had gone to giving sour milk, of bad weather coming – all of it stopped. Never sighed inwardly. Don't do it, fellow. Please. If things got out of hand, the man might die. And despite the drunk's demeanour, Never didn't truly want that.

Futile.

The man leant forward and the stench of his breath thickened the air. Somehow, it was worse than the capital's sewers. It also seemed something had died on the front of his tunic. "I said, you're sitting in my seat. Move."

"I'm really quite comfortable here; how about we share?"

His brow furrowed. Perhaps the man was unable to comprehend what was happening, how someone could refuse him. No doubt he was used to getting his way. Or at the very least, to people getting *out* of his way. Some of them fainting probably.

"Custom would suggest you get angry now," Never offered.

"What?"

"Why don't you sweep my drink from the table?" He smiled. "Or you could roar something obscene, that's always fun."

The drunkard finally realised he was being toyed with. He growled as he reached for his blade, raising it level with his face so it caught light from one of the torches. It did look wicked. "Last chance, funny-man."

Never sighed. Another evening ruined – thanks to his own pig-headedness no doubt. Yet why couldn't the drunk have chosen another time to stumble in? Just one night in a bed would have been enough.

And now this wreck of a man had ruined it.

One of the serving girls was gaping; spiced sausage and red peppers sliding to drip from her tray. Time to put an end to all the fuss. Never winked at her then whipped a knife free from beneath the table. He slapped the cleaver. The flat side of the weapon smacked the drunk in the face. The man blinked then dived forward with a growl.

Never had already slipped from the seat.

The slob crashed into the table, floundering and cursing. Never leapt onto the man's back, eliciting a grunt, and grabbed a handful of greasy hair. He jerked the man's head back with a grimace, placing his knife against an unshaven neck. Yet he did not draw blood; not if he could avoid it.

"You had to ruin things, didn't you?"

"What?"

"Tell me, do you live here in the charming village of Petana then?"

"Get off me," he gurgled.

"Don't be a fool. Just tell me where you live and I'll let you go." Never glanced over his shoulder. The rest of the inn was standing now, men with hands by their own weapons and women with wide eyes – all save one woman in a green cloak with hood, who merely watched, arms folded. Curious. He addressed the crowd, pitching his voice to carry. "Worry not, good patrons, I will be swift. And because I'm feeling magnanimous – I won't kill this poor wretch." He wrinkled his nose and leant closer to the drunk. "Well, I probably won't kill you, if you tell me where you live."

He swore. "Why would I do that?"

Never kept his voice low. "Because you've laid waste to my plans so now I'm going to rob you when I leave – or perhaps I'll kill you now and then rob you. You choose."

"To the Burning Graves below with you."

Never inched the knife in, drawing blood – just a trickle, but it was enough; his own blood stirred in response, veins bulging. Damn it. Always the same. Never gritted his teeth. No. None of that today. Or any other day, ever again, if he could help it. "Tell me."

"Lone house. East end of the village."

"Wonderful. Goodnight then." He switched his hold

to lock the man's head in the crook of his elbow and applied pressure until the fellow went limp. Never stood back, hesitated. No way was he wiping grease on his own clothing. He found a relatively clear patch on the back of the man's tunic to clean his hand. Gods, did the fellow bathe in slime? Never collected his pack from the splinters of the table and turned to the assembled folk of Petana.

"Is he alive?" The barman waved a skinny arm at a nearby patron. "Check him, Juan." To Never he growled. "You wait there."

A dark-bearded man rushed to the drunk, eyes narrowed. Muttering swelled – an unpleasant music indeed. A few men held weapons – mostly scythes or knives drawn from beneath tan robes with multi-coloured stripes. If he was feeling ungenerous, Never had to admit that the Marlosi fondness for colour sometimes cast them as somewhat child-like.

Irrational of him to think so, and there was certainly little child-like about their expressions. Or the steel they held.

"He breathes yet," Never said. He moved toward the door and the barman stepped over to intercept. Never shook his head, pulling his cloak open to reveal a row of knives.

"Gum's alive," Juan announced.

"Fine," the barman said. "Out with you then. Don't want no trouble makers here anyway."

"A pleasure." Never strode from the common room and into the wind. The yellow glow from Petana's windows didn't penetrate too far into the night, and the dirt beneath his feet soon turned blue then black with shadow. Candlelight winked in about half of the homes he passed; the thatched rooves were unkempt hair touched with starlight, resting on squat heads thrusting up from the earth. The poetry of a village.

He was a fool for letting his temper get the better of him. At least none had died.

But Gum was still to pay for his belligerence.

He passed no-one on the street, pausing once to wrestle his cloak from a strong gust, then slowed at the edge of the village. A stand of trees encircled the southern end of Petana, beyond which lay the dark road that hopefully led to the coastline, but no lone house... unless...there, right against the trees.

A shack rather than a house, he decided upon reaching it. The roof was a nest of thatching; the door ajar. Never knelt in the entryway and removed the blue-stone from his pack. He rubbed it in his palms until warmth spread, a blue glow rising. "Wonderful." He stood, took a breath and slipped inside.

The shack reeked of old sweat and rotten food – even holding his breath it was a slap to the face. He sighed, switching to shallow breathing as he stepped over crumpled shirts on squeaking floorboards. The bed was a mound of...unpleasantness and the table featured a half-eaten meal on a broken plate. The pale-blue glow set congealed fat to glistening.

Nothing yet.

A second room looked to be a hasty addition, and held a tall, locked cupboard. Never set the blue-stone down and removed his lock picks from a vest pocket then set to work. The lock soon clicked.

Inside lay a shining breastplate and helm inlaid with the charging stallion insignia of the Marlosa Empire. So the slob had a respectable past. How far he had fallen.

Next, Never lifted a heavy dagger in an ornate sheath worked with a Hero's Seal. He gave a soft whistle. The weapon would have personally been awarded to Gum by the Empress. Before she was driven from her city anyway. Never removed the blade. Beautiful condition. He took the dagger itself but replaced the sheath with a shake of the head. Whatever the drunk had done to earn such an honour, he deserved its memory at least.

Especially when times for the Marlosi were destined to become harder still.

"Now for the stash of coin," Never murmured. Surely there was one somewhere. Moving back into the first room, he placed the blue-stone on the table and stepped over to the bed. If only he had a nice pair of gloves. He lifted the mattress, pushing it against the wall.

A small pouch lay in the centre of the floor, its drawstring tied.

He smiled. "There you are."

Light flickered and he spun, Gum's knife in hand. A dark figure stood in the doorway, stars and the faint glow from the village behind, waiting just beyond the reach of his glowing stone. "What are you doing?" A woman's voice.

Never chuckled. "Robbing the owner of this house, of course."

"No you're not."

"No, I am." He bent without taking his eye from the figure and retrieved the pouch, untying it with one hand and emptying most of the coins into an inner pocket in his cloak. He grinned. "See?" Then he dropped the pouch back into position, which gave a sad clink.

"Put that back."

"My dear, I could never do that."

She shifted, reaching behind her back. The thin outline of an arrow appeared against the starlight. The creak of a bowstring followed.

"Last chance."

He kept his hands raised and moved slowly toward his blue-stone, collecting his pack. The archer's silhouette tracked him. "And now I have to leave. Since the hospitality of Petana is so lacking, I have to find a nice ditch to spend the night in."

"I can thread your eye from here." Her voice was hard but she sounded young.

He took a step closer. "You're not a murderer, girl."

"It's not murder if I kill a thief. It's a service." She paused. "And I'm not a girl."

"Very well, 'young lady', perhaps? Let's say twenty summers or so?" He took another step and raised the stone. Her arrow was knocked and the bow at half-draw. Pale hands held the weapon – not a local then, and not with those green eyes either. And her cloak was green too. The woman from the inn? Beneath her cloak she wore a light blue tunic with no insignia, rank or sword. Not a Vadiya soldier either – how they hated everyone not knowing exactly their rank and family.

"Stop moving."

He paused. What was that accent in her command? "Do people mistake you for the invaders?"

"How do you know I'm not Vadiyem?"

"Because your accent isn't right for Vadiya." Never shrugged. "In any event, I have to leave. People are following me and they'll catch up sooner or later." One more step and the arrow was inches from his chest. "Could you please move aside?"

"No. I'm keeping you here."

"Not providing a service anymore?" He softened his voice. "Come now, we both know that if you were going to kill me, you'd have done it instead of announcing yourself."

She drew the string to full stretch. "Sure about that?"

"Are you sure I care either way?"

She frowned.

Never put gentle pressure on the arrow, moving the bow aside. She let him, though her jaw was locked. Her expression wavered between frustration and curiosity. "You shouldn't be doing this."

"Killing in cold blood cuts both ways. Let me pass, you're not ready."

"Damn you." She finally stepped aside.

"Thank you." Never slipped out of the shack and into the trees.

A Note from Ashley

Hi! I hope you enjoyed *The Last Sea God* and thanks for reading.

I'd like to ask if you could help me out by leaving an honest review of the book at your place of purchase? Long or short, bad or good, it all helps!

AND if you'd like to sign up to my newsletter you'll be the first to know when the next Bone War Book is released. You'll also have first access to preview chapters and pre-release editions of the story, in addition to being automatically added into the draw for giveaways.

Ashley

ACKNOWLEDGMENTS

For Brooke, you make such a difference, thank you always!

Once again, thanks also to both my families for all their unwavering support, to my editor Amanda and also to Rebekah at VividCovers for another superb cover.

And last but definitely not least, the readers who have been lovingly hounding me for the rest of the story - hold tight for number 2 and 3 in this new series!!

Ashley Capes

ABOUT ASHLEY

Ashley Capes is an Australian novelist, poet and teacher. *City of Masks* is his first novel and the follow up is *The Lost Mask*. The trilogy was completed with *Greatmask* in 2016. Ashley is also the author of five poetry collections and various other novels. He loves Studio Ghibli films and strongly believes Nausicaa is one of the greatest heroines out there.

Visit his blogs at *www.cityofmasks.com* & *www.ashleycapes.com* or follow him on twitter @Ash_Capes.

Other titles by Ashley:

The Bone Mask Trilogy

1. *City of Masks*
2. *The Lost Mask*
3. *Greatmask*

Book of Never

1. *The Amber Isle*
2. *A Forest of Eyes*
3. *River God*
4. *The Peaks of Autumn*
5. *Imperial Towers*
6. *The Phoenix of Kiymako (forthcoming 2018)*
0. *Never (Prequel to The Amber Isle)*

The Bone War Trilogy

1. *The Last Sea God*
2. *Forthcoming 2019*
3. *Forthcoming 2019*

Salves of the New World

1. *The Red Hourglass*
2. *The Ruby Heart (forthcoming 2018)*
3. *Forthcoming*